Ex Libris

Paul Francis
Recade

THE CONFESSIONS
OF
PROINSIAS O'TOOLE

THE CONFESSIONS
OF
PROINSIAS O'TOOLE

JOHN MORROW

BLACKSTAFF PRESS

© John Morrow 1979.

Published by Blackstaff Press Limited, 3 Galway Park, Dundonald, Belfast
BT16 0AN, with the assistance of the Arts Council of Northern Ireland.
First published in a hardback edition in 1977 by Blackstaff Press Limited.

ISBN 0 85640 125 0 (Cloth)
ISBN 0 85640 196 X (Paper)

Printed in Northern Ireland by Belfast Litho Printers Limited.

Alternatively, I could have taken the air up at the pitch-and-toss school that Monday — and perished, perhaps, in the flurry of gunfire that broke out over an unusually heavy penny; or sought out Teesy Hagan and touched for a smear of the sailor's itch she was said to be retailing about then. But I chose to go knocking on the door of Meehaul's flat, thereby lighting a long fuse (80,000 words, give or take).

My first knock set off a series of bumps and scuffles inside, my second triggered an explosive curse and the muffled pealing of a telephone. The door flung open and I caught a brief glimpse of golliwog hair, John Lennon specs and jock-strap as the tenant bolted for the kitchen where the phone was.

Wandering in, I came face to fine bare tit with a bird who teetered on one leg beside the bed. Her first reaction was to cover up; luckily she remembered in time where she was and who she was pretending to be, threw back her shoulders and smiled an uncertain greeting. The smell of her reminded me of an empty handbag I'd once swiped from the back seat of a Jag (a long time ago, of course).

'... No Mother... no... I'm not losing my mind... If you wish to speak to me ring off now and phone (61974) in one minute's time... Yes... I can see it from here — it's vacant... All right now?...'

He came hopping into the room, pulling on a track suit. 'Stephanie, this is Proinsias O'Toole — Proinsias, meet Stephanie Hamilton ... Back in a sec...' He cascaded downstairs.

Stephanie had taken snappy advantage of his passage to get into the other leg of her drawers and was half-roads into a sweater when I turned. Disappointed, I crossed to the window and saw him dive into a phone box in front of the University. 'Ah Christ!...' I began to gurgle — but pulled myself together in time, continuing solemnly: 'They're still after him?'

'Yes,' said Stephanie, kneeling on the bed combing long fair hair into some sort of disorder, 'isn't it awful! Fascist pigs! Every time you lift the phone there's this loud click. He has to keep running over to that box at all hours, poor love... But I suppose you know all about that sort of thing, if you're the Proinsias O'Toole he's always on about.'

Could there be another? I shrugged modestly. Of course my real name, the one which has enlivened manys a Petty Sessions, is Francie Fallis. What started as a joke when everything went suddenly Green and Erse a couple of years back has proved a blessing in some ways: that last load of copper, for instance, whereas 'Proinsias O'Toole' got off with a six moon suspended and a twenty quid fine, Francie Fallis would have gone down for five years hard. Easy.

Stephanie was going on: '— and now that Diarmuid and Peter have been lifted... did you hear about that? Yesterday they raided their pad and found — or planted — ten pounds of gelly, two sticks of cannabis and four dozen dirty postcards —'

'— My Christ! Ten pounds! They'll throw away the key.'

'But wait'll you hear... they're not charging them with the gelly, the cunning bastards, only the pot and the postcards!' (Cunning indeed. I had to admit to myself that it would be hard to formulate a 'Speech from the Dock' around Acapulco Gold and a wanker's album.)... 'So now, on top of everything,' said Stephanie, 'Meehaul has to take over the admin. of the WC.'

Meehaul came panting back up the stairs — Michael Clive Grieves, only son of a well-got Prod purdy-hoker in the back country (Michael being one of those OK Taig names used increasingly by Prod golfers to draw a line between them and the 'Willy John' proles). WC means Workers' Commune, a student action group consisting mainly of first-year A-Level casualties, battle fatigue cases who find a sort of therapy in the hairy squalor of revolution.

'You've heard about Diarmuid and Peter?' he asked, picking at his navel. 'Cunning bastards! They're getting warmer, Proinsias — we'll all soon be on keeping.' When he came off with things like this last bit, which was often enough, I always thought of the time during the war when my oul' Republican Da brought home a framed picture of Churchill which bore the patriotic inscription 'He Steered the Ship'. This he scored out, substituted 'He Speared the Shit', and hung it up between James Connolly and the Pope.

'The Special Branch mind is so predictable,' Meehaul fumed on, hurling into the jungle kit he called clothes, '— and so naive! As though lopping off the branches makes the tree any easier to fell! Stephanie will tell you: I go out every day and leave that door open to the wall — but no, never a tickle. They tap the phone, skulk behind

2

newspapers in pubs, break into the car and then try to make it look good by flogging the spare wheel — so far, no further. And then they lift a couple or pawns — mere clerks! — like Diarmuid and Peter. The leaden subtlety of it all!'

'Did you ever report that wheel missing, darling?' inquired Stephanie.

He froze in the midst of a tricky bit of bead and headband adjustment and gazed at her, eyebrows raised pityingly. 'Did you hear that, Proinsias!' he groaned, following up with a laugh which I can only describe as bitter. I guffawed similarly, and for good measure threw a look of despairing contempt — which I was glad she didn't catch (the memory of even a small cut like that could mean the difference between success and failure should an opportunity ever arise to upend her). 'Christ woman!' he wailed on. 'Isn't that just what they're after? To involve me in a web of petty litigation — visits to the barracks to make statements, etcetera — and when they finally get round to doing me they'll have a readymade dossier a mile thick. Use your head!'

Judging by the state of the bed he'd been using a few bits of her himself quite recently. But that's a Prod for you: nooky over, kick her in the crotch; it's all to do with the guilt thing; if Adam had been a Prod, Eve would have got that apple core between the eyes double quick.

Still, the outburst had helped bottle his bile to some extent. Dressed, he now set about the laborious construction of a cigarette — using, inevitably, black paper. When lit up his eyes hooded over in a way that had sent manys a honest burgher screaming for the drug squad. (It was only 'Golden Virginia', but the black paper seemed to have this curious effect — on him, I mean.)

'Well, what's with you, Proinsias?' he asked, passing the 'joint' back to Stephanie — it fell to smouldering fragments in her hand, poor girl, and ended up sizzling in the po, but Meehaul never noticed.

'Oh, not too bad,' I replied vaguely; 'things moving along nicely —'

'— Those six stens should make your column pretty effective.'

For one wild moment I came near to bollixing it all by asking, 'What six stens?' In time I remembered the hundred quid for the venal — and entirely fictional — armourer sergeant... 'Yeah — great,' I enthused; 'the lads love them. They're all up at the oul' brickworks this minute, practising.'

'Be careful about the military,' he advised, eyes scouring the room for concealed shorthand writers; 'we've had the word that massive reinforcements are due in.'

So had I — from the second leader in that morning's *News Letter* — but I said nothing to disturb the Young-Intellectual-Guerilla-Leader/ illiterate peasant relationship I had cultivated so carefully. Anyway, he need not have worried: the 'column' — Punchy Coyne and a couple of nippers to keep dick — would welcome a drop of fresh loot around the tumbling pennies up in the brickfields. (The KOSBs, though lucrative, had proved troublesome in adversity)... But what worried me was the inquisitive turn the conversation had taken, and I was relieved when a diversion occurred before Meehaul could probe further into the 'column's' activities — even though it took the generally odious form of Mr O'Halloran Burton...

He greeted Meehaul in the tongue of the heathen Spud God, scowled at me, and had a quick grope at Stephanie's bum whilst nibbling her cheek. If the curse of Ireland in the 19th century was absentee landlords, in the 20th it's absentee agitators. Until recently Burton, a well-camouflaged forty-two, had not laid foot on the Soil since the age of seven. A Prod, a Cambridge man, a poet of some notoriety, he had been one of a panel of Anglo-Gaels unearthed in troubled times to mouth about Irish affairs on the box. His distaste for me dated from the day of his arrival behind the barricades two years before — with TV camera team in attendance. The fighting had ceased weeks previously and we had organized a bit of entertainment for the locals in the Parish Hall. In the middle of it some idiot Maoists had got hold of Burton and hoisted him up on the stage, shouting, 'Recite, recite...' He did — but never got beyond the first verse, which contained the word 'quim' and the phrase '*crêpe-de-chine* knickers'. He said afterwards it was because his revolutionary collection was not then complete, and that anyway he had been stoned. I didn't hear him recite myself, but I did hear his screams as Father O'Driscoll started dragging him by the sideboards across the lawn in the direction of the sacristy. The Father is a six-foot-three Tyrone man and I think his plan was to get Burton inside, stick a couple of candlesticks in his hands, kick him to death, and plead attempted sacrilege. I and a few others had managed to rescue him in time, but Burton still insists that we allowed the Father to trample him a bit in consolation. Since then, indeed, the Confraternity has figured in his fantasy life in much the same way as the Special Branch in Meehaul's — gombeen men in twenty-two inch trousers lurking round every corner with lead-loaded rosary beads.

4

Until now I had managed to keep Burton — or he me — well beyond spitting distance. At first, whenever I ran across him in pubs he gave the impression of having little time for frivolous chatter, always drawing people aside to mutter conspiratorially in an earhole before gulping his jar and darting off to weld another link in the revolutionary chain elsewhere — or so I thought. Then one evening I caught sight of a furtively palmed note and realized he was on the tap, professionally, dawn till dusk! Dirty verse and dirty shirts I could thole — but this was competition. (Which was what I was supposed to think. Poor deluded mug me!)

'Putting an arm on' it's sometimes called. Burton now acted out the phrase literally, manhandling Meehaul into the adjoining room and heeling the door closed. Stephanie, still reclining in long sweater and short knickers, wrinkled her nose and murmured: 'That's what's known as a financial squeeze. Mangy brute!'

His approach had been brutally direct — a fault, no doubt, of his Anglo-Saxon upbringing; the more civilised Celtic manoeuvre I had planned would have taken us through a wet lunch and most of the afternoon. Still, only success counts, and I had been well and truly beaten to the honey jar. A lesser man would have retired in the sulks: Proinsias O'Toole began to blaze an alternative route...

'Yes indeed; Meehaul has a lot to stick,' I sighed, slumping nonchalantly onto the bed beside her. 'And I suppose his people are on his back because of the publicity? That was his Ma on the blower, wasn't it?'

'Oh God — don't talk! They've threatened to drum his Da out of the Lodge and she's on every day pressurising him. And in case that doesn't do the trick she's trying to bribe him! Every post brings something — a transistor, a portable telly, a watch, a shaver — look...' She leapt off the bed (a heart-stopping flubber of flesh) and pulled open a full length cupboard. It was like discovering Aladdin's cache in a Viet Cong dug-out: every chromium bauble of filthy affluence you could imagine — all she had mentioned and more — some, I noted, with price tags still dangling... ' — Would you look!' cried Stephanie, brandishing an electric toaster; 'and he lives on rice and stout!'

Closing the cupboard, she plumped back on the bed, not really looking where she was going, and sat on my hand. She sighed 'Whoops!' with encouraging restraint — but followed with, 'What about the wife and weans, Proinsias? Still down in Gormanstown?'

which was a bit of a damper. At that tense moment we were rejoined by Meehaul (big mouth!) and the literary leech.

Burton still had a firm grip on Meehaul — who, fortunately, had his nose in a sheet of typescript and so did not notice the hasty sundering of his bint and I. Burton wore a satisfied smirk.

' — Fantastic!... Tremendous!' Meehaul criticised.

'Oh, it's not in the first rank by any means,' boomed Burton modestly; 'but the Running Dogs of old Auntie might well find it acceptable.'

'— Marvellous!' Meehaul was crooning when his knees struck the bed-end, causing him to surface from the sewage... 'Oh — Stephanie darling, O'Halloran and I have to scatter down to the Beeb about this. Proinsias, I'm sorry...'

'— Notatall,' says I briskly; 'I was just telling Stephanie here about the wife and kids coming back from Gormanstown next week and what a state the oul' chalet's in, and she's volunteered to come up and give us a hand at the clearing up. A woman's touch —'

She hadn't time to draw breath — as I had anticipated — when Meehaul cried: 'Good girl, Steffers! Mutual aid's the thing! I'll see you...'

Burton dragged him away through the door and downstairs.

'Well!' exploded Steffers, on her knees in the bed, little fists on hips, big eyes round and lips clamped tight — for all the world like Doris Day in an early fifties comedy (and just as hammy).

'Well what?' I drawled, Robert Mitchum to the life, picking a hankie-sized garment from a chair and throwing it at her. 'You're coming, aren't you? Get into that bum-curtain and I'll show you how the fut sodgers live.'

I realize now that what followed was the highpoint in my political career. (I write this on a lined sheet headed 'Mountjoy Prison. Laundry List', each of which costs me ten tailormades or fifteen rolled.) Had I employed a slick of PR men to stage-manage our progress through the ghetto that afternoon — with a view to impressing Steffers — they could have done no better. I was hailed jovially from all sides by friend and stranger alike; lovable pensioners with problems sprang up all along the route as though planted strategically; vigilantes (mine) rattled collecting-tins in greeting; even the Right Hon Rory O'Lig MP — in whom I had only a part share — came out of the Golden Calf lounge to

6

say a not very coherent word. To compare it to Kennedy in Wexford or De Gaulle on the Champs Elysée may sound big-headed, but to the underprivileged lad in the centre it felt like that. And Steffers, I could see, was overwhelmed: the pressure of her prow on my elbow increased noticeably.

The only awkward moment was a brief, glowering confrontation with Father O'Driscoll, who had a damn good try at turning Steffer's bare thighs into snakes. Against this there was Sergeant McNinch — known locally as 'Pig' long before Black Power — touching his cap and apologising when I reported seeing one of his underlings nip out of a patrol car to buy fags in flagrant contravention of 'Wheels only' agreements. (Four fat young Peelers to a car, all killed with constipation, developing green liver like *foie gras* geese.) Finally came Major Giles ('Banger') Wilkington-Pike, leaping the fence at the sports field, calling Steffers 'Ma'am' and begging me to kick-off at the Vandals v. Hooligans Derby organised by the 'Hearts and Minds' Committee of the regiment. And then, at last, the chalet...

To her credit, Steffers did try to make a show of it. She surveyed the piles of empties round the roulette wheel, tutted, and made a few unconvincing passes with a yard brush. But I put a stop to that... 'Lave that down, you kinky thing,' says I, couping her onto the sofa.

I shall not attempt to describe what occurred thereafter and intermittently into the small hours. In my present situation the telling might tend to corrupt me; and it would be of no interest to those already corrupted by the sexual fantasies of poove novelists. It was all very simple and direct (but repeatedly so), devoid of talk, surgical appliance or tiring athletics. I have, you might say, a one-crevice mind.

I awoke to the sound of somebody's boot on the front door and him shouting: 'Francie, ferfrigsake, Francie, ferfrigsake, Francie —' and I knew by the speech rhythms that it was the Cavan man from the boozer opposite. Wrapping my belongings in my shirt-tail I went out and opened the door to the morning sunlight and him in his Pioneer Pin and Priest's trousers, purple faced... 'Francie, ferfrigsake — there's an eejit on the blower keeps sayin' he's number one an' that it's terrible urgent.'

Meehaul. I tore an old raincoat from the back of the door and sprinted across the road...

'Number one?'

'Proinsias — it's happened — no, say nothing, just listen, I have to

7

be quick. The bastards were in sometime yesterday and turned the place over. They took nothing relevant to the movement — photographed it perhaps — but they did the same simulated thievery bit as the spare wheel. This could be a pattern for their strategy in the future, so I'm contacting everyone vulnerable —'

'— Did they take much?'

'I don't really know; mostly a lot of trivial junk... but it's the same "bait" idea —'

'You're not going to take it up with them, are you?'

'Christ no! And there's no need for that sigh of relief — you don't think I'd fall for that after sitting out the car ploy, do you?... But look — I can't linger — what I want you to do is to get hold of Stephanie. Do you know where to contact her?... Good. I think they'll be watching my place for a while to see how this particular hare jumps and I don't want her to get involved. So will you do that, Proinsias? Thanks a million. Up the Rebels!'

Our cheery milkman was depositing the usual fifteen on the step when I scampered up behind and goosed him thoroughly. 'That's an oldie you're whistling,' says he, thankful it wasn't the Cavan man, and we finished the verse in harmony: '— and skies are sunny / We gotta lotta what it takes to get around.'

But then, from the semi-darkness of the bedroom, duty summoned sleepily. Therein lay my mission, curled up under the Starry Plough counterpane tailored for me by a patriotic aunt with a passion for martial interment — the muffled drum, the Last Post in Gaelic, the furtive firing-party... And so, hoisting the flag like a good soldier, I laid hold of, and made contact with, as per standing orders, Stef-f-fer-rs.

The next relevant phase began with a boom on Thursday morning. I awoke at eight-thirty and had a vague notion it was Friday until disabused by an Englishman some time later. Two days, thirty-two bottles of milk and almost continuous nook since Meehaul's phone call; the only other interruption being a nocturnal visit from Punchy Coyne with loot from the disposal of certain items (Example: £3 for a toaster with price tag for £12 attached! A fence's market.) Also, he had drawn my attention to sharp cracking noises in the near vicinity and a red glow to the west that had fuck all to do with delighted shepherds... 'Them Prods are blatterin' away like mad over there,' he whinged.

'And them's not pages from *The Lives of the Saints* the Faithful are flinging back,' I observed, catching the familiar boom of Mickey Close's 1916 Parabellum. 'Where's the troops?'

'The weemin and childer are holding them off behind the chapel. They say this nigger corporal did a terrible thing to Tessy Hagan with a rubber bullet.'

'If he did what I think he did I'd give no odds at all on him getting it back... Never fear, Punchy,' I assured him. 'Away home to your scratcher and try reciting, 'Every roun' a half-a-crown / Five bob for "Every Proddies"' — take it from me, it's better than sheep.'

Propping myself up on the pillows I lit a Sweet Afton (a perk, by the way, from a German business friend over the line in Dundalk and much more acceptable than the party pamphlets with which the Russians and Chinks pad their merchandise).

Steffers snored. She lay on her front, the Starry Plough covering her to the waist, one hand hanging out of the bed, the other grasping me for the same reason a nervous householder ties a string from a doorknob to his toe — an alarm system which had not prevented her being thoroughly burglarised in the recent past, I might add. She stirred and whimpered as I retrieved my battered possessions. Poor Fagan. It had been hard to realize, during some hallucinatory moments in the last forty-eight hours, that he had still been wholly attached to me and not some, if not separate, shared entity; six inches(?) of disembodied gristle over which we fought, with Steffers gaining ground at every engagement.

'It'll teach you,' I murmured, giving an admonitory shake, 'that your master is not dead yet. Thought you were on the pension, did you? — lolloping about in your lawful tunnel —'

My mind shied away from thoughts of Kate and Gormanstown. I assisted it by running my hand along the switchback of Steffer's spine, humming an old folk air the while...

> Tight as a drum, never been done,
> Queen of all the Fairies.
> Maggy Maquiddy had only one...

But not Steffers. Oh God no, by no manner of means Steffers. All there in shapely super-abundance; handy-packed for quick access; odour-free; matt-finished in glorious non-skid light-tan; easily disposable(?). Pound for pound, bulge for bulge, there was as much of Kate, the package that had taken me two long years to unwrap — button by button, zip by zip, a sexual snakes and ladders. (Black mark! — Go three inches below stocking top and stay until favour restored.) Every button a mortal sin, every zip fifty Hail Marys, culminating in one great spiritual orgasm against the graveyard wall — 'Jeezus, Mary and Jo-o-o-siff!' — precipitated by a dozen stout on one side and six brandy-'n'-ports on the other

Not that the result, a splendid white wedding and our eldest girl (Concepta!) had altered the rules one whit so far as Kate was concerned; the brandy-'n'-ports, she considered, had been loaded dice. (Go back to base!) But domestic privacy had meant that, starting early of an evening, I had a fair chance of running a telescoped version of the two-year obstacle course and reaching goal before either sleep or exhaustion overcame me. There had been other brandy-'n'-port, 'Jeezus, Mary and Jo-o-o-siff!' times of course; four in all — Kevin, Sean, Roisin, Mary and...

That last one, Malachy, had a definite Culchie look about him. Brandy-'n'-port, Gormanstown, class of '69?... More likely an extra bowl of stirabout from some bog-reared cook sergeant. In the three seasons since, she had taken off well before spring manoeuvres began. My telegram via Punchy — 'Prods rampant. Town on fire. Stay put.' — might stave off her return for a week or two yet.

My hand swept down under the Starry Plough and Steffers, still sleeping, groaned the short lay term which is her ecstatic rosary... Easily disposable? I hoped so; indeed was beginning to look forward to Meehaul's repossession. It's the oul' criminal element in me, I suppose; the rapist under the skin...

The blue fag smoke hanging in the sunlight moved suddenly — followed, it seemed, by the entire chalet.

Boom — rah — rah — rah —

The blast sprung open all the doors, smashed the front windows and moved the bed a foot nearer the kitchen. Steffers snored. Too close to have been meant for anyone else but yours truly, was my first thought. The Billy Boys! I visualized a platoon of priest-eaters poised in the garden, ready to storm in and catch such a notorious Taig baby-farmer in bed — with a Prod! (We'd hardly talked at all, but I'd ascertained that much.) They'd cherish my severed crigs as a lodge trophy!

Clutching those precious items to me I ran through to the front of the house and peered guardedly from an empty window to the roadway outside.

Relief!

Blast is a peculiar thing: I'd have sworn it was at least ten pound of gelly, yet it had been a mere pipe bomb, a simple do-it-yourself contraption consisting of copper tube, weed killer and detonator, of a type favoured by the lower age groups in the district.

A dozen or so twelve-year-olds stood admiring their handiwork, half-heartedly throwing broken pavers at Major Giles ('Banger') Wilkington-Pike, whose armoured car it was of which they had just demolished the entire front suspension. The Major had been standing in the pennanted turret when the front wheels had gone their separate ways — one coming to rest only feet from my front door. The effect had been as if a camel had suddenly decided to sit without first letting its tourist burden know its intention. When I first looked the major's toecaps were hooked in the map-reading fixture on the front of the turret while his face rested on the bonnet near the radiator.

As I watched, a coal-black head emerged from the turret behind the Major's boots; Corporal Cyril Masimba, the Major's driver and wireless operator. The sight of Cyril was enough to send the kids into xenophobic convulsions; they danced around the fractured car on bandied legs, scratching their armpits... 'Black Proddy monkey...' 'Away home to Bellevue!' (the zoo)... 'Throw him a nut!' etc. (The stock of the blessed Martin had slumped badly since the advent of the Army.)

11

Cyril's reply was to flash his teeth, cock his 9mm automatic and call back: 'Fetch us yer sister, Paddy the pig. I've got something she likes.' In broad Cockney, I might add.

'Now, now — we'll have none of that, Corporal.'

The Major had managed to slide down from the bonnet and had retrieved his tin hat and leather-coated swagger stick. The latter he shook at Cyril severely. Turning to the kids he said: 'Now be off with you, children, and we'll say no more —,' at which point he was himself rendered incapable of saying any more for some time by a half-brick which hit him just about where his flak-jacket ended.

I could foresee it developing into something really nasty. Mad, becurlered heads with fags attached were beginning to poke out from caves along the street. (Ladies capable of atrocities that would have blanched the hair of Zola's Northern peasantry.) Also, the young gentlemen who attended the nearby Christian Brothers academy were due to pass by shortly — and life with the Brethren is as good a grounding in urban guerilla warfare as you'll get anywhere. The last thing I wanted at this stage was the martyrdom of Wilkington-Pike on my doorstep, with consequential TV coverage and the Military Police knocking down doors to make enquiries. ('Now Sah, just leave your teeth on the floor and answer the question.') Reluctantly I decided I must act.

Still starkers, I dashed into the kitchen and plunged my hand into a full and evil-smelling slop bucket kept festering for the purpose (soldiers are hygienic bastards), extracting the polythene-wrapped lock and vestigial stock of a shotgun. From there to a small shrine to the Sacred Heart in the living room where, loosely set in a wooden stand and containing the stumps of two mass candles, were the 12 inch sawn-off barrels with cartridges already in the breech (they're also touchy about religious *objets d'art*). Then on with the raincoat and out the front door with the compact little weapon held across my bare belly out of sight, the pared stock fitting my palm like a hand gun.

The Major was still on his knees, helmeted head bowed, clutching his jewels, for all the world like some General hamming it up at the Cenotaph. Corporal Cyril bobbed up and down in the turret, trading racialist obscenities with the kids.

When I came on the scene, knowing me of old, they tended to drop their current missile or hide it behind their back, though still keeping up their abuse of the Corporal. I laid a hand on the Major's shoulder

12

and he raised a green mask to me...

'Francie, old chap,' he groaned, 'thank God you're here. I was on my way to see you when this lot —'

'Wait now,' I said, grasping him under the oxter with my free hand. 'Can you manage it to the chalet?'

He had just got his feet under him when what I most feared came straggling into view: a swarm of apprentice Priests on their way to the mercies of the Brethren. They spotted the car and Corporal Cyril and came running with howls of patriotic zeal, stopping to pick up ammunition en route. The young ones left off baiting the corporal and ran to meet and join this fresh element, the whole forming a rough skirmishing line across the road. Stones began to bounce all around the Major and me. Corporal Cyril retired into his turret.

Wilkington-Pike leant .on the car's mudwing and said, weakly: 'Let's get under cover, O'Toole. There'll be some of our lads along presently... My Christ, man!... What are you doing with that?'

This last could have been his reaction to either the sawn-off or Fagan, for I had pulled open the raincoat and was checking the breech. Ignoring him, I faced the mob with sawn-off presented — Fagan very much at ease in the chill morning breeze — and shouted: 'Bugger off!'

The young bucks, being local and knowing me, did so quickly, scattering into adjacent gardens and waste ground. The Priesteens, from another ghetto mostly, faltered but then rallied, those with sharp eyes taking up a new battle-cry... 'Dirty British Jew!' (It had been a must because of a lesion when I was ten. Mother had to have the Bishop's assurance regarding the immortality of my soul before she'd permit it.)

I cocked the hammers.

'My God, you can't, O'Toole!' cried the Major. 'You'll rip them to shreds!'

But I did... Aiming at a point on the road midway between us and them, I let fly with one barrel. The load was of my own composition: large pellets made from a mixture of fine salt and bonding cement, an old gamekeeper's recipe. On striking the hard metal of the road they broke up into a spray of sufficient force to penetrate the skin's surface slightly, causing a stinging rash like that which comes of being whipped with nettles, and filling the eyes without doing permanent damage.

The effect on the Priesteens was electric. They ran, scratching frantically, falling over one another, squealing unprintably. I helped them on by bouncing the second barrel into their backs. In one minute

13

flat we were alone.

Looking up, I saw the Cavan man and his favourite potboy leaning out the bedroom window above the bar, clad in matching purple pyjamas, gaping. At them I flourished my other armament cheerily, causing the potboy to scream and duck inside and the Cavan man to groan, predictably: 'Fer frigsake Francie!'

'Salt, you say,' exclaimed Wilkington-Pike, lowering the level of his second tumbler of Islay Mist by a good inch. (I kept an all-round stock: Islay for officers, brandy for bints and squaddies, Powers for Priests and politicians and bottles of stout for Peelers.)

'Aye,' I replied from the kitchen, watching a seething scum of well-stewed tea leaves mount up the pot. Leaving it to simmer I returned to where he sprawled on the sofa, helmet off, flak-jacket undone, puffing a Sweet Afton.

He was a gingery, short-back-and-sides thirty-five and he spoke with the blimpish boom of a septuagenarian Field Marshal. Of course they all do, from the cradle it seems. In the old days (a year ago!), treating across' a night barricade with a battle caparisoned commander who sounded like Churchill at his ripest, it had been hair-raising in daylight to hear the same voice issue from a bit of a lad you wouldn't have trusted with a box of matches.

'Salt pellets,' I said. 'Manys the time I've caught a load up the arse trying to get out over an orchard wall.'

Clothes felt strange after so long. I'd managed to extract shirt and trousers from the jumble on the bed without waking Steffers. The shirt was off-white nylon with porter stains and a collar which had never known tie, the trousers part of my navy-blue ensemble, well-bagged and with faulty fly-zip: in all the trendy uniform of the Urban Guerilla as seen in pseudo-furtive TV interviews. ('If we could just place the fag-end behind the ear, sweetie... so!')

'Extremely effective, I must say,' mused the Major. 'Automatic shot-guns loaded with salt. H'mm. I may put it up to HQ, y'know. They're ready to try anything in the present situation. The *sansculotte* appear to have become inured to CS — or addicted. And rubber bullets have become trophies to be solicited. I hear the nuns up at St Sappho's have a weekly target board!'

I wondered if it had been Corporal Cyril who'd been unspeakable to Teesy Hagan. He squatted on his heels outside the front door, fondling his 9mm and crooning quietly...

> 'If you want it
> here it is
> Come and get it...'

Across the road a breakdown gang from the Scots Borderers fucked and blinded over the removal of the Major's wrecked car. Little old ladies passed by townwards, shopping bags abrim with incendiary devices for planting in stores where they owed money. The postman staggered from door to door with his usual load of intimidating letters, ('Git out or be brunt (*sic*) out you taig/prod basters'), which each recipient had posted to himself to boost his position on the new housing list. A local Priest — not O'Driscoll — and the Protestant vicar moved along making their daily joint appeal for calm and restraint, between calls walking in stony silence, taking care not to touch one another when entering narrow doorways... Not exactly Camberwick Green — but it is home.

'The purpose of my visit is to beg a favour — two, in fact,' said the Major portentously. 'I'm loath to impose upon your good nature, O'Toole, for you've been more than helpful in the past.' I pooh-poohed the various items — lorries, guns etc — recovered in the last two years. 'The first is similar to your other efforts on our behalf. This time it's a sentry — a Private Briggs. Last seen by us he was waving jovially to the Backward Boys bus as it approached his position — as you know, all our chaps are under instruction from the "Hearts and Minds" Committee to wave jovially at everything native that moves. We've had various garbled reports of legs seen dangling from the bus window as it proceeded through the ghetto afterwards, so we must presume that the Backwards have him — and his rifle. We'd be most grateful, Francie, if you'd use your good offices to recover Briggs — and, er, that rifle.'

'I'll do my very best, Squire. Might be a bit dodgy though,' says I, putting on my 'Local knowledge' face — the trusty scout telling Custer it's all clear up the Little Big Horn. 'The rifle, that is. Briggs'll be no problem — or what's left of him — but you know as well as I do that Header Hall is a sort of Sandhurst for snipers in this quarter. That last eighteen-year-old Lieutenant General your fellas knocked off the mill roof was one of theirs. So,' I said tentatively, 'it could mean a few quid.'

'Spot on. No bother,' said the Major, holding out his empty glass.

'Between you and me, Francie, the rifle's the thing. Losing Briggs entirely would even our score with the Coldstreams — I suppose you've heard about their Adjutant being murdered by the Marrowbone Darby 'n' Joan club last week — damnable thing — upped them to five this year — but that rifle could cause one hell of a din. My second request concerns the Right Honourable O'Lig.'

Oh God! Our Member, everybody's member, the biggest prick since Parnell; Rory O'Lig, sage of the Golden Calf.

'What or who's he at now?' I groaned, pouring myself a jam-jar of blood-red tea. All the cups were coated with stout glaur from the last roulette school.

'Well, he's been putting the boot in a wee bit much of late. As you know, that stated policy of the Secretary-General in the present situation is "Containment" — that is, holding the ring until those fucking burglars in Whitehall get round to sorting things out between the various factions. But O'Lig appears to have a misconception about who is containing who. Up till now I've gone out of my way to comply with his outrageous demands. That time, you remember, when the vigilantes set Sergeant Steen alight and then discovered he had "For Queen and Country" tattooed on his arm — a provocation, O'Lig called it! Well as you know, Francie, I had every manjack in my company parade stark naked for inspection by O'Lig himself, the vigilantes, the Republican Maoists and the Knights of Columbanus. "Mum", "Dad" or "Sweetheart" were deemed innocuous, but there were two "Death or Glory's" and a "Britannia" on the boat for Aldershot that night, let me remind you — not to mention the poor sod on the stretcher whose "Lady Godiva" the Knights mistook for King Billy! Francie, I have left myself badly understrength because of O'Lig, and this latest demand of his is the final straw. My second-in-command, he insists, must either have plastic surgery or be out of the country by Good Friday! Now a drain on Other Ranks is one thing, but Captain Levy is —'

'Good morning.'

The Major and I sat side-by-side on the sofa facing the fireplace. He now bounded up, twisting like a diver as he went, scattering helmet, tea and whiskey all over the shop. It was as if she'd barked 'Hands up!' She stood in the bedroom doorway, hair falling down over the Starry Plough counterpane which she clutched about her, smiling sleepily. La Pasionaria of the permissive revolution; Cathleen Ni Yorgenson, the wild bitch of the bogs; one five-second TV colour spot of the oul' rag

16

being used so and there'd be no recruitment problem.

'Morning — ah — Ma'am...' stuttered Wilkington-Pike, flailing at a smoulder in the crotch of his trousers caused by his decapitated Afton.

Steffers puckered her brow at me in a way I interpreted as meaning: 'What the bloody hell is this Capitalist Imperialist lackey doing here?' I replied with a surreptitiously pursed mouth, closed eyes and upturned thumb meaning: 'Don't shop the meeting. He is an unwitting pawn in the devious game I am playing on behalf of Irish Workers and Small Farmers.'

'You've met the Major, darling,' I said aloud.

'Yes,' she replied tartly, but seemed reassured by my brilliant mime. 'Proinsias, what time is it?'

'Half past ten or thereabouts.' The Major confirmed this with a glance at the mini-computer on his wrist.

'What day?'

I was at a loss. The Major gave as near a snort as I've ever heard and said: 'Thursday — the 24th.'

'Oh Christ!' She lunged back into the bedroom.

'What's up?' I enquired, sauntering casually over to the door, anticipating a sport of pleasurable voyuerism. But I had barely time to catch a flash or two before all was covered and she came bursting past me.

'I've got to be at the University this morning,' she panted, hands up the back of her choker adjusting the hawsers.

'She's a real bull for the books,' I informed the Major with an air, I hoped, of avuncular pride.

'Bugger the books!' snarled Steffers: 'My grant's due through to-day. Look, I'll meet you in the Prince this afternoon. I'll have to see Meehaul anyway. 'Bye, Proinsias darling.'

We guzzled a bit and I treated myself to a farewell fiddle while the Major made a great show of looking the other way (refilling his glass as he did so). On her way out, with a third party present, you'd think that even an emancipated woman would have other things on her mind. But no; mild advance was answered by brisk counter-offensive and for one wild moment I thought she really was going to take it with her...

'And the best of luck, Meehaul,' thinks I, waving from the empty window as she ran a gauntlet of Scots lubricity from the breakdown gang. I heard Corporal Cyril moan quietly outside the front door, polishing his 9mm lovingly.

17

'Grand gel,' declared Wilkington-Pike, again recumbent on the sofa.

I could see he intended staying for the heel of the bottle, but I didn't mind. It was dole day and I didn't have to sign until twelve-thirty. The bona-fide unemployed — more every week as the boys became more efficient with the gelly — were all through by eleven o'clock, but the thoughtful chaps in Social Welfare recognise that activists, like showpeople, sleep late. Also, the Major had settle into an interesting condition: that half-bottle, slightly slurred stage out of which, I knew of old, a profitable indiscretion or two might well blurt...

'Grand gel,' he repeated. 'Reminds me of a cameo in Pike Hall of the notorious Sybil. You've read about her, of course?'

'Wasn't she — ?' I strained, snapping my fingers in simulated frustration. I hadn't a clue what he was rambling about, but I've had enough experience of bar-room bores to know all the responses.

' — the greatest horticulturalist of the last century. British Museum chock full of her stuff. My paternal Great-Granny, married to Redfers Wilkington-Pike, Chief of the General Staff in his day. That's how she got the stuff; travelled everywhere with him, y'see, collecting specimens!... Haw, haw!' (He convulsed.) 'She was a holy terror! The Pathans shot up old Redfers during the retreat from Peshawar in 1840. And do you know what she did?... Haw, haw!' (It actually sounded like that) '... Went out with the Sepoy women after dark... cut the thingummys off twenty dead wogs! Snip, snip with her secateurs... like she was pruning rosebushes! There's a legend in the family that she had them strung on piano wire... haw, haw... like a necklace... and wore it to the Quorn Hunt Ball!'

I had a mind to tell him how the similarity between the 'grand gel' and his great-granny did not rest on looks alone. My thingummys tingled at the thought of her waltzing in the Prince with them bouncing between her boobs, threaded like a black-headed worm on the hook! (Hippy fashion being what it is thingummys would be fetching a tenner a set in no time... short, squat men being hunted like seals.)

But I knew my 'Waffle-ing-puke', as he's known to the rank-and-file, and let him ride his shaggy dog unhindered — 'turned up in all sorts of odd corners in the Hall when I was a nipper' — utilising the fixed appreciative smile and breathless guffaw I had perfected while listening to hearty Priests telling their one gynaecological story for the umpteenth time — 'There was a terrible din when Father caught a maid using one to polish the family brogues ... Haw, haw ... thought it was

18

an old chamois leather!' — until it dropped dead at the sight of the empty Islay bottle.

'Dear me!' he exclaimed, bottle in one hand, empty glass in the other. 'I'm afraid I've made rather a pig of myself, Francie. Remind me to send you a replacement from the mess. My God! Is that the time? I'll have to get my finger out.'

He rose to his feet, swayed, and grabbed my shoulder. His face was brick red. He spoke slowly and very distinctly. 'I'll leave the matters I mentioned in your good hands, old boy — 'specially friend O'Lig. Becoming increasingly difficult to control the men when he's about. Kicked the Sar'nt Major in the kneecap the last time. I uncovered an incipient murder gang in C company the other day, and we don't want anything like that just when things look as if they're on the change, do we?' (Wait for it!) The Major glanced around furtively, reminding me of Meehaul. 'For your private intelligence, Francie, the next few weeks could see a substantial withdrawal of troops to the mainland.' (Did he really think he was on the Isle of Wight?) 'The lead-up to this General Election looks like being a bit crunchy. The grapevine says there's been some trouble in Bradford and Wolverhampton. If this Baden-Jones shit gets in there'll be hell to pay, mark my words.'

These last observations he puffed while corseting himself in the flak-jacket. Then, the rest of his accoutrements gathered, he drew himself upright and flung me a teetering salute with the swagger stick. 'Mum's the word in the meantime, Francie. All the very breast.'

The Major exited, walking unsteadily, and fell headlong over Corporal Cyril, still squatting faithfully on the step outside.

'Cunt!' chanted the Major, 'black, hairy cunt...' like some sexual fetishist as Cyril lifted and linked him down to a Land Rover provided by the Military Police. What with the bomb, the half-brick, the whisky, the fall and now the fresh air, Wilkington-Pike had had a traumatic morning. I watched the Red-caps strive hard to preserve decorum as they saluted the figure supported by Cyril; he shambled, hen-toed, as though his knees were tied together; a life size 'Action Man' puppet. It was like the surrender scene in the last reel of a movie about one of America's gallant defeats in the Second World War — starring Walter Pidgeon and Rochester — up to the point, that is, when the Major leant out of the Land Rover as it swept past the breakdown gang around the armoured car and screamed: 'Filthy Jock sheepshaggers!' Walter Pidgeon would never have done that.

19

Never one to welsh on a quid-pro-quo, using the Cavan man's blower I despatched Punchy to Header Hall in pursuit of the rifle — and what remained of Private Briggs. Then, on my way to the dole, I called in at the Golden Calf to beard O'Lig.

He was in the midst of being human for an American TV crew; Mammon grilling under the arclights, the point of his cropped skull spangled with sweat.

It was as near repose as I've ever seen him — outside a prison cell. Standing at the bar behind the lights I tried to seek out, beneath the great pitted, tufted cheeks and ponderous dewlaps, the cadaverous features of the young revolutionary who had shared my po in '56. In vain: the only thing wayward glands and a gargantuan thirst had not obliterated was his bile...

'... and as I've stated before with regard to your question, my colleagues and I in the RSVP are totally at one with regard to the question of total withdrawal of troops, abolition of the border, the forcible deportation of all non-Catholic provocatives to the Scotch highlands and an immediate fifty million pound grant from Westminister to help with the reconstruction of devastated areas and subsidise the dole until such times as we set up one for ourselves.'

'But Mr O'Lig sir, I have here a completely contradictory statement issued last evening by your Vice-Chairman, Mr Rarity —'

'Fuck you an' Mr Rarity!'

Probably forewarned, they were quicker off the mark than some of their predecessors and saved the camera. But the flying table caught two lamps and left marks on the interviewer, a trendy-left draft dodger by the look of him, that would have earned him a Purple Heart and pension in Vietnam. It was the signal O'Lig's resident platoon of free-loaders had been waiting for — bonus time. They fell on the tardy ones and extracted contributions for various local charities, the more experienced hands in the crew simply flinging loose change over their shoulders as they galloped for the door. (Later in the day, on seeing an ancient wino clad in the interviewer's buckskin shirt I had one of my

'Custer' moments — 'God sir! It's a Seventh tunic! They've massacred C troop!')

O'Lig continued to kick things and people for some time, pausing frequently to toss off a half-pint from the huge water jug which he had whisked from the table before upending it. Raw Gin, of course; but for all his cauterized taste-buds cared it could have been anything from Pernod to piss. At birth a defeated Providence had rewarded this last in a long line of notable drouths by leaving out that impediment to consumption, the swallow. He had no 'thapple', as they say locally; along with which gift he had developed a method of breathing through his nose (of necessity, having suffered the-kiss-of-life from a few unsavoury bar-flies) which enabled him to lower half-a-gallon plus in one go. To stand beside Rory when his head tilted back to form a straight drop from mouth to sump, and then to hear the merchandise hit bottom, was an eerie experience.

He caught sight of me.

'Did you hear that, Francie?' He punched a passage through the throng to swing on my lapels, blue lips spraying a fine foam. 'Mr — friggin' — Rarity! Tell me, Where was Mr — friggin' — Rarity when you an' me was in Crumlin? Eh...?'

I could have replied, truthfully, that Liam Rarity had been in short pants, still grinding away in the Brother's forcing-house from which he was to take a scholarship to the University. But that would have been a direct provocation.

'Ah shure, Rory oul' son,' says I, with just a trace of the Joxer Daly's about the adenoids, 'he was probably helpin' his Da scrub the pit dust outa the half-crowns.'

Rory roared and slapped my back. My reply had been just right, implying that Liam Rarity PhD (Econ) was the overprivileged offspring of a money-grubbing 'Castle' Catholic, a gombeen man who had used wealth and influence to advance his son's academic career while the childer of the working classes trudged to the mill in bare feet at four in the morning, etc... Both Rory and I had known Rarity senior, a hard-wrought, dawn-till-dusk coalman; but the current trend is to denounce anyone who works — who has ever worked, in fact — as a tool of the Capitalist Imperialists. The only sure way of being accepted as a member of the 'working class' (as in 'movement') is to have a proven, unbroken dole record since leaving Borstal.

'Me hand on it, Francie,' wept Rory, 'yer one of the oul' stock. Them

21

were the days — no fart-arsein' about with political wings an' chains of command an' social programmes. Eh? Just bang-bang, them or us...'

> Give me oul' Parabellum
> An' a coupla han' grenades
> Take me to the firing line...'

And so on for six full verses and choruses. That Jackeen Behan has a lot to answer for; bad enough when pugs like Jack Doyle and Rinty Monaghan warbled 'Irish Eyes' through blood and broken teeth, but since *The Hostage* it's been impossible to have a conversation of more than five sentences with any political punter without giving a cue for a selection from 'Our Cultural Heritage of Song'. Worse, O'Lig's hanger-ons responded to his lead like a chorus in a Jeanette MacDonald/Nelson Eddy spectacular, humming and swaying like a claque of Uncle Toms round the old plantation door. I had two Powers down me and was starting on a third before they guldered the last stanza.

'What in hell am I to do about him?' groaned Rory while his backing group rushed to the bar for their traditional fee. 'I niver wanted any art or part of the bastard. He wallops in here slabberin' about ''Meaningful Dialogues'' an' ''Power Bases'' an' things, an' telling these idjits they need committees an' executives — as if I wasn't doin' all right on my own! Now every time I open my bake he's on the blower to one of them Prod puffs in the BBC he went to college with an' the next thing he's on the box cuttin' me to ribbons, the sly bastard!'

'Why don't you duff him up?'

'Christ Francie, I dream of it! A good, old-fashioned, honest-to-God boot up the bollocks!... But it's not on nowadays, oul' han'; the friggin' media would be on it like a shot, an' Rarity knows how to make the most of that shower if nothing else.'

'What have you tried?'

He glared a hovering barman out of range and hissed through rigid lips in the best prison chapel tradition: 'Twenty-five poun' of gelly buried in his back garden an' an anonymous tip-off to the bulkies. No go. The gelly disappears an' the next night the Prods blow the Hibernian hall. Sergeant Mc-friggin'-Ninch musta had a nice wee turn outa that one, I can tell ye... Then I tries circulatin' the Bishops with photostat copies of his University Young Communist card. Fucked up again; it turns out he was a spy for Catholic Action, the devious bastard!'

'Crude, Rory,' I chastised sagely. 'Crude. Think it through, mate. Even if they had charged him with the gelly he'd have been a martyr overnight — and you'd have made him! The same with the Party card — the lefties would have canonised him as a victim of clerical oppression. No; that's not the way, Rory. In my experience the most effective approach is the quiet one. And that's where I might be able to help. Is he on the phone?'

'I think so... Yeah, he is.'

'Good. Give us a bag of tanners and I'll get Punchy on to it the night. What's his Missus like?'

'A stuck-up convent school bitch if ever there was one!'

'Dead on. I wouldn't like to turn Punchy loose with the heavy breathing on a dacent woman. He was a bit of a knicker-ripper in his young days, so I'm told. What do you think then? — one on the hour day and night, threatening if it's him, breathing if it's her. I've known better men to be down begging in Australia House after a day of that.'

He gave me a short, painful jab in the kidneys, denoting approval. 'You're the divil, Francie! You've a mind like an Englishman. God, I'd give a million to see her ould bake when Punchy starts droolin'! Australia, here they come. Con...'

He summoned the barman and gave instructions for the bag of tanners to be made up.

'In return, Rory oul' son,' I said, 'there's a small favour you could do me. This morning I had a visit from the Major —'

'That fruit merchant!'

'Now, now, Rory — wait'll you hear...'

I passed on Wilkington-Pike's request for a suspension of aggro. Then, when the torrent of obscene derision had subsided, I threw in the leak about the troop withdrawal. His little eyes glittered evilly. 'Wigs on the green, Francie! We'll have them Prods swimmin' for the Mull of Kintyre in a week! It's a terrible thing for a Convinced Socialist to say, but I hope Baden-friggin'-Jones gets in with a hundred per cent.'

A hair appalled at this gleeful acceptance of wholesale slaughter I said, dryly, 'You realize, of course, that there's a right few non-swimmers among them. The Duncher, for instance. He tells me that if the troops were out of the way he'd be looting Dublin in a week.'

'Bluff, Francie; pure bluff,' scoffed Rory. 'That psalm-singin' bastard's on his last legs. He has broken the unwritten law, Francie, a sure sign he's badly rattled.'

'And what law would that be?'

'The one that's kept fellas like him an' me alive this past three years when the fut sodgers were droppin' like flies, just. An' now the holy huer starts sendin' his bully-boys to take potshots at me!'

'You're joking!'

'Cross my heart. Ask the boys there. Lucky for me he sent a bad workman. Somebody knocks the door the other mornin' an' when I opens — bang — there's the Pru man dead on the mat. Two Sundays ago I'm kickin' off at a match up at the Brothers — bang — the referee gits one up the arse. Now you can't call that coincidence!'

I certainly couldn't. I knew the workman. Tully!

I said nothing to Rory — was, in fact, incapable of saying anything for some minutes, my insides cramped with bottled guffaw...

Tully! Oh my Christ, Tully!

If the rest of our society mirrored the truly ecumenical spirit of the dole queue the likes of me would be forced to work for a living. Here citizens who had driven one another from factory and building site with bomb and bullet mingle in good fellowship, all venom uniting against the pleasant young men and pretty girls behind the counter. Also, it is the only building in the city where one can loiter for an hour in the certainty that one will not emerge as a jig-saw for jovial morgue attendants. The most fanatically filthy bird never shits in its own nest.

This morning, unfortunately, the conviviality of my weekly pull at the udder was marred when, on leaving the hutch with my ha'pence, I was buttonholed by a pair of Prod dwarfs.

'The Duncher sent us.'

They were doing their undercover bit, scoop-peaked caps pulled down over the eyes like guardsmen, hands thrust ominously into dexter pockets. The speaker obviously meant to be conspiratorial, performing the frozen lip mime in a manner that owed more to late night James Cagney than practice in defying H M prison regulations; but what came out was an ear-splitting rasp that echoed round the hall like a Tannoy in a railway station. A victim of 'Shipyard Ear', I diagnosed, that industrial ailment, caused by excessive noise, which make every East-end bar on pay day reverbate like an aviary of overgrown, belligerent mynah birds.

I could see the streaks of red-lead on the crown of the spokesman's cap. 'Poison dwarfs' the Cypriots called them. If we Irish are 'white wogs', these mannikins are the Gurkhas of Ireland.

'What's he want?' I asked, hoping they weren't an escort.

'To have a word,' they howled furtively.

'When?'

'In yer own time. Same place.'

Relieved, I watched them off the premises before myself heading for the Prince.

You know the one about the Brighton Pavilion being a pup out of St. Paul's? By the same figure, if a Victorian railway station were to get up on an underground lavatory of the same vintage the result would be something like the Prince.

My most vivid childhood memory is of travelling with my Mother on the top deck of a bus along a route which lay past the almost ecclesiastical frontage of the Prince. In those days it was known locally as 'the plantation' and, although only mid-morning, the entrance was draped with the bodies of American negro troops in various stages of collapse either from drink or the rigours of an overnight train journey from their camps in the tubercular hinterland. A few were being supported by well-dressed ladies. This scene I took in as our bus drew to a halt at a loading point opposite the Prince's half-glazed side windows ('Gin Palace' they stated frankly). My eager gaze tracked over the glazing to the rows of private snugs inside. In one of these, briefly, I saw a black man with a cigar in his teeth, and a white lady, all tangled up in a curious way. Then Mother screamed, clapped her hands over my eyes and began reciting a litany of Saints.

The snugs are still there, and the massive square pillars with gold-leafed *fleur-de-lis*, the mosaic ceiling depicting the Rake's Progress, the three-inch thick marble bar-top from which spout brass gorgon's heads spewing gas-jets to light your Sullivan; all still there to the chagrin of the man who had risked life, licence and good name in the wars years by selling watered whisky and renting out the snugs to 'fast weemin'. On many a rough Saturday night in 1943, when razors cleft the marijuana fumes and the white helmets of the Provost's men came battering through the mob, he'd day-dreamed of the gutting he'd give the kip when it was all over: a back-bar quilted like a film star's bedhead; ankle deep carpet (where there were no spittoons, he reasoned wrongly, men would cease spitting); banquette seats, concealed lighting, piped musak...

Peace came — but so did the Architectural Heritage Society. At the first rumour of his intentions he found himself surrounded by a host of tweedy, teetotal nuteaters who threatened economic ruin and grievous bodily harm if he so much as cleaned a window, let alone modernized.

He now slid my pint across the hated marble and groaned: 'Things is bad, Francie.'

'Couldn't be worse.'

'They were at it again last night.'

'Man they were.'

'The Bunch of Grapes got it, I hear.'

'An illuminated address.'

'D'you think they'll ever get this length?' he queried, wistfully.

'You're one fly fucker, O'Toole.'

This last came from behind me, the fruity bray of O'Halloran Burton. But for it I would hardly have recognised him from the hairy, bebaubled puff I'd last seen shepherding Meehaul to the Beeb. Now he was dressed in keeping with his years; well cut light tweed, dark green shirt and saffron tie; the uniform of the 30's Left, right down to a pair of lethal-looking brown Veldshoen. His thick black hair was combed back, à la the Tony Curtis 50's, to reveal a pair of startlingly large white ears standing out against his facial grog-blossom like fungus lilies on an ancient monument. Later, I noticed that he'd filled in the ring holes in the lobes with make-up.

'I'll allow you to buy me a jar out of the loot,' he said, grinning craftily.

'Out of my dole, you mean,' I corrected, wondering if Meehaul had twigged. 'What sort of bottled stout would you like?'

'Black and Protestant. Bring it over to yonder snug.'

Doing so, I wound my way among the various groups on the vast area of terrazzo between bar and snugs. I tried not to meet the soliciting eye of a short fat man in golliwog wig and velvet flared trousers — not what you think, but Mickey Close, erstwhile sewage worker and now No 1 on the Special Branch wanted list, in disguise. He was being closely observed by a member of the Vice Squad (they're easily spotted — young, televiewable, the only people who smoke pot in public) who was thinking what he was supposed to think. Nearby, a gabble of French TV men were being briefed by an up-and-coming entrepreneur called Slack McGuigan in relation to their forthcoming 'secret' interview with Mickey (fifty quid for the interview, plus fifty if Threatening Military Presence required, and fifty more for culminating mini-riot — rates unchanged since I'd founded the business). Crammed against a pillar, a well-known Special Branch sergeant allowed his person to be fondled by a drunk, homosexual trade union official... 'You must tell me more about those gay commissars you met on your Moscow trip.'

'Ah,' exhaled Burton. 'Always refreshing to sink one's nostrils in the bottled Ganges of the race. My one regret is that Mater took short with me during Galway race week; Airdrie would have been much more palatable.'

'Save that guff for the arse-banditti and let's hear what you're after,'

I growled. Not knowing what to make of him, I decided to stick to first impressions.

'Oho... a touch of the Behans, is it,' he sighed wearily. 'Y'know, you don't really have to with me — though I must admit you do resemble the late boyo on one of his better days. But, as you request, I'll zoom to the point... Francie O'Fallis, you are no dozer. When I had pieced together your small caper with mutual friend Grieves I went on to make further inquiries into your interests and was suitably impressed. So much so that I — and others — have decided that you are ready for better things.'

'You sound like the man from the Prisoners' Aid,' I sneered. 'Does Meehaul think I pulled a caper on him?'

'If you went to him now and made full confession he would smile bravely and refuse to believe one word of it. Last seen he was in a state of what I can only describe as *pre-internment euphoria*; he'd already completed the preface to 'Notes from a Prison Cell' and was putting out feelers to the trendy mags with regard to serial rights.' Burton grinned lewdly and sighted at me along his forefinger. 'So if you're feeling guilty about throwing the leg over his mot, you needn't.'

'Look mate,' I growled, hackles up, 'guilt has fuck all to do with it. The only reason I want him sweet is so's he'll take her out of my hair. Anyway, if you've been nosing about all you say you'll know he's a very wee sprat in my pond.'

'But it is a wee pond, Francie, don't you see? Which brings us back to the point: either you continue to act the pike among your homicidal sprats or decide — as I hope you will — to evolve into a shark. I don't know if you've had the word or not, but if this forthcoming general election goes a certain way your bucket of mad worms could boil over — and being a big one wouldn't save you!'

'Christ! that's a right mixture — sprats, pikes, sharks and worms! I suppose you mean if Baden-Jones gets in and they withdraw the troops,' I said, a trifle smugly. 'I hear tell they're having a bit of trouble in the Midlands already.'

I relished his arched eyebrows.

'Where did you get that from? They've clamped down on the entire media.'

'Oh, us small fry have our sources.'

'Hm... impressive,' he said. 'As I told them, Francie, you're no dozer.'

'Who's them?'

'All will be vouchsafed you in time — if you decide to take a hand in our game. Suffice to say that we are a few spirits who would manipulate the manipulators. In the meantime, for your further enlightenment, and without prejudice, I should like you to join me for a week-end at the seaside.'

'Oh, what a bold sailor you are! Will I bring my overnight bag?'

'Have no fear, darling,' he said blithely; 'though my school was private the Matron was free... I say, isn't that your bit of booty?' He nodded in the direction of the bar and I saw Steffers the moment she started towards me. No Meehaul.

'Remember, Francie,' muttered Burton as she came pushing through the underworld: 'the seaside; Saturday morning; I'll pick you up.'

Steffers, white faced, slumped down beside me — and burst into tears. 'Oh Proinsias, I am glad you're here... something terrible's happened...' She began to sob violently. I put my arm around her and told Burton to fetch a whisky from the bar. This he did, heaping cultured curses on the head of a slothful barman. I got her to swallow a gulp or two and she became coherent again.

'Oh God, Proinsias, I feel so awful about it...'

'About what? What's happened?'

'Meehaul. He's been shot... while you and I were... Oh the poor darling!'

Meehaul had been shot — twice. He was in a private ward in the City Infirmary, closely guarded by his mother and two plainclothes men.

This much only we gleaned from Steffers between bouts of tearful self-laceration which both Burton and I were quick to recognize as purple patches in the pulp novella she was creating around herself. We encouraged her to make a meal of it, he with whisky, I with the sort of loaded assurance — 'How can you blame yourself?' — which tended to send her off on another point-by-point indictment. Later, in her new role as the brave young war widow, she was to support the instant-propaganda theory that Meehaul had been gunned down by a duck-squad of Cameronian keelies; but my favourite eye-witness, the ubiquitous Punchy, had a different tale to tell...

The Chapel fields after dark is a no-mans-land between opposing ghettos and even Punchy could give no satisfactory explanation of Meehaul's presence there, armed with a 9mm automatic. (I must here state, not for the last time, that I had nothing at all to do with it. My own theory is that someone had doctored his Golden Virginia with the real stuff and sent him on a trip — Messianic or Kamikaze, depending on the grass used.)

Traditionally, each evening after tea and the Magic Roundabout the local residents take up firing positions on the rooftops from where, until the Epilogue and bed, they snipe companionably at one another. Most evenings it is a desultory affair — especially on the Prod side, at five bob a load — evlivened only by the appearance of a stray dog or cat among the hillocks of builder's rubble and husks of burnt-out cars from old barricades. In the early days, while domestic pets still survived, great bitterness and one minor pogrom had arisen out of the slaying of a Protestant dog or a Fenian cat; now all were treated as pagan and fair game by the rooftop marksmen. Of course, the legend accepted by both sides is that the pets had been eaten by coloured troops; similarly, both sides gave equally vivid descriptions of the raging gun-battle between Meehaul and the duck-squad despite the forensic facts that one of his wounds, the head crease that knocked him unconscious, was caused by a

.22 — the army use nothing under 9mm — and that his own weapon had been fired but once; and that, according to ballistic evidence, into his own kneecap...!

The word according to Punchy is that at ten o'clock on an evening that had been overcast and therefore quiet because of poor visibility, the moon leered down briefly to reveal Meehaul standing on the crest of a mound halfway between the ghettos. Both sides opened up gleefully and he was seen to fall just as a cloud again shuttered the scene.

Now he was seen to fall by at least one other than the rival snipers. At her back bedroom window on the Catholic side, a vantage point she had manned hopefully for three years, Mrs Bernadette Keegan gave a shriek of mingled horror and excitement. (Punchy informs me that she is the grass widow of one 'Bum' Keegan, a gas meter robber turned gunman-on-the-run whom he and I had met on our last Dublin trip. I have only a hazy memory of 'Bum', who had tapped me for quid at the tail-end of a wild night in McDaid's, but I do recollect the dolly-bird courier he was shacking up with.)

Mrs Keegan, a much-childered bolster of a woman in her sagging forties, grabbed her beads and bin lid from the bed and headed for the street. The bin lid was a highly polished, non-utilitarian affair — her real bin is plastic — and she used it mainly for signalling the approach of Crown Forces, laying into it with a hefty wooden spoon. This she now proceeded to do vigorously, and was soon surrounded by a dozen or so other ladies of the confraternity, all blattering away on their own personalized bin lids and chanting in unison: 'British basters, British basters...' But they soon quietened when Mrs Keegan acquainted them with the nature of the emergency, dispersing swiftly, some to swap bin lids for black head-scarves and mass candles, Mrs Keegan herself to collect her makeshift, portable altar complete with plastic lilies, Mrs Joyce to phone the TV crews in the BBC club and Mrs Hagan to fetch Father O'Driscoll.

The Father was not at all pleased. He'd had a hard day in the confessional and had just settled in front of the Chapel house fire, a huge foot on either hob, the warm air circulating pleasantly up his cassock, a short cheroot in his teeth, a long Powers in one hand and a volume of calculus in the other. (This is my own creative reconstruction, mind you; I've often seen him thus when delivering a small sweetener — twenty Dutch Darks and a half-bottle, say — for some favour begged. Yet even these he had accepted in much the same way as he did Mrs Hagan's summons: with a roar and a curse — in Erse, of course.)

Curiously enough, I suspect that the root cause of O'Driscoll's legendary ire, which I've mentioned before in relation to Burton's porn, is to be found in his other pastime: higher mathematics. A frustrated genius, though you'd never guess it. In his youth he had been hailed as a prodigy by his tutors; a budding Einstein of the bogs with a gift of total recall wedded to a natural bent for pure maths. So, via the string-pulling of his mother and Parish Priest, he had gone on to join the flower of Ireland's intellect in a seminary on the Belmullet peninsula, there to spend seven years pondering such timeless problems as the capacity of hell and the latitude and longitude of limbo.

He was in such a mood, Punchy swears, that had it been anyone else he'd have thrown them his 'beaming-up' kit and told them to get on with it. But Mrs Hagan, forby being in everything bar the crib, happened to be the mother of the notorious Teesy, and O'Driscoll was feeling guilty about Teesy just then. (A week before, in a fit of ungovernable rage brought on by a ten-minute earful of Teesy's hair-raising doings, he'd darted round and dragged her out of the confessional in midflow, planted his boot in her precocious arse and told her to wash out her mouth with black soap and say 500 Hail Marys.)

When O'Driscoll arrived at the field the ladies were grouped around Mrs Keegan's lath and hessian altar, which she had set up on the boundary footpath well out of range and beneath a sodium streetlight to facilitate the TV men when they arrived. Black-mantled, kneeling, they were being led by Mrs Keegan in a rendering of 'Faith of Our Fathers'; but this she nicked in the second verse on spotting O'Driscoll, quickly cueing the others into 'Soggarth Aroon'. A great one for the niceties of production, Mrs Keegan: Soggarth Aroon himself was not impressed…

'Where is it?' he growled, meaning the cadaver.

'Out there, Father; near thon oul' breadvan,' pointed Mrs Keegan. And as though to underline her directions a burst of tracers from the Prod side rattled off the gutted landmark.

O'Driscoll looked long. When he turned again to face the ladies his five o'clock shadow stood out against his sudden pallor like a Hallowe'en mask. He knew what they were up to. Playing for the jackpot: a dead hero Priest, Murphy's best Mercedes, the lone piper, the

Cardinal, the Bishops, legions of fellow Priests and a thousand marching men; the funeral going and the riot coming back would make it a day to remember.

A series of mouth-watering alternatives must have flashed across his mind at that moment: to kick the ridiculous altar to pieces and choke Mrs Keegan in its ruins; to drive them all out into the gunfire with boot and fist; to run for home and plead insanity... But like the good Priest he tried to be, O'Driscoll turned on his great brown heel without a word and made off into the darkness of the field. (A few weeks later he got his revenge on Mrs Keegan by simply bribing a platoon of the hated Paras to deposit, ostentatiously, a tray of cups and saucers, provided by him, on her windowsill with a note of thanks. The fury of her ladies was such that she was forced to do a moonlight flit that very night.)

Sanctity had its reward. The rooftop Prods could hardly believe their luck when the unmistakable figure came stumbling into the line of fire. Word of the big game in view went round like wildfire, bringing other sportsmen from bed and box to add their contribution to the barrage which, by all accounts, was phenomenal. Yet when O'Driscoll tottered back to the boundary footpath some ten minutes later, cassock riddled, biretta and the heel of one boot gone, eyes starting from their sockets like a throttled rabbit's, the only punctures in his hide were some barbed wire scratches on his ankles.

It was a moment of screaming hysteria — which, for the ladies, more than made up for lack of corpse. Afterwards, they tended to gloss it over by saying: 'The Father had a wee bit of a turn, poor man.' But one outside source, a TV rigger who had been setting up gear on the footpath, has left a terrifying description of O'Driscoll's passage with boot, fist and blistering tongue through the crowd of well-wishers. Breaking clear, he headed for the Chapel house leaving in his wake a trampled, smouldering altar and half-a-dozen berserk ladies wallowing on their backsides like upended turtles.

But where was Meehaul? What had happened out there?... Punchy's informants among the military, who arrived in time to disperse a rearguard of the ladies with a few well-placed rubber bullets, could supply only the aforementioned forensic facts: they'd found Meehaul lying half-conscious in a sheugh between the hillocks, head creased, kneecap shattered; and they'd found his gun, minus the round which was later extracted from his kneecap, *twenty yards away from his resting place!* Further light on O'Driscoll's ten-minute safari — and that last

33

curious fact — had to await the professional indiscretion of one Jeremy, a comely RAMC male nurse who had tended Meehaul in the feverish hours following his ordeal and who is now, coincidentally, a temporary mount in the Cavan man's stable.

Meehaul, it seems, had regained consciousness and had been about to make for safety when the barrage in honour of O'Driscoll broke out. Terrified, he flattened himself in the sheugh and cocked his pistol — but, he swears, never fired it. What happened next all but unhinged him. Out of the crashing darkness a panting, snuffling something came crawling to settle on top of him full length, squeezing the breath from him and pushing his face into the mire, covering him like a huge randy dog! Rigid, shrieking soundlessly in terror, he then heard the thing begin to gibber incomprehensibly close to his ear and felt a moistness seeping over his head and neck. Summoning all his strength he heaved... O'Driscoll rolled over, screaming, his Holy Oil bottle flying off into the night. The rooftop snipers homed on the altercation and bullets whipped and thudded all around, causing both to cower deeper into the sheugh...

At this point must have occured the short-lived dialogue which I here creatively reconstruct from Jeremy's report of Meehaul's ravings:

O'Driscoll (*accusative*): 'You're alive, my son!'

Meehaul (*enraged*): 'Yes — so you needn't have bothered. Anyway, I'm Presbyterian.'

Imagine it! This man of Herculean fury — a fury already well-stocked by Mrs Keegan and ladies — running a pitchblack gauntlet of murderous fire to shrive the Faithful, only to be ticked-off by a grazed Blackmouth!

Famous last words — or very nearly. Meehaul uttered them many times in his ramblings, Jeremy insists, and always as a prelude to a spasm of howling and knee clutching. Yet once out of the coma and on the mend he appeared to have no clear recollection of anything after the initial head crease. Shock, said the Medical Corps head-shrinker, had erected a permanent barrier in the mind. As soon as he was able Mummy spirited him away to convalesce in the country; later, he went on to finish his degree at Strathclyde University, and that's the last I heard of him.

Meanwhile, in the Retreat House of an obscure flagellant Order not far distant, O'Driscoll administered his own therapy. For forty-eight hours, according to Miss Conaty his housekeeper, he wore out scourges as fast as the merry Friars could construct them. And Miss Conaty should know, she having a long-standing arrangement with the same merry Friars concerning the disposal of such used materials which, at five bob per bloodstained thong, she retailed to the ladies of the confraternity. Mrs Hagan swears that a mere snippet of O'Driscoll's gore dunked briefly in the family broth not only cured her lifelong sciatica but also was the cause of arresting certain alarming symptoms in daughter Teesy.

Pardon the digression (which was very much better in the first draft used by my cell-mate to wipe his overproductive arse) but I wanted to set the record straight for posterity. Allegations have been made in the public prints about my part in the Meehaul affair, not least by a certain young lady whose mammary glands have been hanging out of the *Vicar's Gazette* every Sunday for weeks in an attempt to stir up interest in the serialisation of her book *My All For Ireland*. My hands are clean; I will say no more. Let us now return to the mainstream of Irish political life, bed and boozer.

In the Prince, Steffers, encouraged by Burton, kept up the bleeding heart bit throughout the long wet afternoon. I provided a comforting arm, but lost interest at an early stage. To be frank, I've never had much time for social intercourse with any woman who has neither Fagan or a frying-pan in her hand. (I recall one occasion when Kate managed both, pulling on one to bring me within range of the other.)

Punchy came in about tea-time while I was still reasonably compos. I left Burton to carry on his avuncular bit with Steffers and joined him at the bar. It being dole day there'd been a big take at the toss, which we now divvied up. After that there was his report on negotiations concerning Private Briggs and the rifle up at Header Hall: six Jeroboams of scrumpy had secured the rifle, still unused, and a further three Private Briggs, well used in every way imaginable, who was now on his way to the regimental health farm in Sussex. We decided on the total cost of the operation to be invoiced to Wilkington-Pike (twenty-five quid) and I then produced O'Lig's bag of tanners and outlined Operation Rarity and lady wife.

Punchy did not like it.

'Why not just bump him off?' he suggested. 'I'll do it for the tanners.'

And so he would; neatly. That archaic terminology is no affectation picked up from late-night gangsters on the box; nor is the slight Yankee accent, a whinging, nasal overtone that always reminds me of W C Fields. In 1922, aged fifteen, he'd been caught with a warm gun up his jersey and sent down for two years. In prison he'd taken up boxing to avoid hard labour and had emerged a useful flyweight with an introduction to a professional trainer. In the following three years he'd fought over a hundred matches and at the age of twenty had sailed for America in search of the Golden Gloves. There, in the quarter finals, a squat negro had gutter-fought him for eleven rounds and, with a head butt in the 12th, had sent him to the vegetable ward for six months. The quacks there had been so certain he was a goner that they never bothered fixing up his face, which is why his eyebrows sag unevenly and his nose, a cache of splintered bone, spreads across one cheek. Also, in the 9th, he had bitten off and swallowed a fair-size segment of tongue, which is why he articulates slowly. He left that Chicago hospital looking and sounding punchy — but he wasn't. A few days later, standing in a queue for a soup-kitchen, he had been hailed from a large limousine by two chaps from back home, fellow activists with whom he had shared many a fag-end in Crumlin. They were in the service of a Sicilian entrepreneur who was always on the lookout for lads with just Punchy's background and qualifications. And so for the next five years Punchy led an affluent life abrim with excitement and adventure, in the pursuit of which he collected a number of other injuries. Sadly, it all ended in 1932 with the repeal of Prohibition and his deportation as an undesirable alien caught in possession of no less than five concealed weapons. He had arrived home just in time for the big depression, joined the dole queue, wangled an IRA pension for wounds caused by FBI bullets and, on forged papers and for the same dishonourable scars, a British Legion allotment.

Oh he's far from punchy is our Punchy. He is also a believer in that motto common to American hunters and Irish patriots: when in doubt, shoot it. I found myself pleading for Rarity's life, not because Punchy had anything against the man — did not, in fact, know him — but because 'bumping him off' would be less trouble and, in our anarchic times, much safer...

'Three-quarters of the damn phone-boxes in the city are wrecked,' he moaned, 'an' anyway, I don't fancy the thing with the dame.'

'You've done it before. I've seen your record, mind.'

'That's a long time ago. I started with them ATS broads during the war, part of the Movement's psychomalogical campaign, only them dirty bitches loved it!'

'And you loved it too, horny oul' ghett!'

37

'But it's not the same...'

'Ah, Christ save us from arty-crafty perverts! Next you'll be telling me you need inspiration!... Well, let me give you a bit: if we do do him in O'Lig will have us by the short hairs for life; but if we do only what I'm telling you, whether it succeeds or not, it'll keep Rory sweet, and we might be able to use a sweet Rory in the near future. Get it?'

He did; reluctantly.

'Another thing,' I went on, 'a couple of Duncher's wee fellas tackled me in the dole this morning. He wants to see me. We haven't been lumbering him with duff ammo or anything like that, have we? I wouldn't like to think we were letting partiality get in the way of profit.'

He assured me not... 'Course there's always the oul' gripe about not gittin' enough of them Swedish dum-dums. They like them for writing on, y'see. Buxy McManus was showin' me two the quacks dug out of his brother. One said: 'FTP' an' the other: 'John 3 & 16'; a lovely bit of minature engraving.'

'Christ! They'll have us in the *Guinness Book of Records* next. The first man to score an entire gable wall, including King Billy's horse, on a 9mm dum-dum!'

'The only other thing I can think of is Duncher's 'Monster Revival Campaign'. There's some funny people been sniffin' roun' that tin hut of his — Teesy Hagan, for one, ever since O'Driscoll put the boot in.'

'And Tully? Have you seen him about?'

It was worth the expression of horror on the mangled old face.

'Ah Christ no! Don't tell us he's on the go again. It's enough to put you on the boat for friggin' Saigon or somewhere safe!'

'I'm not sure yet; but keep your eyes skint. Now away and start giving Mrs Rarity the benefit of your bad breath.'

I had noticed Burton skulking up to another part of the long bar and when I rejoined him and Steffers in the snug he was 'there, there-ing' away, coaxing her to finish a short, darkish drink.

'What's that?' I inquired.

'Brandy and Port,' she wept. 'O'Halloran thought it might steady me.'

'O'Halloran' grinned at me and patted her hand. 'I was telling Stephanie about our projected journey on Saturday. A whiff of the ozone might be just the thing to buck her up. What do you think, Francie?'

I wanted to tell him that if he continued feeding her brandy 'n' port he would be very welcome to cart her off and reap the benefit. Already she'd begun to rub her frontage on my arm like an itchy cat.

Evidently mistaking my glare for jealousy, he went on: 'My wife will be there, of course. I'm sure Stephanie and she would hit it off nicely.'

I'd forgotten he was married. I remembered the photo and blurb in the Willy Hickey column — about four years ago — Lady Chloe Vane-Paraffin or something, an uppercrust pop-novelist who had lived with drug-addicted, black homos in some sewer and cashed in on the experience. About fifteen years younger than Burton, if I recalled aright. But if I knew Burton a wife of four long years standing would not stop him humping Steffers if he had a mind and the opportunity. Certain he had the one, and vowing to do everything in my power to present him with the other, I muttered: 'We'll see on Saturday.'

'I must away now,' he announced abruptly, getting to his feet. 'I'm giving a lecture to the WEA entitled "Underground lavatory and gable wall — the sub-human predicament" — illustrated, of course. See you both Saturday. I'll call with transport — early.'

He wasn't right out the door when a barman dumped a large brandy 'n' port and a small bottle of stout in front of us. 'That English fella sent it,' he snarled.

'Isn't he fabulous!' sighed Steffers, eyes brimming, snatching the drink. 'You really can misjudge people, can't you?'

'He's a friggin' scud, for my money,' I said, watching her swig the three-star aphrodisiac. Her fingertips bit into my thigh adjacent to the centre of things. 'You're an old grouch,' she crooned, her head on my navy-blue shoulder. Then, remembering her role, she burst into tears... 'I don't know what I'd have done if you hadn't been here, Proinsias...'

In the next couple of hours I tried hard to dampen the fires in her puddings with half-pints of draught stout — but I could do nothing about the tears. (I was reminded with alarm of the legend of 'Melville' O'Rourke, so nicknamed after a well-known firm of funeral furnishers, whose appearance and general demeanour had been so lugubrious that the IRA General Staff in 1922 had chosen him to be the bearer of bad tidings to the wives and sweethearts of the fallen. A decent man at heart, it was said that he'd been so shaken by the bizarre effect his news had on some women that it had turned his mind. Long after hostilities had ceased he kept turning up on suburban doorsteps when the moon was full and the man of the house out, his long grey face a caricature of grief, his brief speech — 'Yer man's kilt' — a prelude to an inept frontal assault.) However, I found that an occasional 'there, there' and sympathetic grope kept her prattling away at her tragic life story as though doing a run-through for 'Panorama', leaving me to give a free eye to the floorshow.

The mad ballet featuring Mickey Close, 'Slack' McGuigan and the French TV men was approaching a climax. 'Slack' had been darting back and forth to the phone and now the venue for the interview seemed to be settled, the military laid on for the promised 'Threatening Presence' and a score or so of Header Hall's worst for the mini-riot. I'd done it so often myself I knew every move; I also had a fair idea of how much loot 'Slack' had tucked away in his top pocket, give or take a fiver.

The fact that Mickey was now speechless and footless was no deterrent to the Frenchmen, who weren't far behind him. The man from the Vice Squad was chatting amicably to a warty veteran of the 1939-45 campaign who still wore rouge and ankle-straps for the nostalgia trade; the Special Branch sergeant, green-faced and drowsy, was being led away by that other veteran... 'We'll have a wee and then go on to my place for coffee and I'll tell you about this dishy commissar in Vladivostock...'

I watched until 'Slack' had shepherded his entire cast off the premises. (Why 'Slack'? His real name was Liam, but since childhood he had lived in the sartorial shade of an older and very much bigger brother, whose clothes he had been forced to inherit long before he had grown into them. Hence 'slack'.) I then made for the phone and acquainted a certain sub-contractor with Slack's affluence and approximate whereabouts — thus again, e'en at this late hour, living up to that life-philosophy succintly outlined by baddie Lee Marvin to goodie John Wayne in *The Comancheros*: 'Never let the sun set without showing a profit.'

Then back to the chalet where, under the 'Starry Plough', Steffers administered a brisk course of physiotherapy to a sad case of brewer's droop. Successfully, I might add. I kept myself to myself and let the pair of them get on with it.

On the main bridge spanning the river which splits our city topographically, politically and religiously, we idled in a queue of traffic towards the military checkpoint. The tide was out and, upstream, thousands of the world's most pampered gulls stalked vast, ponging mud-flats in search of a morning corpse. Downstream, where river becomes harbour and the iron gibbets of the shipyard tower dizzily, a party of gloomy-looking souls were boarding the Isle of Man steamer under a banner which proclaimed: 'Christian Endeavour Day Trip — Ye must be born again'. They were singing, ominously, 'Nearer My God To Thee'.

As we approached the barrier I prepared myself for a severe groping. At the wheel, Burton hummed to himself and tooled the big car very close to the toes of a gesturing sergeant... 'H'm — the Life Guards,' he murmured, braking: 'augurs well for our little mission, Francie, if you knew the whole of it.'

Before winding down the window he had a leisurely sort through the contents of his wallet. A kneeling marksman on the pavement sighted his SLR at the windscreen on my side. The sergeant bent down and glared through the window on Burton's side, the muzzle of his Sterling automatic tapping impatiently on the glass. I felt myself slipping into one of my Celtic slack-lower-lip turns and, looking straight ahead and smiling weakly, hissed: 'For frigsake hurry! I'm touching cloth!'

In dark glasses, spray-on tan, light-grey worsted, pale blue shirt and matching tie, Burton looked every inch the Maltese white-slaver. Gold flashed on his wrist and fingers when he at last let down the window and cut short the sergeant's set-piece — 'Naw then sah...' — by shoving a small card in his face. The sergeant looked briefly and straightened up to wave the barrier aside. He bent down again, but Burton had already closed the window and whatever the sergeant said, if anything, was lost in our slipstream as Burton booted the car over the bridge. I came away with the distinct impression that had there been a forelock handy the sergeant would have tugged it...

Travelling through the Prod heartland I marvelled at the relative unscathedness of it all — relative, that is, to the battlefield across the water. Even at this early hour the pavements were alive with the sort of people who, one knew, still paid rent, had a current TV licence and taxed their cars on the first week of the quarter. Young families in colourful leisurewear promenaded the shops before taking off for a day at the seaside. (Average number three; to promenade the average family in my part of town would require the giving of twenty-four hours notice to the security forces under the Special Powers clause relating to processions.)

A handful of Commandos lounged around the bullet-scarred remains of a chapel — shirt-sleeved, at their ease, surrounded by a giggle of admiring girls — the only military presence we were to see this side of the bridge. The only other evidence of three years civil strife was an abundance of children's playgrounds — at the end of every other street, it seemed — with brightly coloured swings, chutes and see-saws, marked off neatly with white painted chain loops. These were on sites previously occupied by public houses belonging to, managed by, or employing, Catholics. All had been burnt or bombed in one week-end of loyalist ire two years ago — after being thoroughly looted, of course, by hordes of young families in colourful leisurewear.

It's not a part of town I've ever frequented, but one pub I had known in peace time (I was going to say 'better times', but that's a relative term) and when we passed the site, an unusually large one with room for a bank of twelve swings instead of eight, I couldn't restrain a guffaw.

'Curious the sight of a dry waterhole should amuse you,' remarked Burton.

'That one belonged to a fella I knew — at least I knew his people. Vinny Burke...'

'One of us or one of youse? Cowboy or Indian?'

'That's the laugh... how the hell they winkled him.'

I told him about Vinny's six war years as an Officers' Mess steward in the RAF; about his buying the pub with his gratuity and accumulated perks; about the montage of crossed flags and Vinny's medals above the bar (topped by a photo of the Queen Mum beckoning to guardsmen from the balcony of Buck House); his Protestant wife; free drinks for the Billy Boys every Twelfth of July; and about his annual day-trip in a false beard to do his Easter duty in Dublin's Pro-Cathedral. And they'd twigged him! We guffawed.

'Could it have been his "Wee button nose"?' suggested Burton. 'As the Orangeman said to Brendan in Millisle.'

'Or maybe they noticed, after all those years, that he "had a down look about him",' I offered.

'... or detected the underlying speech rhythms of the native Celt in a phrase such as "Six halves of Haig, fourteen stout by the neck, a Wee Willy, an' the keys of the jakes for the lady".'

'... or that he pulled his ear when passing a chapel, instead of spitting.'

'... or that his hammer hung down the left side instead of the right...'

Our laughter brought Steffers' dishevelled head into silhouette against the back window, eyes staring wildly. She'd been snoring under a rug even before Burton had started the engine outside the chalet.

'Where are we?' she demanded in a voice that deserved a more dramatic response ('Bound for Buenos Aires, my lovely, where you'll dance like you've never danced before — or else!') than Burton's: 'On the road to Comber, darling.'

'The setting of that wistful old drum solo, you'll remember', I amplified: ' "Who kilt the fifer on the Cummer road..." ' and Burton, sensing my desire to deflate, joined me in the chorus: ' "Billy Ma'dowl, Billy Ma'dowl, Billy Ma'dowl..." '

'God Francie,' wheezed Burton, 'what a wealth of native culture we do share!'

'For just a moment there,' sighed Steffers, 'I was completely disorientated.'

'— as the Geisha remarked after her operation,' murmured Burton.

If she meant her wits were scrambled, little wonder. Friday had been another session of deep-litter lust in the dark chalet, and this time there had been a large carry-out of whisky and stout to add another dimension of unreality to the goings-on. But for the stout, purchased with part of her grant money, I think I'd have kicked her out about midday. Like all Prods, she bangs better when oiled; but in her case this mutually enjoyable liberation was accompanied by a side-effect which, for me, all but cancelled it out. Between bangs she talked, about banging in general but primarily about the preceding bang and how good it had been for us emotionally, physically, morally, socially and economically. By teatime I had been prolonging the bangs to ridiculous lengths just to stave off the talk-in — a ploy which proved counter-productive, as you can guess. Give me a bout of karate with

43

Kate or a bit of slap and tickle with spotty Tessy any day.

Once clear of the city Burton swung off the main drag in case of more road checks and we spent the next hour clipping hedges along the sunlit boreens of County Down.

Viewed through closed windows and a protective haze of fag smoke it all looked peaceful and well-ordered enough, each fleeting glimpse of chequered downland a coloured illustration from a Senior Infants' reader. And there indeed, was Farmer Giles himself, though not, alas, a rosy-cheeked yokel in pork-pie hat and gaiters. His name was probably McNulty or suchlike and he wore a flat cap and boiler suit, had a canister strapped to his skeletal back and wandered in a field like some plebeian Martian, spraying chemical death on all God's small creatures. At the sound of our engine he turned and waved automatically in the way of countryfolk. Burton's reply was to reduce speed, wind down his window and howl: 'Less of the picturesque peasant stuff and get on with the graft, you slothful bastard!' A few hundred yards further on McNulty, if it were he, had the last word in giant white lettering on his barn-end:'Prepare To Meet Thy God. No Pope Here.'

We came on the sea suddenly, emerging onto a narrow coast road only a mile, Burton said, from our destination. Water sparkled in the warm sunlight, deceptively inviting. Four or five super-tankers and the Isle of Man floated on the horizon. We sped past a beach black-rimmed at the high water mark like a coalman's bath. Kamikaze gulls swooped to put diseased fish out of their misery.

At a place where the road is crammed tightly to the water's edge by a high estate wall we turned off through immense ornamental gateposts and proceeded up a tree-lined driveway. Before turning off I observed, directly opposite the gateway, a long jetty marching out over the waves on concrete stilts. The driveway curved through the trees for a good quarter-mile before spanning out into a cindered clearing in front of a Big House.

Capital letters, you'll notice; a three-storied, uppercrust bunker the sight of which caused a warm glow of nostalgia to spread throughout my usually imperturbable tripes. Blindfolded, I could have found my way along every passage to every room and cellar without putting a foot wrong. For in such a house — as uniform in design from Cork to Malin Head as the labourers' cottages which make up the set — I had spent my last holiday by the sea, the happiest six months of my formative years, in the good company of twenty-nine other juvenile delinquents.

44

Memories of good old Galwally Approved flooded back to me as I fell out of the car and stretched myself, breathed the salt laden air and gazed up at the homely old pile. I began to feel that I just might enjoy the week-end.

Steffers again snored in the back seat. We decided to leave her unmolested in the meantime and Burton led the way towards the main entrance.

'A grand shack,' I commented.

'Built as a country cottage by the wife's great-granda,' said Burton. 'My sister-in-law and her husband run it as a sort of Outward Bound for burnt-out bank managers.'

As though on cue a waddle of elderly anglers, expensively encumbered, came down the steps as we approached. A large man with a head, face and chest of flaming red hair posed on the top step with a cigar and wished them a loud good luck. They chuckled senilely as though he'd told them a dirty joke.

' "O", dear boy,' exclaimed the red giant ("O" is the abbreviation used by Burton's close friends and family); 'just in time for a pre-luncheon scoop. And this must be the terrible O'Toole you've been telling us about. A thirsty looking huer if ever I saw one. Come on on in.'

We followed him through the big mirrored hallway and into a lounge which had, incongruously, a small chromium 'n' formica bar in one corner. He went behind the bar and, without asking our choice, poured three large measures of Scotch. Raising his glass he glared fiercely at me and toasted: 'Up yours.'

'This,' said Burton, 'if you haven't deemed it already, is my brother-in-law once removed, Toby Mann.'

He was my first Toby in the flesh — a name I always associate with pipe-smoking goodies in the nursey novelettes consumed by my pubescent sisters, or Regency Bucks of the Pimpernel era. This one too I'd read about quite recently in the Sunday gutters. To mark the twenty-fifth anniversary of some bit of carnage in the Western Desert they'd done a piece on the SAS — Special Air Service, long-range assassins — in which they'd mentioned that the barbarity of one of its founder members had shocked even the public school sadists who were his comrades: Toby Mann. The ensuing libel action had been settled out of court for a considerable sum, I recalled, while the injured party had been about other barbarous business in the Congo — a mercenary.

('Bloody Mann!' the Mirror had screamed, predictably.)

All that made him at least fifty, but with all that hair it was impossible to judge what marks the life had left on him. Physically, clad in open-necked, dove-coloured drill with tit pockets and cartridge loops, he looked a virile thirty-five — and aggressive with it...

'You're carrying, O'Toole,' he said conversationally. I noticed then that his eyes too were red — and very steady.

Burton spluttered over his whisky... 'You're mad, Toby!' he squealed. 'You're in one of your niggling moods, I can see. Francie had his coat off in the car so I'd have noticed any hardware. Do you think he'd chance it through road checks on this side of the country!'

'Now, now, "O",' soothed Toby, 'don't get in a lather. No offence meant, Francie, but you'll have noticed that posse of geriatrics on your way in. They're a nice front for some other activities which you'll no doubt get to know about, and when one of them passes away on the premises it causes a hell of a lot of unwanted stir. Only last week a big tope took one overboard out beyond the island and had the place tramping with Peelers for days. Now, any kind of explosion indoors could set off a chain of heart seizures and land us up shit creek sharpish — which is why I really must insist on confiscating your fountain pen.'

Burton gaped as I unclipped the pen from my top pocket and handed it over. Toby received it reverently, eyes glowing... 'Lovely job. Single shot .22. Made in the shipyards, I should imagine; I hear they're turning them out by the hundred undercover.'

I knew a gun nut when I saw one and was glad to disillusion him. 'Shipyard *type*: the Japs got hold of one a year ago, copied it, and are turning them out by the thousand at half the price. Another example of the decline in cottage industry, I'm afraid.'

'Christ!' Is nothing sacred to those yellow parrots,' groaned Toby, extracting the single load and pocketing the pen. 'So far, without fear, favour or prejudice I've shot, gutted and choked Wogs of about every hue under the sun — including a half-breed Navajo in the Kennedy Peace Corps — but never a Chink or a Jap. After this, Francie, I promise you that failing all else I shall pick a quarrel over the sweet and sour pork and bloody well —'

'Shut up, Toby!'

Burton was trembling with rage. He rounded on me... 'You might at least have told me about that thing. You realize that if we'd been searched it would have meant the Paras' urinal in Holywood barracks,

46

dangling by our thumbs like so much dirty washing!'

'Ah yer arse,' I said colloquially; 'don't believe everything you read. If you've done so much snooping into my background you'll know that I've been in Holywood, and the most damndable thing they did to me was an untipped fag that had me coughing lumps of lung for days. Anyway, it was me that sweated at the road block — and after seeing you flash that wee card at the sergeant I reckoned the risk had been worth it. How the hell do I know you're not a Judas goat for some Intelligence murder gang? After all, brother-in-law here has a bit of a record in that line of work.'

Toby laughed and re-filled the glasses all round. 'I see you've been reading my press-cuttings, Francie. Still, you must admit he has a point, "O",' he said to a still glowering Burton. 'Best show him that card and confirm his forebodings.'

'I still think it was a stupid chance to take,' grumbled Burton, but filched the card out of his wallet and passed it to me. They watched in silence as I inspected it. Under a celluloid sheath was a youngish, short-back-and-sides photo of Burton in a high white collar; the rest of the card was taken up with printing imbedded in a mess of coloured curlicues like those on banknotes, 'OHMS' on top, then 'Military Intelligence 12. Capt O'H Burton'.

A shiver passed over my scalp. I looked up and the pair of them burst into howls of laughter.

'Ah God — your face, Francie!' giggled Burton.

'Wait'll you see it,' roared Toby, 'when he hears it's not a forgery! And for good measure, Francie, here's mine.'

I saw why Toby favoured whiskers: in his photo bald chin merged imperceptibly into neck, both shadowed by a wet-looking, pendulous lower lip; the printing was similar to that on Burton's.

'All I can say,' I brassed bravely, 'is that you will need no electronic device, fag-end or ball nipper. I will tell all, gladly, in blank verse if required.' But at that moment I really was shit-scared. Not of torture: any Intelligence man worth his bribe would know my previous record of fulsome co-operation (at least two huts in Long Kesh internment camp should be named after me). So why lure me down here?

'Spoken like an Irish Patriot,' cried Burton, slapping my shoulder, 'but you needn't worry, Francie. Toby and I are Old Boys of the same academy for young empire builders, one of its traditions being that every pupil is automatically enlisted into the great Intelligence Mafia

47

on leaving; one finds one's card stuck in the flyleaf of one's presentation copy of *The Life of Cecil Rhodes* on one's final speech day.'

'Even I,' said Toby proudly, 'who was expelled for gross indecency and Secret Sin in my fourth term —'

He was interrupted by the door bursting open to admit a scuffle and yelp of hounds and a woman with a riding crop in her hand. 'Toby,' she shrieked, evidently in high dudgeon about something, a ripe Katy Jurado figure in tweeds and surgical-looking brogues: 'they've scoffed another beagle!'

'Ah Christ!' Toby responded, hurling the dregs of his glass down his gullet and coming out from behind the bar. He booted one of the half-dozen canine neurotics that were barking, peeing and snuffling all over the shop at a terrible rate. The lady advanced into the lounge and shouted an incomprehensible something which seemed to further agitate the beasts but had the effect of drawing them to her, whereupon she laid about with the crop, driving them, howling lamentably, outside. 'I'll have to go down, "O",' said Toby, following, 'and you'd better come with me. Help yourself to the liquor, Francie. Back shortly.'

From the window, glass in hand, I watched the trio and dogs cross the forecourt and disappear into the forestation opposite. It was all very strange. I thought about Toby and wondered if the no-chin and beard were symbolic. He came through as the sort of forthright lunatic I usually get on well with; but he was a big man, and where I come from big men are either Peelers, bailiffs or not to be trusted.

The walls of the lounge were decorated with the stuffed heads of slaughtered animals. To pass the time I was reading the brass plaque attached to one — 'Thompson Gazelle. By Major the Hon Picton Vane-Paraffin; East Africa, 1901. Shortly after the kill the Major disturbed a nest of the deadly Mamba snake and died of poison.' — when a voice from behind commented: 'I've often wondered just what aspect of Great Uncle Picton disturbed the Mambas so.'

'You're Proinsias O'Toole, I gather,' smiled Mrs O'Halloran Burton, allowing me to hold her hand briefly. (Regrettably, this is the most intimate physical contact I've had with her to date. If I thought for one moment that being a black, homo, drug addict would break the stalemate I'd start taking the pills now.) A tiny, dark, slim thing, draped in something short, black and silky, she looked up at me and I felt suddenly huge and ungainly, a buckskinned Gary Cooper at bay before a crinolined Susan Hayward. To one whose success has been largely with robust ladies, she appeared as an emissary from a third sex. Yet, curiously, her voice was low and resonant, her tongue rolling the vowels as though they had a tangible bulk, like an announcer on a TV programme for the deaf.

'I'm Burton's old woman,' she said; 'call me Chloe.'

For want of something to say I confessed: 'Mine's really Francie —'

'I know — Cox or something!' she cried, the dark blue antenna of her falses lashes splaying upward in goggle-eyed delight. 'Fabulous! I remember "O" telling me —'

'Fallis,' I corrected.

'Better still! "O" has a habit of getting things wrong... Oh God! I've made a ghastly pun, haven't I. Where is everybody, by the way?... Here, let me freshen your drink.'

Following her to the bar I explained about the irate lady with hounds.

'Sister Meg,' she groaned, passing me a bumper, 'and her friggin' dogs. With Toby being away so much and having no kids, she's developed this maternal thing about animals. That's the second gone for elevenses in a fortnight. Can't blame her for blowing up, I suppose.'

Mystified, I asked: 'Scoffed? Elevenses? Where, and by whom?'

She laughed and slyly tapped one nostril with a silver-lacquered claw. 'You're jumping the gun, cock — oh God... sorry again... Now let's converse about other matters, if you don't mind. Where, for instance, is the choice piece of crumpet "O" told me you were bringing?'

On learning that Steffers still kipped in the backseat of the car she insisted on going out to waken her... 'Can't have that. It's not often we get female company down here these days,' she said brightly, heading for the door. When I made to follow her she quickened her step and cried: 'No, no, Francie — you finish your drink.'

I went to the window facing onto the car-park and watched her open the rear door of Burton's limousine and poke her head in. She then stood back and held the door for the sticky-eyed ragbag that tumbled out on the cinders. Coming towards the house they looked like some sort of Beauty and Beast circus act; or the Matron of a with-it private asylum welcoming a dangerous guest.

Chloe breezed into the lounge and headed for the bar, crying over her shoulder, 'Come and have a drink. I'm sure you're dying for one after that journey.'

From the doorway Steffers shot me a nostril-flaring look of hatred that heartened me considerably. She looked like a poster for a double-X movie — 'I was a Victim of a Gang-Bang'; her hair hung in tatted ropes; black pearls of coagulated stout glistened at the corners of her mouth; dark splashes of the same marked the shelf of her yellow T-shirt; the fly-zip of her jeans yawned halfway open. An aura of old, damp mattress preceded her to the bar.

'You're a pair of right bastards, aren't you!' she hissed at me, passing a totally inadequate hand through her thatch. I said nothing and kept well out of reach. Chloe, in the act of pouring her a whisky, patted her hand and soothed: 'There now, don't take on. Francie's not all to blame, if I know darling Hubby. The idea was to keep you out of Toby's way as long as possible, I'll bet.'

'Is there anywhere I can wash up?' asked Steffers after demolishing the liquor in quick time.

'On this floor, no less than three,' boasted Chloe; 'I'll show you.'

They were halfway to the lounge door when the outer door slammed and Burton's unmistakable guffaw rang out in the hallway. The two pair met in the lounge doorway, Burton and Toby (Meg and hounds nowhere to be seen) Chloe and Steffers. Burton screamed: 'Darling!' and launched himself at Chloe, hoisting her to a reachable position on his paunch, her feet a good six inches clear of the floor — the sort of carry-on I'd previously witnessed only in TV ads for tinned soup or fish fingers.

Toby drew up in front of Steffers and said, gruffly: 'You must be Stephanie' — his outspread hand moving forward to meet hers — 'I'm Toby. Get them off.' This last phrase was accompanied by a quick downward deflection of his reaching hand just before it met Steffer's. Her back was towards me, but I heard her gasp and saw her dungareed buttocks arch... Toby broke off the engagement almost at once and came striding up to the bar. Steffers swung round, fumbling madly with her now fully gaping zip, her face a study in dumb shock. I knew then that whatever Toby turned out to be, or whatever he did to me in the future, I'd forgive him a lot for that moment.

'You're a swine, Toby,' chided Chloe (but I could see she was anything but annoyed), ushering Steffers over the threshold. Steffers's exit line was 'Bugger!'

'You really are the concupiscent limit, old boy,' stated Burton at the bar (and he, I could see, really was piqued). Turning to me he went on: 'You'll have to forgive him, Francie. Our satisfaction will come when he appears in the *Vicar's Gazette* some Sunday for terrorizing old ladies in railway carriages.'

'Fuck all to do with me,' I spoke out stoutly; 'the same girl is well able to look after herself.'

Toby beamed and grabbed my hand, squeezing painfully. 'Good man, O'Toole! Spoken like a right bastard. And as for you, "O", you poetic con-man, fight your own brand of undercover sex war and let met get on with my siege tactics. Who was it, after all, who discovered that ex-Colonel of the Bengal Rifles travelling in drag on the *Brighton Flyer* in 1964? Francie, I cannot begin to describe the look on that poor old chap's face when I —'

'Toby, I swear that if you don't shut up and let us get down to talking about serious matters in hand, I'll tell Meg.'

Toby winced as though in a spasm of pain — like the cut of a riding crop across his arse, I surmised. He glared at Burton, but he did let his matey arm slip from my shoulders as he growled: 'All right, bloody dry boke, I suppose we'd better get started before the women get back.'

'Where's Meg, by the way?' I inquired innocently. 'Preparing a dog for dinner?'

They looked at one another slyly and laughed.

'You're a cute kid and no mistake,' said Toby.

'But it's none of your bloody business as yet,' added Burton, 'so let's begin at the beginning, shall we?'

Toby filled the glasses and Burton talked. He used his hands a lot, not in the erratic way of a Frog or a Wop, but in a precise geometric fashion, tracing squares and rectangles in the air and then clapping and squeezing the sides as if each idea expressed was moulded plasticine. His delivery was in the aggressive, pecking style of the BBC school for Talking Heads...

'First of all, the hinge of the matter: next Wednesday's General Election. Your intelligence, Francie, agrees with ours: *i.e.* that if a government headed by the Right Hon Peregrine Baden-Jones, henceforth to be designated "B-J", is returned to office there will be an immediate and substantial, if not total, withdrawal of troops from the six counties to deal with ensuing uprisings among the immigrant population. Already this week there has been minor clashes in places like Wolverhampton and Bradford — caused by a rumour that B-J is so confident of success that he has placed a charter order with Nicarios for five jumbo oil-tankers... Not a bad idea when you think of it; with judicious packing he might be able to clear out a place like Brixton in one go! Anyway, firearms were used, though not very effectively, it seems. Of course we've all known for some time that they've been buying in substantial quantities, as have the Welsh and the Scots — and Womens' Lib. Marvellous what effect our handful of mentally retarded recidivists have had on the political scene — 'If you wanna get ahead geta gun!' More to the point, at the first shot the 'Spirit of Grosvenor Square' deserted the British Bobby for good, and when the Powers panicked and ordered a mass issue of firearms every manjack from Sergeant Dixon down refused, quoting the recent case of a constable in Shropshire who shot a gun-toting bank robber and got two years for malicious assault because the robber's gun was empty at the time of the shooting — a technical point in eighteenth-century Salop law relating to duelling. So, if B-J gets in, it's troops. There's rumours about a call-up of First Reservists this week-end; but if it blows like we think it will they'll need every squaddie of the fifteen thousand over here.'

'So,' Burton went on after a long swig, 'withdrawal. You more than anyone on this Godforsaken rock know what that could mean, Francie. With the troops out of the way Duncher's lads would backlash with a vengeance. Facing them would be O'Lig's RSVP aided by the Provos and the *Saor Eire* bank robbers. Sniping at both would be the Marxist Officials, the Irish Democrats, the Wolfe Tone Society, the Catholic Ex-servicemen's Guild and others too numerous. And the Maoists, of course, agin everybody. On top of this you could very well have Fred Carno's Army from the Free State blundering over and getting slaughtered by all sides. All in all a recipe for at least ten year's sport among the ruins, wouldn't you say?'

I nodded agreement, but added: 'You forget to mention the factions on the Prod side: potentially one for every tin tabernacle. And on both sides the townees hate the culchies worse than they do each other, and the culchies hate everything that's not from their townland.'

'Then you'd agree that anyone seeking a strong power base in this bedlam would be wrong in the head?'

'Mental. Withdraw the troops and within a year there'd be a republic in every parish and it'd all be back to where it was seven hundred years ago — only this time they'll not be murdering each other over such sensible things as fields and cows and women. Still,' I said contentedly, 'roll on anarchy; there'll be grand pickings for fellas in my line of work.'

In an emphatic gesture, Burton drove an invisible nail into the bar-top with his fist. ' "Fellas" — plural — meaning you accept that there'll be one like you in every parish republic, and half-a-dozen at any given moment trying to get over your corpse to the honey-pot. You're thinking like a sprat again, Francie. Come Wednesday next the entire future of two countries will go into the melting pot: what we're offering you is the opportunity to be one of the cooks rather than an ingredient.'

'So far,' I retorted with some heat, 'you have offered me fuck all but a ride in your motor and a few jars, which I have accepted. Whatever else you've got up your sleeve, I wish to Christ you'd stop beating around and spit it out. But if all depends on yer man getting in next Wednesday, wouldn't you be better saving your breath till then? It is an election, after all, and they can go either way.'

I had given a cue for a brace of smirks and, from Toby, one of those ostentatious throat-clearings that usually precede either a naughty revelation or a phony leak. 'Not this one, old boy,' he said, 'if the poll is taken anytime after tomorrow's papers have hit the streets I'd give terrible long odds on the present incumbent of Chequers losing his deposit. What do you think, "O"?'

'That's about the height of it,' agreed Burton, gauging 'it' between flattened quivering palms, oozing with self-congratulation: 'a landslide.'

After an expectant pause I decided to say, off-handedly: 'Well, the Sunday rags'll be worth it for a change, if what you say is right. But sure it matters little either way; I'll still have to scrounge for a mouthful... And talking of grub, Toby oul' han', I could scoff the balls off a beagle myself if it was handy. Any chance of a bite soon?'

Burton's hands had fallen to his sides as if someone had snipped the strings. 'With your apparent lack of curiosity,' he said coldly, 'I find it difficult to imagine how the hell you've managed not to starve.'

Toby groaned. 'Ah for Christ's sake "O"!... He's having you on. The object of this preliminary chat, as you know well, Francie, is to impress you not only with the seriousness of our intent but also with the scope of our planning. To do this we must now give you a preview of tomorrow's big story and the background to it. No one's eating until thus far has been achieved, and as I'm ravenous too, and as "O" is inclined to make a bit of a production out of it... Now don't sulk, "O" — it's your artistic side... Anyway, Francie, I shall now give you the initial dirt straight...

'Last Tuesday, at 3pm precisely, a gob of London fuzz who specialises in such things came upon two males being unspeakable behind a bush in St. James's Park. One was a city gent in early middle age; the other, in keeping with tradition, a drummer of the Blues. On Wednesday morning at Bow Street the city gent — a Mr Smith — was represented in his absence by expensive counsel and fined twenty-five nicker; the trooper got six months hard chokey. A routine case; barely worth an inch in the most salacious evening daily, and certainly not near graphic enough for the *Whore's Gazette* on Lord's Day — until it was — er — revealed that Mr Smith is none other than the Right Honourable Tarquin Gordon-Smythe, Junior Minister of the Environment in HM Government and close hunting — foxes — friend of our fun-loving PM!'

'Poor little otter!' laughed Burton. 'I bet he's in bed with his bunny now, crying his eyes out! And the beautiful irony of it is, Francie, he was once Baden-Jones' fag at —'

'Steady, "O", steady,' rebuked Toby; 'I'll let you do your Willy Hickey bit later. Just now I'd like to have Mr O'Toole's reaction to our little Sabbath bombshell.'

'Yours?' I exclaimed, all eyebrows, knowing it would please him. It did — Burton and he hoisted a smug little toast to one another — and I concluded that their delvings into my past hadn't been as thorough as they'd tried to make out.

'To the very bush,' purred Toby; 'the whole thing timed like a Whitehall farce.'

'Grand work,' I mused, 'but hardly to the scale of Profumo — and the Permissive Society has come a long way since he started it on the road. The last poll, remember, gave the holders a twenty-five percent lead. I think it'll take more than a bit of buggery in the Cabinet to wipe out that kind of margin. I may be wrong, but I've a strong notion that your good old run-of-the-mill British voter has a secret yen for the kinky — look at all the working-men's clubs, female impersonators the whole go. Now if it had been the drummer's horse...'

'Or,' suggested Toby coyly, 'the drummer was black?'

Oh my God! Bingo!

'Black Bugger!' screamed the *Mirror*, predictably, in half-page headline. Someone had propped it against a lamp on the bedside table, meaning it to be the first thing my waking eye lit on. It wasn't; the first was the great ornamental rose in the centre of the ceiling, here outlined in Wedgewood blue but as familiar to me as the rest of the house. For a split second I wallowed in the joyous illusion that I was again snug in my wanking pit in good old Galwally — then the morning sunlight struck, revealing a painful condition never experienced in those Spartan days. When I moved, sharp things tumbled about inside my skull; my tongue was an ulcerated nerve-end, my nostrils as firmly plugged as though a fairy embalmer had prepared me in the night. Whisky; Irish whisky; unadulterated Irish whisky, washed down with innumerable bottles of the most fart-making stout I'd ever lipped.

I knew by the constriction around my crotch and armpits that I was fully clothed under the blankets. I pictured myself, elephants, being carted upstairs by a bearer party of Toby's tame geriatrics clad in thigh waders and oilskins. I remembered them returning from the kill, crowding round the bar, wizened caterpillars peeking out from wet, crackling chrysalises. I also remembered the staring eyes of a dead fish being measured by Toby; a rhapsody on the delights of colonic irrigation delivered into my ear by a retired stockbroker; Steffers complaining about being groped by everybody; a screeching match between Chloe and Burton from which a vivid phrase (hers) remained with me — 'Frig you and your stinking drawers!' Meg pouring beer into a basin for the beagles and punching Toby playfully on the mouth — several times — and drawing blood; whisky, stout and more whisky — but not one morsel of food did I remember... And Lambeg drums! — sitting up in bed in the darkness and someone — Burton? — rhyming: 'Blackbird on the gate, Blackbird on the gate...' But the name of the tune was 'Pigeon on the gate', wasn't it?

Looking round for a glass of something in which to cool and shrink my tongue I saw, outspread on the counterpane, a pair of knickers. I use this evocative word with discrimination, the article being pale green, voluminous, elasticated, and having a heart-shaped hanky pocket low down on the left leg. Closer scrutiny revealed stains and a brutal stench that caused me to flop back on the pillows abruptly.

Whose? Steffers I knew to be innocent of pants, panties or briefs under the skintight denim. Chloe? — never. Hard to believe that even Meg... Before dozing off again — the only sensible alternative to the agony of getting up, at least until help arrived in the form of strong tea or stout — I decided that I must somehow have got hold of a particularly dirty and gargantuan tinker woman.

My return to semi-consciousness was caused by the creak of an opening door. Through a film of eye matter I observed Burton crossing to the bed. Hope stirred; a pot of tea, a piece or two of toast; thoughtful of him... But no. In my comatose state his movements took on a stealthy, dreamlike quality — a fuzzy-edged flashback in a foreign movie — as he folded those terrible bloomers with almost reverent care, stuffed them up his sweater and exited on tiptoe. Refusing to believe it, I shut my eyes and cast off for another hour or two.

But when it came the effort of rising was as I had expected: mind turning. The geriatrics, or whoever, had neglected to remove my shoes and my feet and ankles were dead and swollen. I had a notion that if I removed them now I d find my toenails black and festering, so I didn't. Groaning upright, I felt accumulated liquid rushing to my bladder, which has always seemed to operate on a convenient gravity principle, precluding either bed-wetting or nocturnal rising even after a marathon on draught porter. But once started it couldn't wait; the short hobble from the bed to the adjoining bathroom seemed endless, the first spurt of orange-coloured stale a relief beyond words. I held my nose (whisky!) and moaned luxuriously. And from the bath along the wall to my right came an echoing moan...

The explanation of my next move is, I suppose, jaded nerves and mid-flow muzzle velocity. I swung to the right. In the bath, Steffers, in the act of jacking herself up on her elbows, took the full bore in the face and jerked to a sitting position, dripping, eyes closed tightly, hands flapping loosely at shoulder level, shrieking very loudly.

She kept saying 'Bastard, bastard...' as I helped her out of the bath — she had a pillow, a quilt and blankets in there — and assisted her to strip off her soaked sweater. She kept spluttering it as I poured water over her bent head at the wash-basin until I was forced to protest: 'You don't think I deliberately pissed on you — do you?'

She did, and explained why in detail. Later, sitting on the bed drying her hair, she kept up the abuse — while allowing me, incidentally, to dab other damp areas of her upper person with a small hanky — and now she tended to include Burton...

'What the hell had you in the bath anyway?' I asked.

'Your kinky friend Burton, that's what,' she snarled. 'You lying there snoring and him running around like a bloody mental case.'

Apparently it was she and the colonic irrigationist who had helped me to bed. She had then taken off her jeans and lain down beside me, falling to sleep almost at once. At about four o'clock she awoke, she swears, to find Burton craning over her. He had the bedclothes pulled back and was trying to thread her left foot down the leg of...

'Green and smelly, with elastic and hanky pocket?' I queried.

'Yes! But how...?'

I told her about my waking apparition and she went on to describe her struggle with Burton and eventual flight to the bathroom, there to lock the door until he departed, giving her a chance to nip out and fetch blankets and things in case he came back... 'I didn't close an eye till dawn broke,' she said bitterly, 'then I unlocked the door in case you took short. How the hell was I to know you'd rush straight in and pish on me!'

The grandfather clock on the landing struck eleven as we passed on our way to find breakfast. By this time we had come to a sort of truce — aided by a certain amount of coarse boisterousness on my part, to which she had responded sulkily but without hostility — and had tried unsuccessfully to rationalize Burton's bloomers. A fetish? — perhaps, but hardly the pick of the clothesline.

Breakfast was being served in what had been the Screw's recreation hall in Good Old Galwally; a large, bright room, here curtained in white chintz, carpeted in floral red and set out with small tables. Only three of these were occupied when we entered, two by lone geriatrics who chewed their cornflakes laboriously and lifted ghastly faces in greeting, the other by Toby, Burton and Chloe.

Toby beckoned us from behind the *Sunday Times* ('The Strange Affair of Mr — Smith') and we took our places at the adjoining table. Burton nodded briefly and, I thought, sheepishly, before taking cover again behind the *Telegraph* ('PM Silent on — Smythe Incident'). Chloe didn't bother to raise her eyes from the *People* ('We Know You, Mr Hyphen Smith!')

I had my breakfast consumed and was starting on Steffer's — she'd settled for orange juice and a fag — before anyone spoke. The man Toby called Fred, a broadbacked punter in a white bum-freezer who had dispensed drink throughout last night's binge, was clearing away the debris from Toby's table. I noticed now that Fred had most of an ear and two fingers missing and I was speculating on the nature of his industrial injury when Toby cried out, flourishing his paper triumphantly: 'Lo, Francie, is it not as I said it would be?'

'Looks like it,' I said; 'go to the top of the class.'

'Save your kudos,' he said, 'at least until after lunch, by which time you shall have had a short — I hope — lecture from "O" and been for a short walk in the woods. So get the face filling over as fast as you can, old son. I'll see you out front.' He ambled out to where I could see Meg, in jòdhpurs and shirt-sleeves, giving the 'cruel to be kind' treatment to a trio of beagles anchored by their leads to a sapling on the lawn.

It was a beautiful sunlit morning; the yelps of the dogs echoed like a woodman's axe in the stillness; a straight pipe-cleaner of white smoke stood up from behind the distant trees. I imagined the brickworks; the sparkle of the pennies as they birled off Punchy's fingers, the circle of silent faces turning upward, slit-eyed, and down as the pennies landed to howls of delight and execration. A sun-trap, the brickworks: lookouts drowsing over molten gun-barrels... I was homesick.

Presently, Burton pushed back his chair and said: 'We'd best get cracking, Francie; I want to be back in town by four.' And Chloe, casting aside the *Times Supplement*, followed up with: 'Stephanie darling, there's a delightful swimming hole down by the jetty and I have a spare bikini upstairs... No "buts", girl, as my old gym-mistress used to say; come along and leave these male chauvinists to play with one another.' She actually took hold of poor Steffers under the oxters and forced her, protesting, to her feet. I had a notion that Chloe would enjoy turfing her in the tide, and the water in these parts was notorious for its iciness even in mid-summer.

'Knickers,' I muttered in Burton's ear as we dandered out to meet Toby.

'Matron's,' he grinned disarmingly; 'another souvenir of the oul' *Alma Mater.*'

'They'd hardly fit under the fly-leaf of *Cecil Rhodes.*'

'Everyone gets *Cecil Rhodes*; and quite a few take scholarships to

Oxbridge. But only one each year gets what has become the prestige equivalent of the Sword at Sandhurst; a symbol, Francie, of heterosexuality asserted against all odds, practised in the very maw, nay, cheeks of Sodom. Remember Kipling — 'If you can dip your wick when all about you / Are punching turds or playing wanker's whist...'

Toby was sprawled in a deckchair, smoking a ridiculously long cheroot and watching his good lady at her work. Sweat sprayed from her brow as the riding crop rose and fell, forearm muscles writhing like snakes under the brown skin. As we approached Toby got up and joined us, calling out: 'Cheerio, dear heart; back for lunch.' Meg broke off for a moment to smile and growl deeply in reply (barring that first dramatic entrance I had yet to hear her speak, I realized, even when assaulting Toby in the small hours).

Burton led the way towards the track down which I had watched them disappear the previous afternoon and Toby again circled my shoulders with his comradely arm. 'Now for the final session of your week-end seminar, Francie,' he chuckled, giving my collarbone a hearty squeeze. I had bruises to show from his affectionate mauling of last evening, a habit of his which had tended to become more frequent and bearlike as his liquor level mounted. Luckily, it was a single-file track, in places almost overgrown with brambles, so he had to disengage and fall in behind me. Burton, blazing the trail, began the lecture immediately...

'Continuing on from yesterday, Francie, when we agreed that the way things were heading all roads lead to at least a decade of religious, political and military punch-ups. Right?... Fair enough. So the conclusion must be that Irishmen are totally incapable of governing themselves. Yet for centuries Irishmen have been going out and pioneering new territories in the four corners of the globe, the mass of them fitting comfortably into society, the few rising to positions of power and wealth, *i.e.* the six or so Scots-Irish Presidents of the United States, the industrial overlords of Canada, etcetera. Why is it then that the Irish emigrant flowers — in the second generation, anyway — into a model citizen and the Irish at home throw up generation after generation of homicidal corner-boys and political Mafioso? Racial inferiority — a collective memory of defeat and subjection — in the Papish breed? A siege mentality, a lack of national indentity, in the northern Prod? It doesn't really matter; the fact is that the Irish neither trust nor respect one another — as individuals, I mean. Only when they are dispersed and brought into contact with other races and cultures do they thrive constructively. So it follows that the greatest good one can do for the Irish is to help them get away from Ireland. Now the British have had some reasonable successes in this field over the years — transportation, starvation, etcetera; even now they bleed off something like 20,000 every year to do the jobs the English worker thinks himself too good for. But if this last economic safety valve is closed — as it almost certainly will be if the British are forced out of the North — and you Papishes go on rutting unsheathed at your present rate, in a short time the situation, you must admit, would be very sweaty gelly indeed.'

At this point he stopped and faced me to make a dramatic explosive gesture with splaying fingers and raised eyebrows — most of which was lost on me; being a city boy I'd been picking my way delicately along the rough track, eyes down, and almost ran him over. The undergrowth had thinned out as we got further away from the house and surmounted a small hill. We were now descending towards the distant sea (the estate, I realized, encompassed the whole of a U-shaped penisuala bounded by the coast road) and between us and it I could see a clutch of smoking chimneys above the foliage. A village?

Plodding on, Burton took up his theme... 'Have you ever heard, Francie, the solution to the Irish Question postulated, it is rumoured, by none other than the late Fuehrer, Adolf? No? Well, it's very simple and straightforward: a complete exchange of population between Ireland and Holland, in which event the Dutch, within a decade, would transform Ireland into an economically viable garden, and the Irish, having neglected the dikes, would perish to a man in the first high tide. As they say in soap circles, how does that grab you?'

'All right,' I said; 'except that last bit. The likes of O'Lig and the bhoys would never wait for a high tide and let an Act of God get away with a propaganda coup like that. A ton or two of gelly with British WD markings — supplied by me — a big boat for the Mafia elite and birds — also courtesy of me — and what's left of the Gaelic Nation would have a focal point of hatred good for another seven hundred years. On the profits of the gelly, the boat and other arrangements I would then join other Wild Geese of my kind in the south of France.'

'So much for poor Adolf,' laughed Toby; 'serve him right if he had got as far as Ireland.'

We came out of the trees at the edge of the 'village': eight ramshackle labourers' cottages, four on either side of what had been a street of sorts, broken kerbstones still visible through the layers of rubbish and undergrowth. Granite-slabbed dolls' houses with two tiny windows and a door and high slate roofs, they are as common throughout the country as the mansions they served. Here windows, doors and roofs were either missing entirely or in a bad state of repair. But smoke poured from every chimney.

'It looks like you might have fairies or hippies at the bottom of your garden,' I remarked, my voice echoing hollowly, for we were now between the first houses.

'Neither,' said Toby. And then he shouted something; an imperative something incomprehensible to me but very much in keeping with what happened next. Once, in my idealistic youth, crouched at the back of a police barracks with a gelly stick in one hand and a lit match in the other, I had heard the whistle and a clatter of boots approaching from both ends of the entry. It had been a moment of decision, a watershed; to light the fuse and go up in a puff of glory, taking a few of the black bastards with me as trade goods to the unknown, or... I had ended up lighting a cigarette presented by an extremely affable SB sergeant (RC), thus beginning a career in that other, always over-subscribed, sideline to the National Struggle... Standing in that derelict hamlet in the back of beyond and watching the response to Toby's summons, my feelings were comparable to those experienced in that dark entry long ago. Only the twice have I had to make a conscious muscular effort to control my bowels.

Black men — some nearly purple men — brown men, yellow men; with high wooly hair, with bald glistening scalps; some wearing turbans, some berets; some in khaki bush shirts, most naked to the waist; in trousers, shorts — a couple in flowered skirt things; all shouting and laughing toothily and brandishing short Chink assault rifles (the guerilla's friend) as they disgorged through the doors and windows of the cottages and ran down to form around us in a chattering, giggling circle. After a stunned moment I realized that I too was nodding and grinning madly, lips curling back on dry gums. Perhaps remembering Stewart Granger in *King Solomon's Mines* I tried to say, calmly, 'Steady men' — but my mouth was like sand — and looked round for a back to put mine to. Toby was busily shaking bundles of pale, waving fingers and gibbering away in strange tongues. And Burton, the bastard, catching sight of my face, flung an arm round the shoulders of one enormous savage and, pointing at me, howled: 'Rissoles à la long Irish pig! Better than beagle!'

To which the jovial cannibal replied: 'Be a mite stringy, mate.'

'Mate' rhymed with 'mite'. A Balubu for Bermondsey!

The next immediate occurrence again confirmed me in the opinion that life is best viewed as a scenario for an MGM movie — preferably of the forties/early fifties vintage. There was a sudden lull in the chatter and heads began to turn in one direction. Turning too, I saw a lane opening in the crowd, a respectful parting through which I half-expected an unspeakable something in mask and leopard-skins to come shuffling, rattling a bag of dry bones. What I was not prepared for was a complete departure from script in the form of a caricature of a City Gent, in black coat and striped trousers, waistcoat and gold watchchain, hard white collar and regimental-looking tie; the tallest, leanest, most black and negroid blackamoor I've seen either off or on a screen, balancing a curly-brimmed bowler over one ear and carrying a flywhisk and a BEA overnight bag.

'Hello chaps,' he greeted, flashing a gold-edged mouthful, halting in front of Toby and Burton and proceeding to lash the dust off his black dancing pumps with the whisk. 'Just off to the chopper pad. Anything I can fetch you from the Smoke?'

'Thoughtful of you, Bertie, but I think we're OK,' replied Toby in a way which gave one the impression that he wouldn't have dared impose even if down to his last match. And he liked saying 'Bertie'... 'By the way, Bertie, this is O'Toole the — er — fixer we talked about.'

Bertie turned the full blaze of gold on me. I dragged my right hand from its trouser pocket lair and had it half-roads extended before I realized that Bertie had no intention of touching me. Instead he threw me a sort of languid benediction with the flywhisk and drawled: 'Always nice to meet another of the Subject Races, Mr O'Toole. I hope you will see your way to assist our little endeavour.'

The chin-in stance of head and neck; the voice — a clipped, nasal Sandhurst; as seen strutting in Sam Browne and gold braid around the platform on Independence Day while glistening politicians lectured tribesmen on the two-party system; a year later — the politician in gaol, Switzerland or heaven — accepting the custody of the State until such times as it was ready for democracy...

'We'll do wur very best, Squire,' says I, 'if the loot's right.' I accompanied this with a brief salute, dipping my forehead to touch a rigid forefinger, a compromise between a Boy Scout's two fingers and the servile knuckles of a culchie ghillie. Bertie appeared to accept it all as his due, dismissing me with a most regal nod and turning away to say something to Toby ('Sound man, that'). But my Killarney jarvey bit had not been lost on Burton, who now seized my elbow and started steering me through and clear of the crowd, which tended anyway to drift along with Bertie and Toby as they moved off, I supposed, towards the 'chopper pad'.

'Acting the Mick,' said Burton, 'could well be mistaken for "taking" it, Francie, with tragic consequences for the actor. Though they giggle a lot, our black brethren are not noted for their sense of humour.'

'Ah shure, Mishter Burton yer honour, I could see right away he was one of the gintry.'

As we walked down between the houses Burton relaxed again and laughed: 'You mean you could see right away he was a prick. He is — but being a white-liberal-anarchist I cannot admit it. Black is Beautiful and Good, even if it is Royal, Wykehamist and Guardee.'

'Royal? Winchester? 1st Balubu — foot or camel?'

'Last of the Watutsi Royal House; fostered in forced exile by the Crown while Unilever and BP rape his hearthland; now bent on action that will lead to his triumphal return to claim his rightful heritage and rid his people of the Western Yoke. At least that's the tale according to his Royal Prickship. I think myself there's as much chance of the Watutsi seeing him again as there is of the Kennedys or Mayor Daly taking up residence in Ballyfermot or Ardoyne. From what I've heard of land-locked Watutsiland it does not abound with yacht clubs, racetracks or white upper-class whores.'

He had directed our steps towards one of the cottages on the edge of the clearing near the tree line: I followed him through the front entrance — rusted hinges on a rotting door jamb — which led directly into the largest of three apartments. Visibility was poor; the one pane-less opening in the far wall was curtained by an old spud sack or something, but I could make out half-a-dozen camp-beds strewn with haversacks and blankets and boots. No racial offence meant, but it did smell like the hospital cage in a zoo.

Burton went over to the door of the bedroom leading off the right-hand side of the room, a new-looking door of unpainted planks hung on shining hinges, barred and padlocked. He produced a key and beckoned: 'Come and see our toolroom.'

I could see nothing at first. Then he switched on an electric torch presumably kept there for the purpose. We stood close together in a tiny square formed by ceiling-high rows of boxes. I didn't have to enquire about their contents; the stench peculiar to fine oil and the foreign stencils on the cases were enough. Burton lifted a loose lid and trained the beam on as mouth-watering a sight as any punter could wish to lay eyes on: ten Chink assault rifles such as I'd seen the darkies brandishing outside, packed head to tail like sardines, gleaming oilily. A grand in one lift! The beam moved around, dwelling on markings — M1 carbine, Luger, Browning automatic, Sterling — finally coming to rest on a pile of four extremely large but unmarked crates. 'Wait'll you see these,' said Burton, hushed, lifting a lid. Mortars!... Three-inch, the sort of bicycle cannon the Viet Cong excelled in... 'and these...' Bazookas!

'Enough for a battalion,' I whistled.

'And plenty more where they came from,' he crowed; 'we're thinking divisions, Francie.'

Just then I was distracted by a familiar sound in the near vicinity, subdued but unmistakable... 'Pigeon on the Gate, Pigeon on the Gate...' and I remembered last night.

'Drums,' I said; 'that's what you were on about.'

'What!!' He had set the torch down to replace the lid on the mortars. He now swirled round and knocked it flying with an unmerciful clatter. Then he was pushing me towards the door and swearing hoarsely: 'For fuck's sake get out of here quick...'

Stumbling into the gloom of the outer apartment, puzzled, I heard the drum-beat clearly now and realized that it was not, as I had imagined, Lambegs being blattered a mile away, but small finger drums being tapped close at hand — probably inside the cottage, for the door of the room opposite the arms cache was slightly ajar. As Burton fiddled with the bolt and padlock I, driven by the curiosity that has been half my success in life, sidled over to this door. It moved as I approached. Black fingers curled round the edge and a pair of big white eyeballs, disembodied, swam in the darkness beyond...

'No Francie!' screamed Burton, and he had me by the arm in a sort of half-Nelson and was rushing me out the front door.

His strength amazed me; only when he had run me the length of the now deserted street did I manage to regain control and shake myself loose.

'What the bloody hell was all that about!' I gasped.

'Keep moving,' he commanded grimly, glancing nervously over his shoulder. 'You've seen enough anyway. I'll tell you when we get along the track a bit.'

A few minutes later we paused on the crest of the hill and looked down on the village. A sound of cheering gusted up on the slight inshore breeze; away to the right, on the seaward side of the village, we saw a helicopter rise out of the trees to hover deafeningly for a moment before veering away into the distance.

'His Royal turdship, I suppose?'

'The Jack Johnston of the Chelsea set, off to the fleshpots,' said Burton, fastidiously clearing a space for his white drills before sitting down and producing cigarettes. I did likewise, but with less care, and we lit up. 'That business at the cottage,' he went on: 'Simbas. Toby brought four back from the Congo. He keeps them in chains, but they sometimes manage to snatch a tit-bit through the door or window — that's how the beagles got theirs. They'd have picked you clean, Francie.'

'Merciful Christ! Imported cannibals! That's going a bit over the nail, isn't it? What's the idea, anyway?... A sort of after battle waste disposal unit?'

'A hair ghoulish for me, I must admit... However, the Simbas are a minor problem,' he said dismissively; 'Meg is quite capable of keeping them on a tight rein.'

'Meg!'

He grinned. 'I'd never have believed it myself if I hadn't seen it. They worship her. And do you know, they seem to understand her every grunt — and even Toby hasn't a word of their lingo.'

He glanced at his watch. 'But now, Francie, the Grand Plan and your part...'

'... which is worth how much?'

'Five hundred — cash — now, and a further two thousand if you deliver the goods promptly as specified.'

Taken aback by the forthrightness of his response and unable to dicker in the dark, I asked: 'What goods? You seem to have everything but tactical atomic weapons back there.'

'Every weapon presupposes a target, Francie; that's your pigeon. Now listen — from the top...'

For the next hour or so, at first sitting in the sunshine on the hill, then dandering back to the house, Burton outlined the caper. Four years ago I'd have listened through the first paragraph and then gone off quietly to fetch the large men in white coats. Since then I had watched the impossible, the unimaginable, happen almost daily — indeed, had had some hand in causing it to happen; I had learnt how easy it can be to manipulate events and people — small events compared to what he was projecting maybe, dozens of people to his thousands — but I had learnt enough to know that the methods were the same whatever the scale: blackmail, rumour, instant propaganda, superstition... A con is a con, is a con...

Baden-Jones would go in next Wednesday; that was now certain, thanks to the Hyphen Smith affair. For years Baden-Jones himself had been the darling of the black-hating lumpen proletariat, especially in the Midlands, because of his oft-stated and sole policy of 'repatriation'. Until recently the liberal establishment of his own party had considered him a bit of an embarrassment, a harebrained backwoodsman bent on rocking the boat. Then had come economic slump, two million unemployed, the consequential increase in racial tensions in mixed areas and, on top of all, the Troubles in Ireland; the latter providing Baden-Jones with another plank for his platform — 'Withdrawal'. 'Repatriation and Withdrawal' was now the rallying-cry: get rid of the blacks, stop pouring money, materials and troops into Ireland, and all Britain's problems, social and economic, would be solved. The party bosses began to think again about Baden-Jones.

Now this Baden-Jones was no mug. He knew the economic drawbacks attached to 'repatriation' — over and above the staggering logistics of actually doing it. All right now with two million on the dole; but when the see-saw tilted the other way — what then? Full employment; shortage of labour; a seller's market; galloping wage claims: the capitalist's nightmare!... Yet still determined to fulfill his promises to the herd and at the same time allay the fears in his own party, Baden-Jones had initiated an intrigue which would not only satisfy both, *i.e.* get shot of the blacks *and* fill the vacuum, but would settle the Irish Question once and for all.

That had been a year ago, as the slump gathered momentum and he saw his Moment approach. As a racialist, an advocate of Apartheid, he had always had good relations with his supposed political opponents in the coloured camp. They too loathed the thought of integration, which would rob them of their power-base in the ghettos; also, as the leaders of a permanent minority in the democratic system they foresaw a permanent frustration of their desire for power — and there was nothing minor about that. So, out of a series of secret consultations had come the outline of 'Operation Starkey': a plan for the 'resettlement' in Ireland of the dissident coloured population and its expeditious replacement by the displaced Irishry.

The first step had been the promotion of a siege mentality in the coloured population, the building-up of Baden-Jones as a bogey man, a campaign gauged to reach a hysterical zenith in the weeks prior to election day, when carefully scored outbreaks of violence would spark off a poor-white reaction at the polls in Baden-Jones's favour. Meanwhile, behind the scenes a military plan was being laid, ghosted by some high-ranking sympathisers in the War House, setting up structures of command, training and communications. To save funds arms had been conned from the Commies by giving the impression that it was to be an internal socialist uprising — on the day, B-J in power, weaponry would be no problem... 'By the most fantastic coincidence,' enthused Burton. 'A battalion of Gurkhas is taking part in the Edinburgh Tattoo that week! The officers and NCOs have been got at, so I should imagine —'

'Houl' hard, houl' hard,' I pleaded, head reeling. 'What week? Got at about what? Where? How?'

'Number one,' he said, thrusting a forefinger under my nose: 'next Wednesday — landslide for B-J. Two: outbreaks of violence in the northern ghettos rapidly spreading south, all carefully produced to look like impending civil war by sympathisers in the media who learnt their trade in Belfast and Derry — I understand rival mobs have already been rehearsed for camera angles. Three: massive, round-the-clock airlift of troops out of Ireland to cope, leaving only a skeleton garrison. Four: the prospect of uncurbed arson, rape and bloody murder in the six counties leads prominent right-wing Unionist to gather the remnants of oul' dacency around him and declare UDI — there's only four or five of them left after all that conscience-stricken hiving-off the last year or so and B-J has promised them villas in Spain and Swiss bank accounts. Five: B-J says that the time has come for the Irish to settle their own squabbles and announces total withdrawal but *stresses the continuation of dual citizenship for all the Irish*. Screams of delight from Vanessa Redgrave, Dingle Foot, John Lennon et al — Yoko wants to paint B-J's bum: screams of horror from Dublin, already bankrupt, at the thought of a million unleashed Orangemen coming their way; extra boats on the

Holyhead/Dun Laoghaire run to cope with fleeing Papists, the sea between pollouted with discarded Irish passports.'

Here he paused, having run through a handful of digits, to ask: 'Get the picture so far?'

'An ambitious production, right enough,' I granted. 'I hope you've everybody rehearsed as well as the rioters.'

'As far as is humanly possible,' he said, quite seriously. 'In Dublin, for instance, we've had agents in every department of government spreading gloom, despondency and rumour for months now. Of course, one can never be a hundred percent certain of a herd's reaction — especially if it's Irish! Be just like them to do a lemming the other way and throw themselves off the Cliffs of Moher... But it's not really this side we're concerned about — except, of course, that aspect of it which will be your pigeon, Francie. On the other side, under cover of the largely bogus happenings of the past week, a carefully planned exodus is already proceeding to schedule. In that time the populations of three holiday resorts on the west coast have trebled, and the Isle of Man has been invaded by a legion of Pakistani bag-men — bags, Francie, that clink... Stop here a moment.'

We were almost within sight of the Big House. Burton didn't sit down this time, but moved off the track and leant his back against a clean tree. Again it was he who produced the fags. 'I want to finish this without interruption,' he explained; 'it having to do with your part in the scheme of things.'

'Now that's just what I've been cudgelling my brains about: what in hell you imagine I can do that's worth two and half thou? Not that I don't want it, like — after listening to you my one inclination is to put the width of the Atlantic between my tripes and them Simbas, and a quid or two wouldn't go amiss.'

'Grand,' he said. 'Now listen —' preparing to chop the air into chunks '— who invented what they now call "Urban Guerilla Warfare"? The Irish, of course. "The Turrible Beauty", as you know well, Francie, was born out of ambush, back-shooting, ditch lynching and the rest, the sort of anonymous, spasmodic violence for which the National Character seems peculiarly suited. And it's deadly, Francie, when used against the disciplined rigidity of a uniformed foe on strange ground. The last time they faced the British as an army, in 1798, they dissolved in a drunken rabble after their first minor victory, celebrating the event by the wholesale murder of their fellow countrymen... But in 1920 they found their *métier*, and none since has bettered them at it. How many men, for instance, are holding down the 8,000 odd troops in the city now? You know, Francie — how many?'

'Say... a hundred at any given time. But I've known forty good'uns to have them standing on their heads —'

'Fantastic, isn't it! And we realize that we could cope no better than the present incumbents. So the answer must be to root out the canker before we plant — and that's where you come in... You've noted the lie of the land here?' His arm swept in the U-shape of the peninsula bounded by the coast road: 'Sea on three sides, and on the fourth, between the roads at the top of the U, impassable bogland. On a night approximately two weeks from now, landings will take place all around the peninsula; it is your job, Francie, to have assembled in this area on that night every sniper, bomber, booby-trapper and pogrom impresario in the city — from both sides, and from the splinters of both sides... O'Lig, Rarity, the Duncher —'

'— the Pope and the Archbishop of Canterbury!' I giggled. 'You're a right cod, Burton — might as well try to persuade bats to sunbathe. The motto of those punters is, "Where two or three are gathered together, draw a bead on the biggest". But go ahead, go ahead — I'd love to hear your suggestions on how to go about it.'

'Simple: as soon as the exact date is set you will be given two copies of a bogus communication, one addressed to, say, O'Lig, the other to, say, the Duncher, or whoever else is at the crest of the respective dunghills at that particular time. Both communications will bear the signature, *bona fide*, of our new PM. The contents of both will be the same — confirmation of a huge arms shipment, invoice attached listing everything from pistols to tanks, a gift from HMG in anticipation of certain economic concessions in the set-up of the New Ireland. confirmation too of the rumour which you will have been spreading thickly on both sides. O'Lig's letter you will, of course, show to the Duncher, and vice versa. The date and place of landing will be given. All depends on your ability to sell it both ways, of course; that's what the two and a half thou's for. Well, what do you think?'

As if I'd tell him!... Naturally, I intended to accept the initial five hundred quid; but after that, once back in the city, I'd play it by ear. After all, for a quick two thou wouldn't I be setting fire to my own profitable midden, cashing in my capital... 'What if I did manage it?' I asked. 'I take it you don't intend packing them off on world cruise?'

'Scruples! Surely not, Francie!'

'God no!... I just wanted to make sure it would be a one-way trip. Once they twig it'll be open season on me and mine. Rest assured there's not one of either lot I wouldn't pour sauce on for the Simbas.'

'Think of it, Francie,' he gloated, finishing his fag and taking off along the track towards the house; 'the pogrom merchants, the Bully Boys with their petrol bombs in the night, maybe the very ones who missed the pub that time and frittered the OAP in her bed. Eh? Or the heroes who got the three Jocks drunk and blew their brains out; or the ones who asked the seven-year-old "Is your Daddy in, love?" and emptied a Thompson into him while she held his hand... The kiddy killers, Francie —'

'— "Where wur yous'uns when we kilt five charweemen in the very heart of the enemy war-machine —" '

'— Them too with any luck. All there, in the dark, the Gurkhas coming in from the sea with their long knives and Bertie's mercenaries and Toby's Simbas closing the neck of the peninsula behind — nowhere to go, no ghetto to lose themselves in.'

He stopped again to face me, eyes bright with excitement, hands weaving and circling to crimp the beleaguered loutery. 'By the sounds of you,' I observed, 'I'd say you have little time for the Standard Bearers of our Two Traditions.'

He laughed and continued walking. 'I've been in a few hot spots around the world — with Toby,' he went on; 'but nowhere have I seen people take to mass murder with such relish as have my own kith and kin these past four years. Toby agrees. But he's a pro, y'see, in it for the loot; the same with Bertie — and you, Francie. Now I married enough loot to do me my time — and besides, I'm a romantic poet; things like retribution and revenge are the very breath of art to me.'

I'd heard everything now!... After gabbling away for a solid hour, methodically building his invisible bricks, he knocks them flying with one fell phrase!

' "Breath of art" you say,' I mused quietly as we emerged from the forestry and onto the cinders in front of the Big House: 'seems an expensive way of getting a few stanzas. Group therapy on a national scale — with you as the head-shrinker in the middle.'

'The Recording Eye, Francie... but well to one side, I assure you.'

I wished then that I'd let O'Driscoll finish him with the hobnails that time. I'd never fancied him much — in any of his guises — but I'd

70

never guessed he was off his loaf. A Jehovah nutter; using the wife's money to prime a small thunderbolt. Now more certain than ever that I would not participate in the caper beyond purloining the five hundred, I promised myself that on our return to the city an Impi of O'Lig's Simbas would be briefed to put the ultimate restraint on Burton without delay.

The house was deserted of all save Toby, who hailed us from the bar/lounge as we entered. He had three whiskies ready poured, which we gulped wordlessly, he and Burton exchanging meaningful glances over the rims of their glasses.

Burton said, 'Aghgh,' pleasurably, and then: 'we saw the black lord ascend. Everything OK?'

Toby frowned. 'Not too bad. But he's a completely mad bastard. After he'd taken off Majuba — y'know, the Senegalese with the scars — he tells me that Bertie staged another of his little happenings yesterday. His valet, apparently — some Paki from Stafford. Another couple like that before The Day could have a shocking effect on morale, so it might not be a bad thing if he gets stuck in some dolly for a week or so... These football stadium productions in Nigeria have turned his head, but you'd think he'd at least have the wit to wait until after his grand coup in Watutsiland, instead of practising with a length of flex and a plastic bucket at every opportunity.'

'Christ! Lynch-law in North Down!' I exclaimed. 'If he's as mad as all that you'd be better without him.'

'Public Execution, Francie,' corrected Toby: 'swords, epaulettes, drum rolls — even the bloody bucket is painted black. They have a flair for that sort of thing, don't you know. As for Bertie, at this stage the more bloody-minded nut-cases the better — but *experienced* bloody-minded nut-cases, mind you. Myself, I'd prefer a rope any day to one of those Swedish dum-dums your bloody-minded nut-cases will be using on The Day — always providing that they're here, of course.'

I answered the question promptly: 'They will be — in strength. Where's the five hundred?'

'Good man, Francie!' yelled Toby, grabbing my hand and pumping it. 'Here, let's have another round to celebrate.'

'Look,' wailed Burton, tapping his watch face, 'I want to be in town by four, so let's get the essentials — oh my Christ!...'

This last, accompanied by a distracted, head-squeezing gesture, was caused by a shrill of female laughter from the hallway — Steffers', amazingly. The remnants of the outburst were still on her face when she followed Chloe into the lounge, both looking windswept and vibrant. Chloe appeared to have pulled her tight silk dress over her wet body — a nerve-shattering sight...

'Hello chums,' she throbbed. 'Back from safari so soon. I'll have a large, undiluted gin.'

Steffers performed a Girl-Guidish hop and skip across the carpet to nestle up against me. There was a salty smell from her lank hair which, along with her face and neck, seemed to have lightened a shade or two since I'd last seen her. It gave me an uncomfortable, avuncular feeling I'd never experienced with the swarthy slag of yesterday — or for that matter, this morning. I had chilling visions of pigtails and gym-slips in the witness box at the Sessions as she gushed: '— the water was fab... and there was this smashing boat — Toby's — twenty-five foot, twin diesels. We went out for miles and this gorgeous black man let me take the wheel —'

'— I'll kick his gorgeous black arse!' roared Toby. 'Have you any idea, young woman, how much a one mile joy-ride in that yoke costs me?'

'Oh... let's see... Perkins diesels at half-revs... I'd say about two pounds, depending on the tide, of course.' She hammed it up in a horrible-Hollywood-child-actor-finger-sucking way, leaning against me and swinging a girlish leg. I wanted badly to kick the other from under her.

'Oho!' crooned Toby; 'what have we here? A bit of nautical nook no less.'

'I was brought up on boats. Daddy always has a couple on Strangford. We used to cross to France and go down the canals to the Med every summer.'

'Fantastic man, her Da,' I couldn't help adding; 'made a fortune selling coalbrick off a cart in the Holy Land —'

'— Oh for God's sake!' wailed Burton; 'we'll be waffling here this time tomorrow. Toby, will you —'

'OK, OK. Come along with me, Francie. Bring your drink if you like — in fact, I insist; you just might need it.' He and Burton traded another of their sneaky grins, making me wonder about that last enigmatic remark as I followed him out of the lounge. Behind me I was glad to hear Chloe drawl: 'Well, my little Knicker knocker, what's all the rush back to town?' and the beginning of Burton's oath-laden retort.

Toby led the way across the hall and down a short passageway alongside the staircase. He unlocked a.door and we entered what had been the Warden's Den in Good Old Galwally, here fitted out with a desk, armchairs and filing cabinets and called, I suppose, a 'study'. The walls, instead of regulation cream distemper, were oak-panelled — or so I thought at first glance. Then Toby went over to a point in the right-hand wall about mid-way between door and desk and, bending down, slid back one of the large panels at ground level. I won't say I realized then that the decor was bogus — a montage of stained chipboard and laths; I was too much taken with the thing Toby had uncovered... 'The end of the rainbow, old lad,' he grinned, hunkering down to shield his twiddling fingers from my prying eyes.

The safe was no dinky, behind-the-picture job; about two feet square, I reckoned; solid, combination and lever, set firmly flush in the thick wall. Toby has a broad back and in opening the door, extracting what he wanted and closing it again, he did his damnedest to conceal the Mother Lode from me. Had he been a hundred percent successful his efforts alone would have honed my curiosity: but he wasn't, making the mistake of rising to his feet before closing the door. The brief flash I caught between his legs was enough not only to negate all his previous efforts but also to satisfy me that they had been necessary.

'Half-a-thou,' he announced, throwing a bonded bundle of fivers on the desk: 'down payment.'

I reached (an inexcusable weakness), but Toby reached it before I did, covering it with one palm, his great hairy head thrust forward, suspended bison-like between stiffened arms. He had that little-red-eyed look I remembered from our clash over the fountain pen. 'A minute, Francie,' he said gently. 'You are still at liberty to say no and I'll put these back in the safe. No comebacks; we have enough on you to ensure your silence. But I must warn you now against having any thought of taking this and welshing on the contract. If when I lift my hand,' he went on, not without a touch of theatre, 'you take this five hundred, be absolutely certain, Francie, that you are bound — no matter what schemes to the contrary may be running through your devious little mind this minute. Understand?'

'Understood,' I said without hesitation, almost adding, 'Scout's Honour', while vowing inwardly not only to welsh but also, for his lip, to shop the entire meeting. They were doomed to failure anyway, if all their intelligence was like that relating to myself. Burton's fault, I supposed, for leading them to believe they were dealing with some sort of glorified cornerboy operating within reach of their Old Boy's network. Had they never heard of barricades, no-go areas, fortified ghettos? — inside any of which I would be as far from retribution, pseudo-legal or otherwise, as in the rain forests of the Congo... Toby lifted his hand and I pounced.

'Can't tell you how chuffed I am that you decided thus, Francie,' he said as I flicked through the bundle. He then lifted the handset of the telephone on the desk and dialled a single number. 'And now to square the hypotenuse or whatever the fuck they do with —' At this point he broke off to stare down the phone and gabble briefly. There was a moment's pause before he grunted and held out the handset to me... 'For you, Francie.'

It gave me the quare turn, I can tell you. By pure reflex my hand went out to take it from him. Who?... Baden-Jones? Toby surely wouldn't ring through to the lounge, a few yards down the passage; and the trio there were the only ones, besides God, who knew my whereabouts... As I put the thing to my ear the expression of barely restrained glee on Toby's face reminded me of the jokers in Good Old Galwally with their palmed frogs, turds and electric shocks.

Someone breathed heavily at the other end (Punchy!).

'Hullo,' I challenged.

'Who's that?' A woman's voice... sharp.

'Proinsias O'Toole here.'

A silence, a deep breath, then... screeching... 'Fuck you an' yer bog Latin, Francie Fallis, you stinkin' bastard! Sorry the day I ever laid eyes on you an' yer bloody schemin'... Where are ye? In some boozer or tart's bed, I'll bet, an' me stuck with six childer in the arsehole of nowhere... What in the name of Christ are ye up to? Was that concentration camp in culchie land not far enough for ye y' had to land us in friggin' Zululand or somethin'!... D'ye hear me, Francie?... this place is crawlin' with black heathens —'

Click.

Kate!

'Kate!' I yelled down the dead phone, shaking off the numbness induced, even in normal situations, by her vocal attack. Nothing: it had been cut at her end.

' "Someone, somewhere —" as they say,' Toby murmured from behind me; 'I hope you got the message, Francie.'

74

Suddenly enraged, I swirled on him, fists clenched — and found myself looking down the wrong end of my Japanese fountain pen. He held it, cocked, level with his right little-red-eye... 'Mustn't forget your wee doofer, Francie,' he said, the bastard.

At three-thirty precisely we re-crossed the bridge into home territory. I'm certain of the time now because, as though in salute, a distant blast went off just as we passed through the military checkpoint. If I could have foreseen then my involvement in the gruesome aftermath of that bang, I think I'd have forced Burton at penpoint to do an about-turn and sought sanctuary with the Duncher rather than face it.

At least it stopped Burton slabbering. Since our breathless departure from the Big House he had painted — and repeatedly re-touched — an idyllic picture of Kate and the kids in their beach bungalow on the estate, well away from the Simbas, tended hand and foot by a cook and two houseboys, the only blacks within two miles. The kids, he assured me, were having a grand time on the beach and were brown as berries; Kate was scoffing all put in front of her and steadily reading her way through the Condensed *Jalna* series, supplied by Meg.

My heart went out to them… the cook and the houseboys, I mean.

Of course I didn't tell Burton that last bit. From the moment I had rushed into the lounge and dashed the glass from his hand — likewise Steffers's — he had taken the attitude that he was dealing with someone 'Spurred by Grief', hence the lengthy and guilt-stricken reassurance. Far from it: my one thought had been to put as many furlongs between me and the townland containing Kate in the shortest time possible.

'And now, Francie,' Toby had ended this briefing, clipping my pen in my breast pocket, 'as a small bonus perhaps I could arrange an interview with your lady wife?' My reply — something like, 'You'll do no such fucking thing if you want my help' — and left him speechless; pondering, perhaps, on the value of his hostages.

He need not have worried: I now had no intention of welshing — but not because of Kate and the kids. Of course I'd never stand by and let them be harmed — if only because of a firm belief that the grave would prove no barrier to her venom — but in those last seconds in the Warden's Den with Toby something that had been niggling me since entering suddenly jelled. In Good Old Galwally there had been another door in that room, a door which led to a small storeroom containing such deterrents as truncheons, birches, straitjackets, boxing-gloves (for chronic nocturnal wankers), and the position of that door, unless I'd got my topography all wrong, had matched the position of Toby's apparently hard-set little strong-box. It made things begin to look a bit more... portable, somehow (if not blowable).

Burton stopped the car in front of the University halls of residence and I gave Steffers a dunt. She had fallen into her usual backseat coma almost before we'd cleared the Big House driveway (only then had I permitted Burton to mention Kate and the kids, for various reasons) and, as ususal, she awoke in a huff. I would have preferred it otherwise, now having a vested interest in keeping her sweet not unconnected with future plans concerning the Big House and Toby's honey-pot therein; but there is only one way of making a waking Steffers happy and that I was not prepared to do in broad daylight.

Completely out of character, I dismounted and held open the back door, grasping her elbow and guiding her away from the car, all the while making furtive faces and whispering: 'It'll be easier to give this chancer the slip if you get out here. There's big things afoot and I've a helluva lot to do. But I'll need to see you as soon as possible to-night. Can you make it to the chalet later?'

She nodded and I completed the de-huffing process — and forestalled an incipient question — by muttering: 'For God's sake make sure you're not tailed!'

So, leaving her in what Burton would term 'a state of conspiratorial euphoria' I rejoined him in the car. I hadn't a notion what I was going to do a helluva lot of — though he seemed to think he did... 'It might be best to work on the Duncher first,' he rambled as we sped westward through a fringe area of homely-looking dereliction: 'less volatile than O'Lig. The one thing we must avoid at all costs is a tendency to jump the gun. As soon as I get the fake memos I'll let you have them; that'll be the time to put the boot down.'

I didn't have to give him the slip after all. All the way he kept skellying at his watch, and as we approached the 'Peace' line which bounds the ghetto he asked if I'd mind being dropped there, confirming me in Chloe's opinion that he was homing on some piece of hair-pie with Matron's drawers tucked up his jersey.

Unhorsed once more, I strode out joyously on my native peat — literally peat, all the pavements having been torn up and flung at the

British army long since — in the general direction of the chalet.

The place seemed strangely deserted for the time of day. The first living thing I came across was roped to a lamp-post and coated with hardened tar and lumps of old mattress ticking. A placard around it's neck bore the traditional inscription 'Informer'; so where better, I thought, to learn the score.

He appeared to be asleep. When I hacked at his ankle and he raised a clabbered head to say, 'Fugg aff!' I recognised the malevolent eyes as belonging to one of O'Lig's twenty-year-old Lieutenant-Generals.

I gave him a drag at my fag and inquired: 'What have you been up to? Singing off-key?'

'You'll laugh on the other side of yer bake some of these days, Francie Fallis,' he girned ungratefully, 'you an' that fat fugger O'Lig. Ma hair'll niver grow again an' all because that pig's arse wanted a patsy for a shortage in last week's collection . Wait'll —'

'— Any more of yer oul' buck and I'll start picking the tar off you now,' I threatened; 'or better still, I'll tell the first Para patrol I meet and they'll be round with a blowlamp to clean you up sharpish. So just tell me where everybody is and I,ll leave you in peace.'

'Didn't you hear that big blow awhile back? Deef if you didn't. Well that's where they all are... helpin' the morgue men scrape five fellas off a wall — it went up in the car... Here... Hi... look... Francie,' he cried out as I turned to go; 'do us a favour —'

'Before you start, mate, it's more than my neck's worth to cut them ropes —'

'— No, nothin' like that,' he assured me. 'Look, d'you see thon bastard of a dog slinkin' up this way —?' I did; a patchy looking, corgi-type survivor, sniffing its way towards us along the gutter... 'I've been here since four this mornin' an' that ghett's been roun' ivery half-hour on the dot to piss up agin me! Would y'ever wait till he gits this length an' hit him a good dunder up the balls, Francie?'

Request granted — evoking barely distinguishable howls of agony and delight from pisser and pissed-on — I moved off.

Passing the chapel I noted with approval that, splattered patriots or no, O'Driscoll's verger was still at his work, shepherding a Protestant-looking gent into the school yard to select his car from the dozen or so parked discreetly in the white-lined bays reserved for the teaching staff (all of whom had been languishing in Long Kesh since the day the lavatory ceiling had collapsed on Sergeant McNinch's head under the weight of secreted ammo). O'Driscoll himself had started the service in a spurt of ecumenical fervour when the flogged car ramp had been at its height in the first days of barricades and no-go — though he now denied all knowledge of it. In that era of jubilant anarchy the lads would whip a car from across the river and drive it back to the ghetto, there to joyride with impunity until the petrol ran out, all without thought of profit. The car would then either be set alight or added to a barricade; and this O'Driscoll considered a sinful waste. So, unofficially, he had organized the whippers. After they'd 'made their protest', which is the 'in' term for joy-riding, they would drive, or push, the car to the school yard and receive a small payment from the verger, who would then circulate the car's number across the river via the underground and await the arrival of the grateful owner to claim his property — grateful to the tune of as much as twenty-five quid, depending on make and year of registration, so I've heard. Certainly it had gone some way to compensate the parish for the fall-off in attendance at Bingo because of the troubles. It also had the blessing of Sergeant McNinch and his merry men who, although not daring to lay a hand on car or culprit within the ghetto for fear of having Lord Brockway and the Gay Liberation Front on the next plane from London, still had to balance a crime sheet bloated by the joyriders. This they did by means of a side arrangement with the verger whereby he removed the tax disc from each repossession and informed McNinch of registration number and e.t.a before the owner set off to re-cross the bridge, thus giving time for the laying of an ambush on the other side and the preparation of a summons for not displaying a Road Fund Licence. And thus each theft was balanced by a conviction.

I dwell on it because it is one of the very few profitable capers I never managed to get a finger in — a state of affairs that hitherto had rankled badly. Now, with Toby and Burton and the big game still fresh in my mind, it all seemed like diving for so much ha'pence in a swill bucket.

I found the Cavan man shuttered, barred and bolted, an extraordinary situation for a Sunday (the Calvinist licensing laws had been the first thing to go and to appear to be keeping them was an invitation to an illuminated address). I hurled lumps of pavers at the mauve-coloured upper shuttering until the bald and blotchy head of the man himself appeared... 'Fer frigsake Francie! Ye putt the heart crosswise in me! We've had a turrible time, a turrible time... Wait'll I open up...'

Sporting the regalia of his particular Masonic, a wide-sleeved blue silk kimono with embroidered dragons, he flung open the door and pawed me inside frantically, for all the world like the central figure in a points Peeler's nightmare. After a thorough bit of slamming and barring he followed me into the snug and shoved Jeremy the renegade medic and Dominic the barman upstairs, both giggling wildly. Trembling, he splashed me a mammoth Powers. 'God, Francie, tongue can't tell what I've gone through these past two days! I've met some bold boys in my time but never the likes...'

He'd been raided, looted and cuckolded by an assault platoon of Lifeguards. He'd been bursting to tell somebody, poor lonely bugger (whoops! as Chloe would say) and was well into an eye-rolling, wrist-flapping description of his trials at the hands of the kinky khaki hun before I could get my spoke in...

'Before I forget — did Punchy ring?' I enquired at what seemed a natural break in his (unnatural!) narrative, not wishing to offend him too much.

'Yes... he left a number. I wrote it down somewhere... aye, here it is Well here dear, Francie, what d'ya think, the next thing I sees —'

'— Houl' hard a minute till I give him a ring — in case it's anything urgent.'

'Oh well... please yerself.'

He flounced off muttering and I got on the blower to Punchy, who was, if anything, in a more 'turrible' state... 'Jeezus! Am I glad to hear your voice! This Rarity job has me near roun' the twist. I'll hafta come roun' an' see you rightaway. Can't stan' the sight of a phone these days let alone talk into one —'

I arranged to meet him in the chalet in ten minutes time and managed to sneak out with a bottle of buckshee Powers ('Never let the sun set') while the Cavan man still bickered in his harem above.

I'll not say that Punchy looked haggard — that Chicago darky long ago had fixed his expression once and for all — but he sounded it. And he was drinking whisky, always a bad sign with him.

As I progressed round the chalet, clearing pathways through debris left by week-end squatters — including a nest of heretical rubber goods on the bedroom floor — he followed me, jabbering... '— It's not him — he's a sucker for it — shits hesself ivery time — offers me hunners of pouns an' a steady job on his bodyguard. But hur! — oh my Christ, Francie, that woman's far from right! I've niver spoke one word to her

— all I do is breathe an' she goes off like a handbell! An' the things she comes off with!... Yid niver believe it. Them WAAFs durin' the war was bad enough — but they were only jokin'. This one's dead serious. She says Rarity's no good till her — all she has to do is give him a flash an' he decorates the ceilin'. Some oul' goat of a Priest up in that posh school gave her a rub of the relic an' she says she's niver overed it... I'm tellin' you, Francie, I'm shit scared of her doin' herself damage. You've niver heard the like of the way she gits on. She says...'

What she said was for the most part physically impossible; yet it was imaginative, testifying to a thwarted creativity that in other circles would have merited a by-line in a posh Sunday and a place in the front rank of literary bawdy-dom. What appalled Punchy — a survivor of a time when sex had been merely one point in the Devil's triangle, the others being Drink and Gambling — amused me.

'You can laugh!' he moaned; 'but it's hard to listen to stuff like that — especially in a phone box with a queue of oul' dolls glarin' in an' you tryin' to look as if yer gittin' the hard word about yer nearest and dearest from the emergency ward. I'm tellin' ye, Francie, we'll hafta pack it or I'll not be responsible for that one's actions.'

I could see he was in no mood for levity. Also, he was brandishing our big breadknife, with which, plus a half-a-loaf, a slab of marg, and a pot of raspberry jam, he was assisting me to prepare our Olde Englishe High Tea. I thought it prudent to provoke no further.

'Rest easy, Punchy,' says I, setting down a pot of black tea and shaking the fag-ends out of two beakers; 'we no longer need to run O'Lig's errands. Rarity will be the furthest thing from his mind after I've filled his ear with a thing or two. We, Punchy, are onto the killing of a lifetime — and here's something to prove it —' So saying, I produced and flourished the hundred fivers in front of his one visible eye. Peeling off four, I tucked them behind the razor in his waistcoat pocket... 'So sup up yer tay like a good lad and listen —'

I gave him the general outline of Operation Starkey — meaning I told him only what was needed to ensure his efficient co-operation while leaving out such spine-draining items as the Simbas, Kate, etc. In particular I briefed him on the two-way rumour-mongering campaign, suggesting that he handle the O'Lig end while I concentrated on the more subtle approach to the Duncher. Whatever it was, the relief of being rid of the Rarity account or the sight of the fivers, I've seldom seen him so enthusiastic about anything.

81

'Just to get shot of this madhouse for a wee while would be like win-nin' the sweep,' says he, stuffing lumps of bread and jam, apparently, up his nose. 'Did you hear about that big blow the day?'

'Aye; five of them. Whose were they and who were they?'

'Mickey Close, Slack McGuigan, Silver Roche, Barney Moore, Liam Conaty; a fifty-pounder —boomf — in the back seat; spaghetti. Then to make it worse them lazy bastards of morgue men start offerin' the kids a tanner a time for gatherin' the bits! — an' you know what the kids roun' that quarter are like... I heard tell O'Driscoll had give the rites to six-bobs worth of skinned cats before he caught on.'

Poor Mickey. I wondered if he'd been wearing his velvet slacks... More to the point, I also wondered if my sub-contractor had managed to relieve Slack of the French TV proceeds before his fragmentation.

The fifty-pounder, it appeared, had been meant for the off-licence premises of one Bo McGookin, who had fallen badly behind in his sub-scriptions to the Marrowbone Liberation Front (Mickey, Slack, two wives and a total of twenty-five childer). On reaching the target Mickey had gone in to have a scout round before planting the stuff; and, lo, should be standing at the counter but Sergeant McNinch and one of his underlings, having a free wet while Mr McGookin made out his cheque to the police Social and Athletic Club. At the sight of Mickey both drew and emptied their Walthers, blowing Mr McGookin's front door to shreds but not touching Mickey, who had taken off like a hare for the car. Slack had put the boot down, but they'd covered barely a hundred yards before it blew... They'd been mates since boyhood, Mickey and Slack; through every vicissitude — Approved School, Burroo School, Borstal and gaol — they'd been inseparable; it was somehow appro-priate that they should end up sharing the same plastic bag...

'If it was as bad as all that, how can they be sure how many was in the car?' I wondered aloud.

'Easy,' said Punchy; 'they picked up five guns. An' anyway, the five of them were seen drinkin' in the United Club this mornin'.'

Other grisly details of the event, too boke-making to relate here, came forth as we finished our tea and lashed into the Powers. I also remember discussing the toss school, the collection for the Internees Book Club, a fresh attempt on O'Lig's life that had cost a reporter from *Izvestiya* his right ear (Tully!) — and then I must have dozed off.

I awoke because Punchy seemed bent on dislocating my shoulder. Someone was trying to leave footprints on the front door.

'It's Duncher's wee fellas,' whispered Punchy. 'I forgot to tell ye, they were roun' askin' after you yesterday. What'll we do?'

It was eight o'clock and still daylight. Might as well start earning some of the five hundred now, I thought.

'I'll go and see him. You stick around here until that bird I was with in the Prince comes over. Tell her I'll not be long — with any luck.'

'He —' they began to howl in unison when I opened the door.

'— Lead on!' I screamed.

'— Enveloped, friends, in the red velvet pantaloons of the great hermaphrodite that squats on seven hills! Never! Never, I say, please God, while there's men willin' to lay down their lives —'

And so on... The Duncher was in grand form; spotlighted, looming over the high lectern, arms held aloft, to launch a spray of spittle on the flowered hats of the ladies in the front row. From where I stood between my escort at the back of the huge Nissen hut, it looked like an angry vulture tethered unwillingly to a perch.

'Hallylulyah!'

'UDI!'

'FTP!'

It had been raining for some time outside, and the congregation of two hundred odd, mostly burly women, reeked like a mob of wet sheep with bladder trouble. On either side of me and along the walls lounged the dungareed forms of Duncher's youthful Mohawks, shoulder-length hair braided back with tartan bands, holstered revolvers tied down à la John Wayne (all licensed to the 'Island Small Arms Society'), ornamental spurs jingling on the high heels of their motor-bike boots. My scalp shifted nervously as I noted the wisps of human hair adorning the jacket of one acned bandit and heard the throaty baying of the old Biddys in response to the Duncher. I began to wonder, seriously, if he had decided to round off his act with the ultimate catharsis — human sacrifice! Was I destined to be the first Pope-substitute?...

The atmosphere was of a camp-meeting on the American western frontier, circa 1870 — directed by John Ford. The Duncher himself, in three-quarter, broadcloth coat and black string tie, bore more than a passing resemblance to Ward Bond in *The Searchers* and tended in his quieter passages to lapse into a folksy Texan drawl. The air was thick with cigarette smoke, and quite a few of the congregation seemed to be in an advanced state of intoxication — falling-down drunk as distinct from the religious *tremens* evident in the behaviour of some of the ladies... All in all a state of affairs that would have been unthinkable in this or any other tabernacle of the Lord three years ago — before, that

84

is, Big Tex DeWinter and his Sagebrush Songsters had passed through
on their World Wide Testimony Circuit.

Burton had said something about 'A lack of National Identity in the
Prod faction'. Whether Big Tex had become aware of this cultural
vacuum and strove consciously to fill it is hard to say; but it's doubtful.
In late middle age, after a lifetime of rodeo roughriding, Tex had taken
to the Gospel Road in much the same way as a boxer takes to
pub-keeping or crime — another branch of showbiz. Almost overnight
— and a very alcoholic night it had been — he had rocketed to fame as
a sort of Hemingway of the Bible Belt, a muscular man of God who did
not eschew even four-letter words in his spirited denunciations of the
Prince of Darkness. ('That fuggin' son-of-a-bitch' had been the exact
phrase.) The Prince himself he visualised as the wild Brahman bull whose
horns had put an end to his rodeo career, and his vivid description of
their struggle, with a slow country accompaniment by the Sagebrush
Songsters, had been topping the charts in the Southern states long
before he crossed the Atlantic.

From the moment he mounted the platform in his big tent on the
opening night of his Mammoth Crusade, the effect this loud ten-gallon
person had on the ascetic Duncher was electrifying. Obviously already
drunk, Tex had started off by taking a long slug from a silver hip-flask;
then, striking a match on the side of the lectern, he'd set fire to a long
black cheroot; a hush-making performance which culminated in a great
collective sigh of disapproval from the ladies, many of whom got up and
headed for the exits with husbands and childer in tow — the cue for
Tex's well rehearsed opening...

'Friends, the first thing you all'll learn about Big Tex DeWinter is
that he don't hedge his bets. Yeah, that's right, Ma'am, I'm sure as hell
partial to a hand of poker — and a coupla other things that'ud burn
yore purty ears! Yessir, when ole Tex is called up to that there big corral
in the sky an' the tallyman in the frilly nightshirt starts cryin' about
them gallons of booze, them millions of seegars, an' all them cathouse
poker schools... waal, ole Tex here'll jest say, real friendly-like, "Jest you
open thet fuggin' gate, Mac — for every shot, seegar an' whore has
been paid for in full by the glorious blood of —"'

'— Jeez-us Churr-ist!' chorused the Sagebrush Songsters with a crash
of banjos and a flash of spangled thigh from the Joygirls.

It was a fine point in theology that had long troubled the Duncher.
In the ten years since he had been Born Again he too had had his daily

tussles with the black Brahman. In his personal testimony — *Soldier For The Lord*, issued by the Protestant Truth Society in tract form — he tells of having done in sixty fags and two bottles a day when available; and the transcript of the court martial which terminated his reign as Quartermaster Sergeant in the Rifle's depot (I once bought a peek at it with a view to putting the bite on him) gives a very full account of his depredations not only at the gargle and puff but also among certain young females on the NAAFI staff. But since re-birth, according to the tract, he seems to have reckoned his chances of salvation on a sort of points system, awarding himself so many for each untouched dram, forsaken fag and, I suppose, unmolested bint. Then — revelation! — along comes Tex with the message that self-denial did nothing but point to a lack of that great spiritual antibiotic, Faith — and who was Duncher to argue with a dollar millionaire!

That very night, at the after-the-show party in Tex's hotel suite, Duncher had celebrated his conversion to butch Christianity with a bottle of Tex's bourbon, twenty Wild Woodbine and a brace of Joygirls.

More to the point, it had marked the emergence of Duncher as a major political force. Until then he and his wee boys had been handicapped in the to and fro of the Irish Struggle by what is best described as 'guilt-overload'. OK, they'd burn a chapel or pick off one or two here and there — but they hadn't the staying power or the heart for the big media-drawing spectaculars their opponents excelled in; whereas Mickey or Slack or any of the boys could plant a fifty-pounder in the Protestant Orphans Home, off-load it into O'Driscoll's lug, say fifty Hail Marys and be planning another for the Cripples Institute half-an-hour later, the worst of Duncher's litter had tended to start looking over their shoulders after dum-dumming a mere couple of stray Sodality men... Big Tex had changed all that; the most heinous action taken against the international commie-pape-nigrah axis, he assured, would have the full blessing of the Big Strawboss in the sky...

'— Smite them, Brethren!... Hip and thigh!' thundered the Duncher. 'In the spirit of our forefathers at Aughrim an' Derry; in the spirit of the great men of our hardy stock that tamed the red cannibal in the backwoods of America; in the spirit, friends, of the Protestant pioneers of Rhodesia that are this very day defying the Bolshevik stooges in Whitehall — smite them! hip and thigh!'

'Hallaylulyah!'

'UDI!'

86

'Fuggapope!'

Throughout the ovation Duncher repeated his last stanza four or five times in descending octaves, preparatory to entering one of his quiet patches... 'Hip — and — thigh...'

Then, raising a hand for silence, he swung round and indicated a member of the platform party seated in the shadows beyond the spotlight. 'We have been priviliged to-night to hear the testimony of this young lady,' he drawled, and the spotlight inched back to illuminate the calves, thighs, hips, gross bosoms and, finally the smirking face of Teesy Hagan! In a little black dress! Her hair in a bun! 'Is there a man among yis,' screamed the Duncher, retrieving the spot, 'whose gorge didn't rise when he heard of her treatment at the hands of the so-called celibate men of Rome? Who now can doubt the revelations of Maria Monk? Are there words vile enough to describe a so-called Priest of God who would defile his own confessional in such a bestial way —?'

Contortionist?

The thought of O'Driscoll taking off through the hatch after Teesy caused me to snort convulsively. The adjacent apache with the scalp locks turned to grind his teeth in my direction while fondling the hilt of the Bowie knife which protruded from his boot top (ominously, he didn't have to bend or even lean sideways to do so — a real swinger, that one, tree-style). An opportune moment indeed for my midget minders to nudge and beckon me to follow, which I did gladly, along the back of the hall and through into the small annexe where I usually conducted my business with the Duncher, the din of whose approaching orgasm rang in my ears.

In the annexe there were two chairs, a table and a painting of Queen Victoria battering a cringing blackamoor with a Bible. Presently, the Duncher himself came bursting through the door, steaming like a spent horse, and was handed a lit Woodbine by one of my minders. Behind him came Teesy and a crescendo of 'Hallylulyahs!', 'Amen's,' 'FTP!s' and stamping of hobnailed boots. The door closed and he stood glaring at me while the other midget helped him out of his preaching coat. The towering presence at the lectern — an illusion created by a foot-high stool behind and judicious lighting before — might impress the gormless groundling: for myself, just to be in the same room with the five-foot-four-inch reality was bowel-moving enough...

I thought to ease the tension with a quip: 'Sounds like they want an encore, Duncher — or should I say "Second Coming"?'

'Shut yer puggin' face!' he reparteed grimly, fag wagging in the centre of his functional little rat-trap, both hands shaking sweat from his ridiculously plentiful hair. In the middle of his rudimentary forehead gleamed a vivid crescent-shaped scar, said to have been made by the teeth of a six-foot-three-inch Head Constable, no less, in his athletic youth. (From a standing position, without so much as bending a knee, the legend goes, he had leapt upward to demolish the Peeler's entire upper bridgework with a sharp dunt of his hard little nut — hence the nickname.) Otherwise he was indistinguishable from the herd of 'wee huns' he led — except when one knew, as I did, what he was capable of doing to those who hindered the Lord's Work.

'Where wur you since Friday? The boys've bin scourin' the place.'

'In the country,' I replied promptly — in this company circumlocution could lead to sudden violence; 'uncovering a plot which I think you should know about —'

'It'll keep for the minnit,' he said testily. 'I got you here to assist in a very personal matter. It wasn't my idea, I can tell ye, after some of the funny tricks you've bin pullin' lately, but Miss Hagan here seems to think you're the man for the job, an' what she says goes. The fact is that hur an' me's gittin' married next week and she feels that some personal contact should be made with hur Ma an' Da before the event.'

Flummoxed, I looked past him to where Miss Hagan had slumped carelessly in the other chair, her vast thighs making a nonsense of the little black dress. I'd been trying hard to avoid her gaze; now she raised it, wide-eyed, to the ceiling in an expression of despair, following up with an obscene gesture directed at the Duncher's back. I got the impression that it wasn't exactly a love match.

'But Duncher,' says I, 'I didn't know you'd got a divorce, and you know that a good Catholic like Miss Hagan —'

'Not that it's any of your fuggin' business like,' he retorted, accompanying each vowel with a forward pecking movement of his lethal skull, 'but Miss Hagan has embraced the Lord Jesus Christ as her personal Saviour and has jacked in the pagan conspiracy of Rome for good an' all. Haven't ye, hen?' Teesy, caught in the middle of another face-making session, this time incorporating fingers, somehow managed to convert it into a nod and simper as he whirled round on her. 'There y'are—'

'Houl' hard, Duncher, houl' hard,' I pleaded. 'I don't want you to think I'm being nebby, but I have to get things straight if I'm to do anything, haven't I? For instance — you say you're getting married next week, yet the last time I was here — and that's not two months ago — your wife and about three grown-up childer were messing about making the tea. Now I don't know a helluva lot about divorce, but I'm certain even you couldn't get one through that fast!'

He had been nodding and grimacing throughout in a smug 'say yer piece' way. 'Oh you're one rale smart Mick, you are,' he sneered. He then took the breath from me by darting forward and starting to poke me in the chest, his scarred forehead dodging and weaving scarcely an inch from my teeth... '— Well, smart fella, just you go roun' an' ask that woman you're talkin' about for her marriage certificate, or any of them ungrateful ghetts for their birthlines!' His voice rose to a screech: 'We were married by the Lord an' him alone, in a Gospel tent on the Bog Meadows, an' she divorced herself from Him an' me when she refused to follow me in the path of Christ Militant!... An' now the Lord in his bountiful goodness has seen fit till reward me with this tender soul, plucked from the jaws of eternal damnation, as he did the Patri-arches in the Old Testament...'

He'd always been dotty, but no more so than ninety percent of people who get their names in the papers regularly: now, I could see, he was over the wall completely. Ordinarily, I couldn't have cared less — would, in fact, have had some hand in promoting a nice little Holy War centring on Teesy's 'abduction' with a view to increased consumption in the ammo sector; but just now, with a bigger fish in the pan, was a bad time for the Duncher to go all cuntstruck.

I decided on shock therapy...

'Well, if that's the case, Duncher, you're a free agent and the best of luck to you both,' I said sincerely, getting up and snatching one of his hands out of the air to shake it heartily. I continued, lugubriously: 'But take my advice and don't you wait till next week. The way things are going who can tell where any of us'll be by then. If I were you I'd forget about everything bar the wedding — do it the morrow if possible, and fuck O'Lig, O'Driscoll, the British and the whole fucking litter —'

It got to him... 'Watch yer lingo in front of the lil lady,' he snarled courteously, wrenching his hand free and wiping it on the arse of his trousers. 'What's all this about O'Lig an' the British? If yer on yer geg I'll gut ye —'

'Sure that's what I was coming to tell you about...' I gave him a brisk resume of the Hyphen Smith affair, the election, black unrest and imminent withdrawal, finishing off with tit-bits from the manifest of weaponry to be handed over to O'Lig. Carried away, I nearly bollixed it all by throwing in a few helicopters and gun-ships...

'Och in the name of Christ! Somebody's pullin' yer leg!' howled Duncher. 'What would O'Lig do with helicopters? Who in that load of jailbait could —'

'Priests,' I adlibbed; 'young mission Priests who have been working hand-in-glove with the Commies in South America. There's half-a-dozen doing courses with the RAF this minute. I know it's hard to believe, Duncher, but they've done it before remember — in 1923 they armed Free Staters to murder their own mates... and forby the manifests, I've seen a copy of a letter from no less a person than the man who'll be in Number Ten next Thursday, addressed to O'Lig confirming their agreement. Now I don't expect you to take my say so — this is just a preliminary warning — but I have it on good authority that very soon after next Wednesday's result there'll be another message in the pipeline between Number Ten and the Golden Calf, and I have arranged to intercept it if at all possible. It should give details of delivery and suchlike.'

Duncher had retreated across the room and was standing behind Teesy's chair, his hands kneading the puppy fat on her upper arms, his chin touching the crown of her head. She made horrific, appealing faces at me. He glowered.

'I'm not callin' ye a liar, like,' he said, almost absentmindedly, 'but I'll wait and see the letter... It wouldn't surprise me at all. It's all been foretold in the Book — somewhere...' His voice began to rise and the tempo of his kneading fingers increased, as though Teesy was some sort of malleable lectern. 'A Commie-Tory-Papish conspiracy agin people whose only crime is loyalty! If it's true I'll have every man jack in the streets in an hour an' once an' for all we'll raze that ecclesiastical kip-house to the groun'! All the airborne Sodomites in the world — even oul' red-socks hisself on his magic carpet'll not stop us...'

As he raved on I realized I was going to have a problem. The ecclesiastical kip-house he referred to was the Retreat House of the Little Flower, a walled mansion which now stood alone in the centre of a small plain close by the river and gave shelter to no more than a dozen senile nuns. Two years ago the plain had supported a chapel, three pubs, two bookies, a repository and four streets of houses: all of which, in one week-end, Duncher's wee boys had sculpted away to reveal the austere lines of the Retreat House for the first time in a hundred years. They'd have pulled it down too but for the timely arrival of a Scottish regiment which had in its ranks a fair proportion of Glasgow Celtic supporters. Since then the House, guarded night and day by a crack company, had weathered many sieges; and its inhabitants, lissom houris who gladly gratified the troops' every wish (according to Prod myth), had taken on a symbolism inversely akin to that of Gibraltar's Barbary apes; governments may fall, political careers crumble, the great United Nations itself tremble at the complexity of the Irish situation: for Duncher and his wee boys the straight road to a Prod Utopia lay over the rubble of the Little Flower.

An ideal solution, I mused, would be to move the Little Flower brick by brick down to the peninsula. But I decided not to chance even a hint of time or place; time enough when Burton's fake memo materialized —

'Yer not listenin' to one bloody word I'm sayin'!...'

His contorted face was only a foot from mine; I realized with a shock that I'd been half-dozing. Teesy was stroking her mangled arms tearfully.

'God I'm sorry, Duncher,' says I. 'I've had a terrible rough week-end. I could sleep on a razor.'

'Any other time I'd give you a hunnerd Aspros myself an' put you till bed,' he growled, 'but as I toul' ye in the first place you've got a job to do for Miss Hagan here. That hen's yarn about O'Lig an' the British has changed nothin' as far as hur an' me's concerned — an' you'll hafta show me chapter an' verse afore I take the word of a Papish about a thing like that. Miss Hagan has wrote a wee note to her Ma an' Da an' she wants you till take it. I wanted to post it, but she reckons that you bein' a friend of the family an' all it'll set their minds at rest a bit better.'

He handed me a brown envelope on which was inscribed 'Mommy and Doddy' in Teesy's fourth form scrawl (the year the nuns had dragged her, naked, from under a visiting school dentist and washed their hands of her). As he did so I glanced over his shoulder. She was nodding frantically, saucer-eyed, her lips pursed as though for whistling.

'Right you are, Duncher,' I said, rising to my feet; 'I'll go round and see them tomorrow. And when I get confirmation of the other thing I'll be back like a shot to accept your cringing apology —'

'Ah fer Crissake!' he roared, waving the midgets forward; 'take him away outa my sight an' lave him in whatever kip you found him! I 'clare t'God you daren't treat one of them half human but he starts flingin' big words at ye. Ivery bloody tinker in the country talkin' like a dictionary! It's all the fault of them so-called "Christian" Brothers — crammin' ivery wine-victim in the country for the Civil Service. Makes you wonder where it's all gon'ta end...'

As you may have gathered, his mind was elsewhere. About to follow my escort through the door, I looked back to see him heading for Teesy — literally heading, pecking, as if he intended battering her to submission with his frontal lobes. She, meanwhile, had settled back in the chair, big legs strewn everywhere, wearing an expression I had seen many times before, that look of shy resignation that had fooled many a triumphant pederast into thinking he was on the threshold of some sort of victory — until, that is, he was clutched inextricably to that giant bosom and her sharp little heels had begun their joyous tattoo on his kidneys.

It was near midnight when the midgets dropped me off at the chalet (I remember because they asked me for the next day's password in case they were stopped by O'Lig's nighthawks. '"Sacred Heart",' I supplied. 'Jesus Christ!' they howled. 'No, no,' I corrected; 'that was Friday's: "Sacred Heart"...'

Punchy was in the kitchen, polishing off the last inch of Powers.

'Did yer woman come?' I asked.

'Aye, she did; pissed as a newt in a taxi from the Student's Union. Then she wallops into the hard stuff here an' flakes out. She's in bed.'

Sure enough, when I looked in the bedroom there she was, under the Starry Plough, snoring.

'Clear off, oul' hand,' says I gleefully, kicking off the shoes; 'I'm due a long kip and I'm going to enjoy it. See you the morrow.'

'If I don't, don't you forget the funeral on Tuesday.'

'Oh God aye — it'll be the biggest thing since the Beatles. Sort out the gear will you — should be worth a few quid... Oh and don't forget about dropping the word about the other to Rory.'

He went; and I, down to simmit and jock strap, crept stealthily in beside Steffers. I entered (the bed) back foremost, gently fitting it (my back) along her warm front, spoonlike... her very warm front?... her very warm, stark naked front!

Punchy! — dirty old bastard!

deer Francy

    just a line too let you no I am going to kill myself if I do not git out of heer he is a nutcase and keeps me reeding the bible all day and has me neerly kilt at you no wot pleese help

and oblige

yours sinceerly

Teresa Immaculata Hagan

It was midday on Monday when I remembered Teesy's letter to 'Mommy and Doddy'. Time to pack it in, I mused bitterly, when even a mindless vessel like Teesy Hagan has you taped well enough to pull a blind like that!

I sat alone in the Cavan man's scoffing the pint and cheeseburger which were my rent for keeping an eye on the place while Landlord, acolytes and customers were up at the chapel viewing the curtain-raiser for tomorrow's big event — the arrival of remains for the Lying-in-State. Steffers had gone off to the University at the scrake of dawn, leaving me to sleep off the hearty breakfast she'd made of me. Punchy hadn't shown yet.

I went to the door, fitted my shoulder in the groove created by the Cavan man, and surveyed the festive scene. A black Mardi Gras. Black flags fluttered from every window (bedsheets?); black-tied men and black-mantled women hurried by with that air of purposeful gaiety seen in Ireland only at funerals or commemorations of mass murder. The inmates of Header Hall trooped past in columns of three (I was going to say 'marched' but this was being made doubly difficult for the poor lads by some martial fool who kept shouting 'left — right' in Gaelic). Still, I was cheered to note that most of them wore the now traditional black beret, sunglasses and combat coat, a sign that Punchy had been up and about early: at a rental fee of ten bob the lot for the duration of obsequies — half returnable on return — it was a sideline not to be sneezed at.

Early on the job too had been the gable-end aerosol artists — 'Slack-

93

Mickey-Silver-Barney-Liam. We shall not forget! Beware SAS Murderers!' — taking their lead from what Prods call 'The Morning Mick', whose editor had cried out for an independent inquiry into the tragic deaths of the five young husbands and fathers, struck down on their way to a confraternity meeting. Four unimpeachable eye witnesses — the Rt Hon Rory O'Lig MP, Mr Liam Rarity PhD (Econ), Rev Father Ignatius O'Faul SJ and Mr Martin Doyle (O'Driscoll's verger) — testified to having seen a Land Rover with an anti-tank gun mounted lurking in a side road near the scene of the tragedy minutes before it happened... 'A case of deliberate provocation,' stated the Rt Hon; 'I have it on good authority that the British are about to embark on an underhand military adventure the perfidy of which will shake right-thinking people the world over. This callous act could be the beginning.' (Punchy had been busy.) A reporter and photographer from the *Washington Post*, intent on tracing the movements of Mickey & Co prior to the tragedy, had been violently assaulted by the combined staff and family of Bo McGookin, publican, and rescued by Sergeant McNinch only to be charged, convicted and deported for promoting a riot.

'No comment,' said Sergeant McNinch.

'Fuggaff!' screamed Bo McGookin.

The occasion had all the makings of a punter's dream, and normally I'd have entered into the spirit of the thing with a heart and a half. But I had an uneasy feeling that the timing was all wrong for the purposes of Operation Starkey. There was the chance that O'Lig, already enraged with Duncher over the assassination attempts and now being primed by Punchy about the British handover, would allow the traditional two-day post-interment riot to mature into a full-scale attack across the river. Also, there was a persistent rumour that the Bishop himself would put in an appearance — and his earnest pleas for Calm and Restraint could always be guaranteed to have an opposite effect on the Faithful.

Then I spotted him!... No, not the Bishop... but a sight as rare and evanescent as the King of the Fairies himself... Tully! A fleeting glimpse through a gap in the line of advancing mourners — a small figure in a long dark overcoat and large Anthony Eden — carrying an attaché-case — like a barber on his way to prep a corpse. Hardly daring to breathe I sank back in the Cavan man's doorway and waited. The mourners came roistering past and then, unmistakably, there he was: that thin, white-stubbled face and its massive overhang of nose...

I let him get a few yards past the doorway before pouncing. Coming up from behind, I bent my knees and encircled him at waist level, trapping his arms to his sides. I then lifted him bodily, rigid as a caber, and ran back into the Cavan man's.

Inside, still holding him off the ground, I extracted a bulldog belly-gun from his overcoat pocket and wrested the attaché-case from him, like a window-dresser working with a dummy. He didn't move a muscle or make a sound until I dropped him in a chair and he saw who his captor was... 'Francie Fallis! God, you fair put the wind up me! I thought you were the Polis!'

Taking care to place myself between him and the door I laid the attaché-case on the table and lifted the lid. Detachable stock, short hexagonal barrel, telescopic sight, pull-through and small pewter bottle of oil, all nestling in their green baize recesses: a deadly antique. 'Still the same oul' Mauser, Tully,' I said. 'You might be a bit more successful if you invested in something more up-to-date.'

Relaxed now, he lit a butt and pushed the Anthony Eden to the back of his head, thus revealing the unshaded horror of his big dark eyes. While being chased by Peelers in his early youth, it was said, he had dropped flat-footed from a high yard wall, the impact causing his pupils to plummet downward and inward, where they've stayed since, forlorn black marbles that seemed to be eternally hunting for a glimpse of one another round the hooky, droopy obstruction of his conk.

'You'll niver believe me Francie,' he said, 'when I tell you that I was just on my way to the dealers to see if I could raise the wind on it. Belonged to the oul' Countess Mark-the-bitch herself, y'know, along with about a hunnerd an' fifty-seven others, like; but that's the only one she ever used — on the Count, I onct heard —'

'Tell that to the Paras, Tully lad. They tend to get very primitive over telescopic sights ... You heard about poor Danny Skillen only a fortnight ago? They caught him on top of the high Flats with an Armalite. A wild, wild sight, Tully... Danny in free fall for fourteen storeys, flapping his arms right into the car park. Wrote off two Minis —'

'Ah now, Francie, enough of the coddin',' he said nervously, the black discs skittering madly along the lower periphery of his sockets; 'yi'd niver turn in an oul' jail-mate —'

'And what about your other oul' jail-mate? — the one you've been taking pot-shots at for money — and Prod money at that!'

'Now look you here, I niver took Prod money in my natcherl — nor

95

British money! An' if it's that gangster O'Lig yer talkin' about, I'd pay to have a go at him — an' so would you, Francie, if it suited your purpose.'

He'd lost the bap completely. Having bounded out of his seat, he stood shaking a trembling fist under my nostrils, orbs birling in an unco-ordinated way that set my own head reeling. But I believed him.

'OK, OK,' I placated, pushing him firmly back into the chair, regaining the initiative by towering over him in the best third degree tradition. To keep my equilibrium I stared him relentlessly in the mouth; 'if not the Duncher, who is it's after Rory? You can't expect me to believe you're doing it off your own bat; bullets for that thing are a rare and pricey item and I can't see you buying many out of your OAP. Somebody's staking you and I want to know who, now, or I'll drop you in the shit, oul' jail-mate or not.'

'Liam Rarity, that's who,' he spat, surprisingly: 'a young fella with more wit an' more of the Oul' Cause in him than a hunnerd like you an' the Right Honourable O'Lig, God curse him! You'll not git him takin' a foreign oath for two thousand a year an' expenses — or floggin' bullets to Orangemen, either!'

Rarity! Who'd have believed it!... Perhaps because of the PhD (Econ) thing I'd always considered him to be above the sort of dirt us under-privileged lads had to stoop to from time to time. Then a thought struck me — why Tully? — and the true deviousness of Rarity suddenly dawned upon me... Everybody hated O'Lig; but nobody wanted him dead, least of all Liam Rarity. Crooked, two-faced, alcoholic and proven coward Rory may be — but he was also televiewable. In the beginning, when the world media trained its lens on the new insurgents, the slaughter had been heart-rending. Tight-lipped hard nuts who had faced armoured cars with revolvers fell gibbering at the feet of studio floor-managers, and that Che Guevara of No-Go himself, the legendary Buxy O'Hoy, after watching a three minute re-run of himself giggling and drooling Nationwide, had staggered off into the night to give himself up to the Cistercians. But not Rory; just one short interview at a barricade (he'd been stealing parts from a hi-jacked lorry at the time, but that didn't come out in the interview, naturally) had established him as the spokesman for the New Ireland — a broth of a bhoy, strong but merciful, articulate, humorous, tolerant — and in no time at all even those in the box-fixated herd who knew the real Rory had total-ly accepted the small screen version. If Rory should go, Rarity knew as well as anybody, so would a large part of the TV establishment that hung on his every oath; and any modern guerilla will, given the choice, surrender half his arms rather than lose the coverage of one camera.

So Rory dead was out: but Rory rattled...? There were a dozen or so areas of power and profit on which greedy Rory kept a heavy finger; and if the fingers started to shake who better placed to insert a helping handful than trusty Lieutenant Rarity? And what better way to rattle even a moderately brave man than to make him the target of a tully-eyed sniper?...

At least, that's how it seemed to me.

I went to the bar and poured two bumper buckshee Powers. Presenting one to him — and even here there was an almost imperceptible lack of sync between my offering and his reaching hand — I said: 'Pack it in, Tully, before you kill something that matters. Why the hell don't you take up snooker — or darts?'

'It's easy to mock the afflicted, Francie,' rebuked the martyr. 'You were one of the ones that used to take the Mick outa poor Yah-yah Burke up in chokey. I mind you callin' him "the chap with a stoppage in his Erse" — couldn't git two words out together without oxygen. An' look at him now, eh? — Head-buck-cat newsreader in RTE! Eh? An' all due to that Scotchman that was the prison head-shrinker when we were in. All Yah-yah wanted was to be a teacher; but no, yer man says, "Stretch yerself! Aim for the impossible!" You'll niver believe this, Francie, but because of that man there's a fella with one leg makin' a good livin' ridin' a one-wheeled bike along a tightrope in Duffy's circus the day —'

'— Evenin' all.'

The large priestly figure stood between us and the door, grinning broadly at our consternation. He made a back foremost sign of the cross with the barrel of his regulation Walther, causing one of the two bulky Sisters of Mercy who had taken up position on either side of the door to choke on his fag smoke.

'Father Luther McNinch, I presume,' I said. 'You're taking one hell of a chance aren't you?'

'A wee walkabout while the flock are up at the candy-apple'll do no harm,' he replied, resting his fist on my shoulder, the snout of the Walther pressing coldly in the soft hollow behind my ear; 'I might even hear a confession or two while I'm at it, Francie — like why you were over with the Duncher last night. But just now I'd like you to tell me the name of thon unfortunate cratur over there and let me have a quick geek in your wee attaché-case.'

In the ensuing silence I could almost hear Tully's balls (optic) cannoning off the cush. Once across the river, that attaché-case could get us ten years apiece. My nostrils filled with the stench of stale piss and Lysol and I said, gesturing nonchalantly: 'Help yourself. Nothing to do with me. So far as I know it's full of combs and razor blades.'

I had replaced the lid but hadn't bothered to snap the clasps. McNinch, keeping the Walther at my neck, flicked it open and whistled... 'Boys-a-boys! That's one quare shooter, lads. If you're lucky and gets a beak who's a gun-fancier he might make it fifteen years instead of —'

He broke off abruptly. The Walther left my neck as he moved round the table, staring at Tully...- 'Wait now... Jeepers peepers! Bingo! I know who our wee man is now. Well, well — I heard tell you were out and about with your thing... The catch of the season...'

'Y'b-black b-bastard ye!' blurted Tully into his gloating face.

'Now, now,' scolded McNinch, holding the cocked gun an inch from Tully's nose. Then, with the forefinger and thumb of his other hand he grasped Tully's ear and twisted, (God! It was like pulling a lever on a fruit machine — pupils looping the loop in agony) pulling him to his feet; 'that's not a very ecumenical attitude. Serve you right if I handed you over to you-know-who — they'd soon straighten your peepers, no trouble. But I've decided to be merciful just this once, so if you'll take that —' Still grasping the little man's ear, holding him stretched on tiptoes, McNinch thrust the attaché-case into his arms and ran him over to the door. With perfect timing one of the Sisters swung it open and the Sergeant, without slackening speed, launched Tully into the street on the toe of his size eleven... 'and the best of luck to you.'

'Well now, Francie,' said McNinch, returning to the table and deftly draining the heel of Tully's Powers, 'waste not, want not. You've been lucky again; God is preserving you for a worse fate, it seems. I only hope I'm around to give Him a hand when He makes up His mind.'

'You realize what you've just done?' I asked quietly, keeping a wary eye on the Walther; 'that cross-eyed blirt is about the most dangerous—'

'Save your bad breath, Francie. You can tell me nothing about that one I don't know already — up to and including his current contract. But sure it all goes to keep the oul' pot boiling. Imagine what my overtime sheet would look like in the weeks following the demise of a household name like, say, Rory O'Lig! It's an ill wind, Francie; a far cry from the peaceful days when the tickmen were wearing out my doorstep. And to think that just before youse huers started up I was thinking seriously of resigning the force and going on a bin-cart!'

There and then I resolved that this, above all, was one for the Simbas.

'If it's overtime you're after, Sergeant, I might be able to put a bit your way very shortly.'

'Oh aye?' he exclaimed sarcastically. He'd taken Tully's chair and now leant across the table at me, levelling the Walther menacingly; 'something to do with you hob-nobbing with the Duncher after hours?'

'No heavy stuff or you'll hear nothing,' I warned. 'All I can tell you now is that it all depends on the outcome of Wednesday's election. After that I'll drop you the word about developments.'

'Out of the goodness of your heart?'

'Out of our mutual interest in boiling pots.'

He stared me out in silence for a moment, weighing the short-term pleasure of taking me in to fall up and down the concrete stairs which so many of his captives seemed incapable of negotiating without injury, against the long-term prospect of getting a tip-off. He carressed the clumps of hair and blackheads jutting on his cheekbones, small oases amid the boil-cratered tundra of massive jowls; in that Roman collar, without uttering a word, he'd have been a shattering success in the mission field.

But before he could render his verdict an altercation broke out at the door and there was Steffers being restrained by the two Sisters — one of whom, I could see, was taking unfair advantage of one or two prominent points of purchase. McNinch's chair hit the wall behind as he launched himself across the floor. A well-aimed running kick caught the groper in the knee-cap; the Walther reversed and used as a knuckle-duster subdued the other. Poor Steffers gaped speechless at the stricken Sisters, one hopping and moaning *basso profundo*, the other slumped against the wall cradling a damaged face in both hands, and at the Rev Father who took her by the elbow and led her to a chair. She flashed me a wide-eyed appeal.

'Sergeant McNinch's idea of the Great Game,' I explained.

'Please accept my heartfelt apologies, Miss Hamilton,' gushed McNinch, transformed into every American's vision of the British Bobby. He even touched his biretta smartly with a stiff forefinger. 'Over-zealousness on my men's part, I'm afraid. I have the honour of belonging to the same Masonic as your father. A bit of a coincidence running into you like this: he was asking me just the other evening at our annual dinner if I'd make a few private enquiries as to your whereabouts. He's very worried. Shall I tell him you'll get in touch?'

Steffers, still bemused, nodded. McNinch again grovelled his biretta. 'Anything I can do to assist you in the future, Miss, just you let me know... And now I'll not detain you further. Mr Fallis, could I have a private word, please?'

The two Sisters limped ahead and I followed him into the porch.

'I'll be expecting word from you after Wednesday,' he said loudly, glancing around outside to see if the coast was clear. He then turned and gathered the lapels of my jacket in one gigantic fist, lifting and pulling me to him. '— And if anything nasty ever happens to that bird in there I'll break your Fenian neck. Understood?'

I did — or thought I did. Not long after his departure I was wishing, for my Fenian neck's sake, that he's at least given a brief definition of nastiness. Was it, for instance, what the 'bird' and I were doing between the black silk sheets up in the Cavan man's boudoir, watched from the walls by generations of posed pugilists from J L Sullivan to Muhammad Ali, half-choked by fumes from the Holy Lamp?

The Cavan man thought so. On returning from chapel, flanked by the barman and Jeremy, he opened the bedroom door in time to view the last furlong of a hard run race (Pat Taafe with Arkle up, if the simile is to be accurate)... 'Ah fer frig-sake, Francie!' he screamed predictably, clapping a hand over the eyes of both his flowers as Steffers and I tore noisily past the post.

From the word go Tuesday looked like being a long waking extension of the nightmare out of which I had been trying to claw my way since hitting the Cavan man's sofa in the small hours. (Though not the sort to keep a pad and pencil by the bed, I do remember a vivid clip from that particular production: a bull terrier wearing a Roman collar running up to me, wagging skittishly, begging me to take the thing he held in his jaws and throw it for him. The thing turned out to be a wriggling screeching miniature of Mickey Close, complete with velvet slacks, which when I threw it in the air exploded into a million miniscule Mickeys, falling like clouds of midges to settle in my hair, my eyes... and so on.)

Punchy, the bastard, hadn't weighed in at all on Monday; and Steffers had buggered off to visit Daddy before teatime — prompted, I think, by the Cavan man's eye-shuttering, head-tossing disapproval of our upstairs antics. The only constructive thing I managed the entire day was a conversation with her concerning boats, in particular the speed, range and capacity of the one moored to Toby's jetty. She had been a mine of information, most of it boringly technical, and when she'd become inquisitive about my interest I'd had no hesitation in recruiting her — for, so far as she was concerned, a fortnight of nooky afloat in the Outer Hebrides which I had already arranged with Toby. Agog, she'd gone off to make up with Daddy and borrow his charts and compasses and other nautical things, leaving me to kill the day playing game after hysterical game of Snakes and Ladders in the Cavan man's ménage. I got very drunk towards the end.

A phone call from Punchy, harbinger of many a nightmare, began Tuesday, bringing me reeling and cursing from sofa to bar. If I'd had a gun I'd have blown it off the wall without stirring.

'Yes!'

'Wha —?'

'Who's that?'

'Francie, is that —'

'Punchy, God's curse ye! Always when you're not wanted. What the bloody —'

'But I thought you were lifted for sure. I was comin' down the street yisterday just as McNinch an' his bullies went into the pub —'

'Well I wasn't. You might at least have rung up to check. Where are you now? And what time is it?'

'Half-eight —'

'Merciful Christ!'

'I know it's a bit on the early side, Francie, but O'Driscoll's stannin' over me here an' he says he'll break my back if I don't git you down here right away —'

'— O'Driscoll, did you say? Where the hell are you?'

'In the chapel. Francie, for God's sake git yer skates on. There's some bother down here — somethin' to do with the funeral today, an' this bloody muckman's liable to do me damage if —' .

Click. Silence. The hand of the muckman, I presumed, while the other one could as readily be throttling the life out of my oul' china.

Two Bloody Marys later I was on my way along streets already a-clatter with pilgrims hurrying down for a final viewing before the big show. A four-deep shuffling queue started a hundred yards from the chapel's main gate and snaked across the yard and up the steps. My passage through the throng and into the chapel itself did not go unremarked ...

'Luk at yer man —'

'Who the frigs 'e think 'e is!'

'Francie Fallis — big head...'

'Pity he wasn't along wi' them.'

'My man says there's a woman that foun' a pair of somebody's you-know-whats in her gutter...'

Inside, they filed reverently past the five coffins ranked in front of the chancel steps, picking their way delicately over a worm's nest of power cables into the glare of arc lights to genuflect once to the fallen and again to the channel of their choice, BBC to the right, ITV to the left.

As I sidled through the body of the chapel towards the vestry, the solemnity of the occasion was being marred by a dispute between the Italian and French crews. In the verger's raffle they had drawn the positions on either side of the Bishop's throne, both of which were the same rateable value in the verger's book; but now both directors had taken it into their heads that the left profile was the Great Man's best and were frantically upbidding for it, with the verger in the middle doing honest broker. The French won, I heard later, and the verger punched the Italian director severely for not accepting his verdict with decorum.

The vestry door was barred on the inside. O'Driscoll himself answered my knock, glaring at me through a six-inch gap, one of my Dutch darks clamped fuming between his tombstones, the lines of his ever flourishing five o'clock shadow etched like a blue birthmark against his prison pallor: the face of a disgruntled Mafioso at the peephole of a speakeasy. (Incidentally, there's a Prod myth which attempts to explain that well-scrubbed baby's bum complexion peculiar to RC clergy: after ordination, it goes, every Priest pays a secret visit to the Vatican and gets shaved by no less than the Pope himself, wielding a cut-throat razor previously dipped in a secret poison! One nick and he's dead; otherwise, a chin like a billiard ball for life — though perhaps that simile would be more appropriate for the nun's heads which the Pontiff does in between times, hence the Gospel tent favourite: 'There's not a hair on a baldy nun / No, not one / No, not one...' Anyway, in O'Driscoll's case the dose mustn't have took, as they say.)

He beckoned me inside and locked the door behind me. The first thing I laid eyes on was Punchy, sitting at a long refectory table, holding his head in his hands. When he raised and turned his old remains of a face to me I saw that his one visible eye was black.

'Who did that?' I enquired.

'That bastard there,' he answered, indicating a third occupant slumped at the far end of the table. O'Lig, in the throes of the most awful Prussian blue hangover by the looks of him, prised himself upright and growled: 'Rat... nark... grass —'

It had the effect of bringing on one of my now rare violent turns. Why, I can't really say — except that it was an unusual and unnatural hour for me to be up and about. Anyway, the next thing I knew I was half-roads across the polished table-top at him, my tobacco knife well in advance. (I have never smoked a pipe, but for years I have carried one, plus a plug of black twist, as an alibi for the five-inch flick blade with which I now intended to carve patterns on Rory's face.)

Surprisingly for the state of him, he moved quickly and was up with his back against the wall, clawing frantically at his armpit, even before I'd begun my dive. (Incompetent ritualists both of us; me telegraphing my intentions with a Peter Lorre knife-flicking act; he, a right-handed man with a big belly and short arms, carrying a small gun in a fancy shoulder harness on his left side.) Still, I think I'd have got to him — but

103

half-roads was as far as O'Driscoll allowed...

He made a flying two-point landing with his elbows on the small of my back, stopping me dead on the table-top. After that all he had to do was catch the knife as it fell from my rigid fingers, but being O'Driscoll he had to put in a bit of arm-twisting-up-the-back before dropping me on the floor. Then, leaving me to survive as best I could (and believe me it's as near death as I've ever been — on a cold morning after a feed of drink I can still feel the indent of his culchie elbows in my kidneys) he turned on Rory...

'Put that thing away or I'll crucify ye!' I heard him roar, lying with my face beside his great brown boots ('The Farmer's Friend'), struggling for breath. 'Conduct yerselves, both of yis... brawling like Turks in the House of God!... Get up out of that and stop making a great eejit of yerself there.' This to me, stirring me briskly with a reinforced toecap.

My recollection of the next few minutes is a bit hazy. I was vaguely aware of Punchy manhandling me into a chair — a whiff of his breath pierced my coma like smelling salts, but only momentarily. He said later that I'd gone the colour of damp plaster and had sagged so grotesquely that he'd thought my back had been broken. Which was his alibi for administering the only form of resuscitation known to him; the pugilistic equivalent of the kiss-of-life: he sunk his teeth in my right ear lobe.

I came out of that chair very much alive — screaming, in fact — with Punchy hanging on my lug like a fox terrier. Shaking him free, I turned with clenched fist and would have smashed it into his bloodstained mouth — my blood! — but for O'Driscoll's intervention (a vigorously applied half-Nelson).

Punchy grinned horribly with satisfaction as I dabbed the ear and heaped abuse on him. (This apparently, was the reaction sought for; the ear bite, when applied strategically to a demoralised loser in, say, the last second before the bell rings for the tenth round, not only revives him mentally but also evokes a surge of rage which the biter can then direct at the guiltless opponent by means of a strong push from behind.)

'There now, settle down and get outside of that,' growled O'Driscoll, setting a tumbler of what turned out to be brandy in front of me. From a man whose meanness is almost as legendary as his violence it was a gesture of remorse equivalent to his two-day scourging marathon for Meehaul. Gulping it gratefully, I had the added pleasure of seeing O'Lig's mouth begin to tremble and dribble, his little eyes fixed on the decanter in O'Driscoll's hand in an expression of dumb craving. But no sooner had I drained my glass than O'Driscoll whipped it away, returning it and the decanter — both Waterford — to a cupboard which he locked noisily and meaningfully. I fully expected him to swallow the key.

'Now then, my good men,' he said, 'we have a problem —'

'Youse,' I interrupted, getting agonisingly to my feet, 'might have a problem. I'm off while I'm still able —'

'Indeed and by God yer not!' he thundered, placing himself between me and the door. 'It's you and the like of you that have brought me and my parish to this pass! So you'll stay — dead or alive you'll stay stock still till I tell ye. D'you hear me now?'

I did — and stayed, stock still.

Calmer, pacing now, he continued; 'Now I'll be the first to own that the events of the past three years have brought benefits to a poor parish — but does any of yis ever give a thought to the burden it has placed on the shoulders of your Priest?... Damn the bit of ye! I'm the one that has to put a face on your divilment for the wide world; for three years I've been heart afeared to pick my own nose for fear of it being bounced off satellites for the entertainment of heathen Japs; and now this... the Bishop due in two hours time, the biggest TV hook-up the world has ever seen —' For the climax of his mounting tantrum he bounded across to what I thought to be a cupboard door and wrenched it open dramatically... '— and I have four corpses and Christ knows how many consecrated dogs and cats out there!'

It was a tiny, dark robing room, little bigger than a cupboard. In it, tied arse-about-face to a chair, was 'Silver' Roche. His black beret had been rammed down over his ears and eyes; the dirty muffler which gagged him covered the lower half of his face, leaving only his nose visible — but that, in 'Silver's' case, was enough for the purpose of identification. It — the nose — was red, raw and running. He made a struggling, grunting movement with his head and a large droplet shook free and fell to join its shattered predecessors on the soaking chairback. On the forearm of his navy blue jacket glistened the hardened nebula from which derived the nickname he had answered to for thirty years. (A hyphenated lady journalist, collecting data for profiles of the 'Freedom Fighters', had once asked me the origin of 'Silver'. I'd asked her to guess. After she'd put up everything from colour of hair to the use of eccentric ammunition, like the Lone Ranger, I'd told her, graphically; whereupon she'd vomited, copiously, over my boots.)

'When did he turn up?' I gulped, bruised kidneys alone restricting my mirth.

'First in the queue this morning. Drunk as a fiddler's bitch,' growled O'Driscoll, aiming a kick at the chair leg.

'Dogs and cats is bad enough,' I mused, 'but has it crossed your mind that there might be a vagrant Protestant or two mixed up with the boys out there?'

'Will you for God's sake make it no worse than it is!' he bellowed, slamming the door shut on 'Silver'. 'And that's bad enough, with that bowsy on his road from Armagh and me about to be traduced for the entire world to see!' (The Bishop was a city man, a fact viewed by O'Driscoll in much the same way as a District Officer might if a Watutsi were appointed High Commissioner.) 'Something'll have to be done, quick, and on your three heads be it, for one of yis, if not all, is behind the whole damn -'

'Not me,' I said; 'you'd be better directing all your enquiries to Mr Roche's brother-in-law over there —' I indicated the bold Rory, slumped again at the end of the table with head sizzling between hands. I don't think he heard me.

'Is that right?' snarled O'Driscoll.

'Isn't that what I was trying to tell you when he lammed me!' said Punchy bitterly.

'Is that right!' repeated O'Driscoll, rounding on Rory and knocking the elbows out from under his poor head. 'Wake up, ye drunken ghett, and answer your Priest this instant!'

'What?' yelled Rory, fists bunched and fairly spitting with rage.

'Is that malingerer in there your brother-in-law or is he not?'

'Yis! He is. An' if anything happens to him I'll have our Bridget an' his nine brats roun' my neck for life. I'll do many a thing for you, Father, but you can forget about any summary court-martial —'

So that was it... O'Lig and me presiding, Punchy as executioner. O'Driscoll's mathematical mind: five had been indented for Above; five was the number on network credits the world over; the entire production was scored for five cadavers ('The Faithful Five — Take One — Chapel' was the chalked inscription I had noticed on the ITN clapperboard on my way in); and five, by hook or by crook, would go...

Taken aback by Rory's bald exposure, O'Driscoll blustered: 'Now, now, what sort of thing's that —'

'But Rory,' I broke in, 'what difference would it make? As far as Bridget and the world is concerned something has already happened to Silver — he's in smithereens in a box out there!'

'Notatall,' said Punchy, the fount of all truth, eliciting a shaken fist and intimidating snarls from Rory: 'Bridget had Silver locked up, full as a po, in the attic since Sunday night, an' big brother here's had ivery collectin' tin in the town on the go —'

'A "Silver" offering?' I quipped.

'Shut up, you,' hissed O'Driscoll.

'Aye, an' not only that,' Punchy bore on relentlessly: 'Bridget an' him were up at the Commission yisterday puttin' in a big claim on the army for malicious slayin' — an' I wouldn't be surprised if they booked sailin' tickets when they were at it. That's when Silver done the bunk.'

'Ah God! And how could he resist it?' I cried, enjoying the sight of Rory's bottled wrath. 'The Patriot's dream: doffing his cap to his own coffin! If he'd been sober enough he might even have wangled a gun in the firing party!'

'By Jasus, if we weren't on Holy groun' I'd blow hell outa both of yis!' Rory erupted at the mouth like a great purple boil. 'An' who are youse to give off about anybody makin' a bob or two outa the Sassenach pigs? Sure an' it's only right an' proper — him that was on ivery job with them out there this last three years — him that set the clock for fourteen Co-ops, five Woolworths an' Christ know how many pubs —'

'— Not forgettin' four of his mates,' added Punchy.

'He was sick, ya punchy fugger! I'll kill ye stone —'

'Shut up! Nobody's going to kill anybody,' barked O'Driscoll; adding, in a note of quiet resignation: 'more's the pity —'

Punchy started to protest — a vengeful huer, he'd have enjoyed wiping Silver to balance that dig in the eye — but O'Driscoll silenced him with the raised palms and closed eyes of a martyr before the stake. The silence, such as it was, lasted a full minute. Outside, above the slow drag of the mourners' crocodile, the verger's angry bass interwove with a fluid, pulsing soprano, a duet which ceased abruptly in the middle of a fine despairing high C from the latter.

Eventually it was the sound of a very splashy sneeze from the robing room that brought O'Driscoll out of his trance (that or the thought of the Holy Mercedes homing at speed along the M1). 'Take him out of my sight,' he commanded O'Lig, pointing towards the robing room, 'and if he's not on the boat for Camden Town this very night I'll devote the rest of my natural life to ensuring that you and yours roast in hell!'

'You'll never regret this, Father. I'll see —' Rory was saying, halfway to the door, when the Priest stopped him.

'— Just a minute now; there's something else to be settled. I will proceed here today as if nothing has happened; which means to say that I will hazard my immortal soul and defile God's Temple by performing a lie in the teeth of a Holy Prince of the church! Not a small matter for an ordained Priest, Mr O'Lig.' While talking he had moved round the table to face Rory. I could actually hear his teeth grinding... 'So you also, Mr O'Lig, will proceed with the things brought to light by Mr Coyne here — the collection and the claim — and proceed vigorously, for I'll expect the church's half of the total to be very substantial, I warn you.'

Rory knew better than to quibble.

Then I spoke up: 'And the twenty-five percent, of course, that'll keep Mr Coyne and I from squealin' to the Commission, Rory —'

'I'm fuggin' sure yer not!' screamed Rory.

An expression of manic delight flooded O'Driscoll's face. He prodded Rory in the ribs and insisted: 'Oh yes they are, Mr O'Lig; twenty-five percent's better than nothing. And if you have any thought of welshing, think long on the fire and the maggots, Mr O'Lig, on the fire and the maggots for all eternity... Now git that in there outa here!'

Freed, the first thing Silver did was to reunite sleeve and nostrils luxuriously. That was about all he had time for before big brother-in-law started dragging him out of the robing room towards the back door leading to the chapel yard. In passing, Silver's big blue eyes, still heavy with liquor, lit on me. He grinned roguishly. 'Hiya, Francie oul' son! Fuck this for a geg.' Appropriate last words from a joker who got as much fun out of planting fifty pounds of gelly in a packed café as he once had tying tin-cans to cat's tails.

I wish to Christ I'd got up and cleared off the moment that door slammed behind them. But, as they say, one door closes and another opens, the latter in this case being the door of O'Driscoll's drink cupboard. Relief of tension, thwarted violence, guilt — whatever it was it caused him to start ladling out the brandy as though the last trump had sounded. And babbling... 'Here, we might as well kill this bottle before the great sponge of Armagh descends on us — so wire in, lads.' We did, with a will, Hennessy's Three Star, balm to bruised kidneys, and with every sip the thought of him cursing his largesse at the sight of the empty bottle in the morning. He babbled on: '— I 'clare to God it's getting harder for a Christian man to travel a day without drawin' blood! Where'll it all end? Beset on all sides by black heathens in armoured cars; murderous Blackmouths lurkin' round every corner armed to the teeth; and this the day — did you ever see the like of it! — the Pope's Bo'sun draggin' his gouty leg the whole cut from Armagh for the funeral of a gang of cornerboys we'd have had to bury out of parish funds if they'd died naturally! I tell you, I'm about sick to death of the lot of it. The other day when I was up with the Friars behind the hill there I was sorely tempted to pack the Parish in and go into permanent retreat. But sure even they're not safe from it all: they had to get the heart machine out for poor oul' Xavier, the Father Superior, after that demented woman came on the phone and started tellin' him the colour of her drawers. It's all right me — after takin' confessions in this quarter for ten years there's not much'll shake you — I just called her a dirty clart and shattered her eardrums with the loudest tongue-fart I could muster — but a saintly oul' divil like Xavier!... I'm tellin' you it's a sick, depraved —'

'When did this happen?' I asked. Punchy's tumbler had frozen mid-way between table and lip.

'What?' snapped O'Driscoll irritably.

'This woman on the blower.'

'Oh her... mine was on Sunday morning after twelve o'clock mass. But the first I heard of it was Saturday — she came off with some wild things to Father Rafferty down in St Bridget's. As far as I hear she must have covered the Diocese by now. Of course we're used to telephone nutcases — religious lunatics of the other persuasion, Jehovah's Witnesses and the like — but this one's a funny kink.'

'Funny indeed,' says I meaningfully, trying to catch Punchy's eye, which he had glued firmly to the dregs in his glass (sounds like juggling tricks in a transplant surgery, but you know what I mean).

'What's the time?' asked O'Driscoll, filling up all round.

'Five past ten.'

'Not so bad. His Beatitude'll be a while yet — if he's out of his bed, that is. Now, Francie, I was wondering if you could make what they call "an educated guess" at the combined total of O'Lig's claim and collection? — Just thereabouts, mind you...'

I don't know how long we sat there, the three of us, waffling pleasantly in the soothing half-light of the vestry (the only window, a representation of St Stephen's martyrdom in stained glass, contained enormous areas of opaque blood). On me, brandy before breakfast had the effect of a tranquillising needle, not only erasing the ache in my kidneys but seeming to insulate those parts of me that met the polished mahogany of the straight-backed chair, until I slumped, incredibly comfortable, savouring the drone of my own voice and marvelling at the way the glass seemed to float from the table to my mouth. I remember it now as a survivor of Passchendale might the last rest before battle; the mouth-organ mellowness of the campfire before the Mohawk comes in with the dawn; England before Sarajevo... Indeed, the last thing I remember clearly prior to the event that fell like a hand-grenade into my Stream of Consciousness (that's right — and to think that only five years ago, when a Frenchman, on learning my nationality, exclaimed: 'Ah, the land of Joyce!' my reply had been: 'Aye, and he deserved hanging...', thinking of course that he referred to the late Lord Haw-Haw. Prison libraries are very comprehensive these days.) — the last thing I remember was the verger coming in to get his lacerated knuckles seen to. One of the Italian TV director's buck teeth had lodged firmly in the valley between his first and second joints. We all fussed, I remember; O'Driscoll with the brandy, Punchy with the first aid kit, I with a pair of rusty pliers: a scene of almost light-hearted domesticity... Then, like the shot of benzedrine that sets the pen squiggling mindlessly across the exam paper, the door from the chapel yard burst open.

O'Lig fell in. Bleeding. Squealing. And behind him, traumatically, the helmeted head of Wilkington-Pike! — hovering in the doorway, smirking deferentially and looking around, wide-eyed, like an Egyptologist entering a tomb for the first time in a thousand years. Rory writhing ('Bless me Father!') on the floor, the open-mouthed gallery of O'Driscoll, Punchy, the verger and myself, and still Wilkington-Pike performed an elaborate ritual with his helmet, from head to heart in five distinct movements, while saying: 'I hope you'll forgive the intrusion, Father.'

My first thought was that the British Army had finally gone ape. So, I think, did O'Driscoll, who fell on his knees beside Rory (an entirely natural movement considering the state of us all)... 'My poor son! What have they done to you?'

The verger, meanwhile, seeing the glaze of death in Rory's eyes, had run to a cupboard and fetched the Holy Oil and O'Driscoll's stole. But as the Priest accepted them, kissing the stole preparatory to donning it, Wilkington-Pike coughed discreetly and said: 'I don't think there's really any need, Father. Look there... you'll see that it's only a flesh wound — just south of his armpit.'

O'Driscoll, lifting Rory's arm to a crescendo of yowls from the owner, looked, saw, and then began to twist... 'You dirty low cur! Comin' in here, messin' up the place —'

'— But there's another,' continued Wilkington-Pike hastily; 'out in the Land Rover. You might wish to do something for him, Father — posthumously, I mean. Somebody opened up on them just around the corner from here. The poor chap outside caught the first round dead on the button.'

Tully!

Silver!

O'Driscoll clambered to his feet and drew himself up to full height. Even Rory, sensing the atmosphere, fell silent as the Priest, hands clasped in front, raised his big face to heaven and breathed: 'God is not mocked this day.' His expression was beatific.

Wilkington-Pike a-hemmed nervously. 'If I could be of any assistance, Father...'

O'Driscoll, back to business, clapped his hands almost gleefully and roared: 'Bless you, Major, you can indeed. It would be a great help if you'd get your people to cart the poor man in here... but before you stir I think a scoop or two might help all round.' He swooped on the brandy cupboard and produced a virgin bottle and extra glasses. Rory burbled pitifully from the floor... 'Aye, and you too, I suppose — so long as you realize that this divine intervention does not release you from certain financial undertakings to myself, Mr Fallis and Mr Coyne —'

Wilkington-Pike, faintly aghast, began: 'I'm afraid I don't quite —'

'Of course you don't, Major!' laughed O'Driscoll, thrusting a glass at him. 'Much more illustrious men of your race have failed to comprehend our little ways. Don't let it bother you. You and your men could render valuable assistance, if you've no objection... Good man! The verger here'll run over to the chapel house and fetch a crate or two of beer while I outline the operation. Right now, men, bottoms up — for we've a brisk hour or two in front of us.'

111

In a work of fiction you'd expect all the threads to start weaving together about now: the election, mobilisation for Operation Starkey, leading up to a grand climax on the peninsula — action packed — with me flogging Toby's honey-pot and making away in Toby's boat with the bird. But this being the God's Irish Truth things tend to get a bit banjaxed from now on; the election result, as you'll see, starts the rot in the main plot —but rot or not there's still a plot. The rot in the narrator begins much earlier, in the 'brisk' two hours between that second onslaught of brandy and the Bishop's first words on descending from the Holy Mercedes and entering the vestry: 'What's the odds, men?' (Appropriate words from the apotheosis of a long line of turf accountants.)

Nevertheless I shall attempt to describe the happenings in those horrific two hours as clearly as possible, likewise the events from then until, five days later, I found myself bobbing about in mid-North Channel. What has to be appreciated is that I never drew wholly sober breath in that time; so if the threads get a bit tangled, and the time factor — to which I have adhered reasonably well in the preceding pages — tends to blur, blame the drink.

Six squaddies of the Royal Scots carted Silver into the vestry and laid him on the refectory table. Two would have done, for he was a light bit of a thing, but they'd spotted the crates of beer lugged in beforehand by the verger — an additional two managing to bluff their way in by dint of performing a dignified slow march behind — making a total of eight, in full battle order, around the crates when O'Driscoll gave the word to fall to.

Wilkington-Pike sidled across to me, looking bewildered. 'What on earth's going on, Proinsias?'

'I'm past caring. Ask the Earl Marshal there,' I replied, indicating O'Driscoll in a huddle with the verger. I think it was then that Wilkington-Pike said: 'Just my luck — this happening today, I mean. I fly out tonight. Been seconded to the 3rd Gurkhas — in the Isle of Man, of all places! What the fucking hell they're doing there is beyond me.' But I can't be sure.

About then O'Driscoll, having finished his collogue with the verger, started clapping his hands like a demented scoutmaster. ('Rally to me!) 'Now men, pay attention. We have one or two problems which I'm sure, with your assistance, we will soon overcome. Our — er — military friends might be in a bit of a quandary, but I must crave their indulgence —'

And well he might.

Briefly, the problems were: (1) to get Silver stowed safely in his rightful coffin — which, by the way, was abrim with pieces of other people and things — and (2) to do so in such a way as not to disturb or infuriate the queueing mourners. (Wilkington-Pike's suggestion that the chapel doors be closed displayed the lack of understanding that had dogged the British operation for four years. Such a move, as O'Driscoll pointed out, would mean a crowd gathering outside, TV cameras panning, interviewers posing loaded questions to selected nutcases — 'It's been said that the army have moved into the chapel and are removing the coffins for burial in unmarked graves. What's your opinion?' — result, a free riot for the networks.) The third problem was a straightforward one of cubic re-distribution as posed annually with symbolic jugs of water in eleven-plus papers. (O'Lig's suggestion that anything displaced by Silver should be flushed down the bog brought a loud rebuke from O'Driscoll, who reminded him that everything therein had been absolved by him at the time of the incident and therefore required decent burial in consecrated ground.)

The logical way, I thought, would have been to hump all five coffins into the vestry, open them up, distribute the contents of Silver's among the other four, insert Silver and Bob's your uncle. But no, said O'Driscoll firmly; the removal of all five at once would still create alarm and despondency among the mourners and, worse, among the TV men... No; it would have to be one at a time; which brought up the subsidiary problem of who would do the actual humping. Not the verger himself, especially with his bad hand; certainly not O'Driscoll; and never O'Lig, Punchy or me, the sight of any one of whom laying hands on a coffin would set the queue abuzz with rumours of vivisectionist's gold — and anyway, we were too drunk.

My one non-horrific memory of that time is of the sullen features of a small Glaswegian Lancejack as the Major and the verger forced a choirboy's surplice down over his raised arms (on his right forearm the inscription incorporated in a tattoo of crossed dripping daggers read: 'Rangers Forever!').

Wilkington-Pike must surely have realised by then what was going on; but he fussed, cajoled and threatened six keelies into the role of pallbearers and, later, continued directing the most gruesome part of the exercise when all around had succumbed save O'Driscoll and the other two jocks, a razor-seamed sergeant and an elderly, bespectacled private, who had been left out of selection for pallbearers because of their villainous appearance. I remember thinking of the Colonel character played by Alec Guiness in *The Bridge on the River Kwai*. And at the height of the horror — three down, two to go — watching the jocks through a thickening brandy haze as they traipsed back and forth to the diminishing heap of plastic bags that had been tipped out of Silver's coffin, I caught a hummed bar or two of 'Johnny Cope' from the sergeant and thought, ridiculously, of Laurel and Hardy in *Bonny Scotland*, dancing with the brushes in the barrack yard.

My last, but most vivid recollection of those two hours is a vision of Mickey Close, wig askew but still there, wafting past me on a Jock's back, a sparking-plug protruding from his nose...

I came to suspended between Punchy and the verger. My eyes were watering because O'Driscoll, his sweaty face only inches from mine, had been twisting my nose. 'Come on now, wake up and look half-dacent. He'll be comin' through that door any minnit.'

There was no sign of Wilkington-Pike or the Jocks, or of plastic bags or coffins. The tiled floor looked freshly scrubbed. No sign of Rory either — until O'Driscoll took a running kick at a pair of boots sticking out from under the refectory table. A low moan and a faint *ambience* of boke told of Rory's distress. The boots withdrew just as the Bishop's pink face appeared at the door from the chapel yard.

'What's the odds, men?' said he as O'Driscoll fell down for a quick nibble at the Holy Ring and the vestry began to overflow with his entourage: the bodyguard — four black-belted Korean Brothers any one of whom, it was said, could kill with a hard look; the custodian of the Holy Jewel Box; the bearers of the Holy Commode; the personal make-up artiste, a novice in blue-tinted glasses who had received The Call while working for Granada.

I passed out again, unremarked, at the Holy Feet.

I spent the remainder of Tuesday on the Cavan man's sofa — to which I had been borne by Punchy and the verger as soon as the show had got on the road for the cemetery — oblivious to the post-interment riot that raged the length and breadth of the ghetto. This was vintage of its kind, they tell me, due to an additional bouquet of grief over the death by heart attack of a much honoured pallbearer, eighty-six year old Paddy O'Quinn, only survivor of the famous 'Burning of the Infirmary' in 1922, who had travelled from Dublin for the occasion. Ten steps under Slack McGuigan's coffin finished poor Paddy, it being the last to be dealt with by the Jocks, who, owing to a distributive miscalculation, had had to stand on the lid while O'Driscoll and the verger screwed it down. The contents, Punchy says, were fifty percent BMC.

Surfacing briefly in the small hours of Wednesday I saw Steffers asleep in an armchair and Punchy curled up round a half-full bottle of Powers on the rug beside me. Outside, the *leitmotiv* of modern Ireland — gunfire, running feet and drunken laughter... Snaffling Punchy's bottle, I quickly submerged.

Wednesday proper began with Steffers and a brimming glass of Bloody Mary — and was there and then nearly ended for good by a glimpse of Punchy savaging a huge plateful of fried egg, black puddin' and kidneys! I sped away again to the lamentation of the Cavan Man on seeing what I had deposited on his pink sheepskin rug... 'Ah ferfrigsake, Francie!'

My next bout of semi-consciousness coincided with the lunchtime news on TV — 'Ulster — rioting continues throughout the principal no-go areas following yesterday's funeral of five young men killed, allegedly, when their car came under sustained fire from a squadron of British tanks. Bishop O'Lowry, officiating, made an earnest plea for calm and restraint and called for an immediate high level inquiry into the use of heavy armour in built-up areas. In response, the Secretary General has issued a statement announcing the setting up of the inquiry board, which will include such notable figures in public life as Lord O'God, the millionaire property speculator, Paul McCartney and

Edward Kennedy. Our reporter on the spot informs us that the situation has been further aggravated by the sudden death in curious circumstances of Mrs Sinaid Rarity, wife of Mr Liam Rarity, Vice-Chairman of the RSVP party. Her body was found in the living room of their home by Mr Rarity, who alleges that she was the victim of high frequency sound waves transmitted via the telephone by British Intelligence Agents. He has called for an immediate inquiry into the use of electronic warfare by *agents provocateur* and the Secretary General has responded by naming Dame Gladys Syne, the well known actress, to head the board. Both inquiries are to be boycotted by all concerned. And now, the General Election. Polling has been brisk —'

At this point Steffers turned from the box in time to see her drink disappear down my gullet, following Punchy's and the Cavan man's from the table beside my sofa. 'For God's sake, Francie! It'll be the stomach pump if...' I learnt later that hers had been gin, Punchy's Gold Label Powers and the Cavan man's Pernod. A powerful octane. It was as though I were a passenger on a train gathering speed out of a station and Steffers on the platform mouthing away silently at the window. I smiled and waved...

But I was never allowed to return to the same strata of coma as before. Though I have no recollection of it, they tell me that Steffers spent the afternoon harassing me in every way imaginable, from shaking and slapping to some underhand tactics the description of which set the Cavan man's eyes rolling heavenwards in disgust. The effect was that around teatime I found myself sitting up in an armchair, wrapped in a blanket, taking in quantities of molten vegetable broth off a spoon wielded by Jeremy. My place on the sofa had been taken by Punchy, I noted hazily, who was in process of being trussed hand and foot by Steffers and the Cavan man (in the extremities of drink or grief he's inclined to attempt the demolition of walls and things with short, right-hand jabs).

'I'm sure Rarity hisself's not takin' on like that,' panted the Cavan man, standing back.

'He must be some sort of relative,' said Steffers, '— or a lover!'

'Durty oul' brute!'

The broth, home-brewed to a Cavan recipe, didn't do the whole trick, thank God, merely elevating me from the role of potential corpse to that of invalid spectator. For afters the barman, knowing my tastes, had thrown together a Gaelic coffee — double Cognac, a touch of hot water, a thimble of instant, the whole topped with whipped cream — which Steffers tried vainly to intercept. I cursed her; she huffed; the barman smirked cattily; and then we all settled down to the most hilarious evening's viewing I've ever had, before or since...

'Election Special'; a cavernous studio stuffed with computers and all sorts of office equipment; manned by an army of bit players 'reposing' like mad behind panels of university dons flourishing slide-rules; 'experts' in shirtsleeves and carefully ruffled hair who jabbed pointers at graphs and did their best to induce an element of drama into the proceedings; and, best of all, politicians.

We played a game — Steffers, the Cavan man, Jeremy, the barman and I — called 'Spot the Poof'. The laypeople — Steffers and I — would make a guess which would then be discussed by the local initiates — the Cavan man and the barman — and then Jeremy, using his encyclopaedic knowledge of the underground Metropolis, would award points. I said hilarious, and you'll have to take my word for it, it being the sort of humour impossible to transmit into print, a feline thing of sly asides, *double entendre* and voice inflection, the sort of group repartee that I'd first heard in the weaving sheds where I used to spend my after school hours with my Mother and sisters. (The nearest I ever came to punching a card. But I imagine the male humour of shipyard and factory floor to be much the same as in Borstal or prison — the deadpan retailing of dirty jokes.) After a while, if one was tiddly enough, watching some pompous elder statesman rabbiting on through a barrack of obscene innuendo, the illusion that he was not entirely oblivious to it, that he could actually hear the awful things being said about him, played a large part in the total hilarity.

Vision only, of course, which was why we giggled through the sensational turn of events that had pollsters turfing themselves out of high windows and colonels leaping smartly off the Baden-Jones bandwagon from Aldershot to Inverness. Only when the news came on at midnight did we learn the drift of things — or rather Steffers did, and retailed a synopsis, spiked with sarcasm, into my fading ear as I sank, like the sun in the final frames of a Fitzpatrick travelogue, slowly under the last naggin of Black Bush...

'So much for buggering about with the democratic processes,' she sneered wittily; 'neck and neck at the last hurdle. The Emperor Baden-Jones's only hope now is if a sudden colour problem has arisen in the Orkneys!'

117

'Stale-Mate!' gloated Thursday's *Mirror*, predictably... But not quite. The Orkneys, by some topographical error, had been invaded over the week-end by a contingent of starving Wolverhampton Pakis! The votes of the irate islanders had hoisted B-J's overall majority to a dodgy seven.

'He'll not be able to go for a crap without the Liberals' say-so,' stated Steffers graphically.

'Say "keek", my love, not "crap",' I chided, feeling myself for the first time in two days and finding all reasonably intact: 'it is our national duty to use the Erse whenever at all possible. We may have no words for such filthy foreign implements as telephones, omnibuses or computers, but we have, let me remind you, fourteen different ways of describing a red-haired heifer in heat and a word for every shape, volume, shade and aroma of turd that ever fell from the cheeks of man.'

'Oh!' groaned Jeremy.

'Naughty!' sighed the barman.

'Ferfrigsake, Francie!'

'— Will yis all for God's sake give over!' shouted Punchy, regretting it immediately, his head sinking back on the sofa painfully. He continued, in a whisper: 'Has the doctor bin here yet?'

'What doctor?' asked the bewildered Cavan man.

'Ach Lord Christ! Have a titter of wit, will ye. I'm sixty-five years of age! If you foun' somebody of sixty-five years of age lyin' in the street in this state wouldn't ye run for somebody —' Punchy tailed off in a babble, and the Cavan man, heart of corn and former First Truncheon in Downpatrick Asylum, began the onerous task of poulticing his tubes with Bloody Marys and black coffee.

'I've never seen him worse,' I happened to say, conversationally, and at once became the focal point of a collective accusative glare.

'It's your fault as much as his.' (Steffers)

'Poor dead cow!' (Jeremy)

'You an' your Psycomological phone calls!' (The Cavan man)

I tried quoting the bereaved spouse on SAS hyper-sonic warfare (God, he was learning fast, that PhD(Econ)!) but it was no use; Punchy, apparently, had raved a full statement during the night, and the Cavan man had been out and about early gathering hearsay, rumour and doubtful fact concerning the 'curious circumstances' of Mrs Rarity's passing...

With the exception of the Trendy Left and, perhaps, the members of the subsequent inquiry board, no one ever believed Rarity's kite about SAS assassination (no one including the two SAS men who were told off to plead guilty). O'Driscoll and the other Priests who had suffered under the phantom knicker flouter put two and two together and formed their own diverse opinions. O'Driscoll, according to the verger, was convinced that having run the gamut of the local RC clergy, she'd made the fatal mistake of starting on the Protestants: she'd been struck down, he swore, by a lewd counter-attack from a C of I curate in Lisburn, a failed medical student renowned for his wholesale debauchery of choir matrons.

The whole truth of the matter will probably never be known. I do know that Punchy, guilt-stricken, made inquiries of his own by way of a contact in the telephone service department; but beyond the fact that the instrument, one of the modern style with a small cylindrical handset, had short circuited — and a dark hint that it might have been employed in a manner never envisaged by its designer — I've never heard any concrete explanation of the mystery. The version accepted by the ordinary ghoul-in-the-ghetto is that Rarity choked her with a pillow on surprising her, naked, with a black, Protestant Paratrooper — and they loved him for it, a state of affairs Liam was not slow to capitalize on during O'Lig's indisposition...

'— Directin' the riot from the lounge of the Golden Calf,' gasped the Cavan man above the farmyard noises issuing from his patient; 'ponced up like some sorta gaelic horse-marine — ridin' britches an' binoculars! An' poor Rory lyin' like Nelson in the bottling store with not a whole inch of skin on him —'

'Christ! — it was only a nick on the arm —'

'— Up till Bridget an' her litter came roun' lookin' for Silver after the funeral, y'mean... When Rory toul' them the truth I believe it was like a pack of bagles roun' a stag. Bridget sunk her teeth in his gullet — God's truth, I seen the marks myself. They had to throw buckets of water to make them let go.'

Burton came in about elevenses — Steffers and I having just killed a bottle of Gordon's curative juniper juice, recommended by the Cavan Man as a palliative for suppurating liver. Steffers, having failed to restrain my consumption, seemed to have reasoned, fallaciously, that what she swallowed I wouldn't.

'Thank Christ you're here,Francie!' Burton exclaimed, puffing and laying a hand on a supposedly pounding heart. His eyes were bulging oddly, I thought. He was back to the hippy garb again — long black wig, leather bum-freezer and mauve slacks. 'Some bugger took a shot at me when I was knocking at your chalet! Has the whole bloody kip gone berserk?'

'Making their protest, "O",' I said. 'Just making their protest. The sudden disappearance of the army from the periphery has caused widespread alarm and despondency. Rumour has it that they've all changed into civvies and are infiltrating, so the current rule of action is to shoot everything on two legs that isn't immediately recognisable as a blood relative.'

'That's what I wanted to see you about,' he whispered, glancing round. Steffers' lip curled at him; Jeremy and the barman ogled him; the Cavan man took time off from giving Punchy what sounded like an enema to size him up. 'Is there somewhere we could talk?'

I led the way to the master bedroom.

'Jesus!' he gasped on viewing the boxers, the Holy statuary and the black bed.

'Think no evil,' I chided, pouring him a share of my bottle; 'the chamber of a Christian athlete who loathes the sight of bug-marks. No more, no less.'

He looked at me suspiciously. 'I hope you're not on a bender, Francie. Things are going to move a lot faster than we anticipated, and if you're —'

'Say no more,' I silenced him sternly; 'if there's still quids to be quarried I'm your sober man. But I'd a notion you were here to tell me it was all off. What happened to your landslide?'

'Where have you been! — Or are you the only man in the world who hasn't heard of Herbie Boal?'

Of course I had — teenage centre-forward for Beaconsfield Centurions and England, owner of a chain of sex boutiques and health farms, escort of film starlets, idol of the underprivileged.

'What in hell's Herbie Boal got to do with it?' I asked patiently.

'Just that he managed to cancel out all the good of the Hyphen Smith thing by being dragged out of a public pissoir in Marseilles and charged with gross indecency and soliciting — that's all! Good God man, the papers were full of it on Tuesday. Result, a massive vote of plebeian sympathy for buggers everywhere — including, by recent association, our Bunny!'

'So what's the score now? With a majority of seven —'

'We know: B-J'll never last — but he's doing his damnedest, buttering-up the Liberals and Independents like mad. As for Operation Starkey, as you can guess, everything has been frozen on the mainland; B-J has switched support to some moderate black leaders who have managed to cool the situation with promises of reform — and the withdrawal from here has been stopped, leaving about half the garrison still in position —'

'It's off then?'

'Not at all — very much on!' he cried enthusiastically, arousing in me the same feeling as when I'd heard him go on about poetic vengeance. I noticed that there seemed to be an extraordinary expanse of white about his eyes. Birdseed?... 'B-J was merely the figurehead, the mouthpiece, just as any politician any time is merely the eighth part of the iceberg; the visible, audible expression of the will of the real establishment. And that will, Francie, does not waver because some snotty-nosed ball player is caught with his breeks round his ankles. Certainly, if B-J has to compromise the outward forms of democracy will be upheld and Operation Starkey shelved — but the will is still there and things have moved to a stage when it would be exceedingly foolish not to take pragmatic advantage. For instance: the half of the garrison still here is spread throughout the country areas — a large part of it being Sappers, REME and suchlike. And the Isle of Man is virtually occupied by hundreds of the most savage black militants, every one a potential detonator of future racial explosion... Are you with me, Francie?'

I was, barely; well down the second bottle of the day, settled comfortably in the Cavan man's black sheets and wanting nothing more than his silence and swift departure.

'In a nutshell,' I yawned: 'you and Toby still want O'Lig, the Duncher and followers delivered for slaughter. And there's still two thou. in it for me?'

'Right. The only change is the time. Within the next five days; preferably Sunday night. It'll all be well hushed up, of course, but if anything should leak in the future we want to leave B-J and the Party an out — he'll be able to say it occurred before his administration had properly taken up the reins... Now, here's the letters I promised — one for O'Lig, the other for Duncher. We had them made up before Wednesday, just in case. All but the date, that is. Do you think you can organize it for Sunday? It's all to do with tides and things.'

I took the letters but didn't open them. 'Mightn't be too hard,' I

121

said; 'with the army gone our side might welcome a diversion. But the Duncher's another kettle of fish: you never know about them Indians of his. Shout the right slogan, wave a pound note, and our lot's all too willing to fall in for a bit of a lark — so long as the clergy do not actively oppose. But with Duncher's boys I always get the feeling that they resent him somehow. They're afeared of him, certainly; and the women love him; but when he's haranguing away they're all glowering up at him as if to say "Pull the other leg, mate!" You're one of them so you'll know what I mean —'

'One of them! How dare you!' screeched Burton in mock affront. 'Let me tell you that I represent a generation of lost leaders. When I was a kid the peasantry used to assemble on the lawn every Eleventh of July; and my father, an atheist pamphleteer, a militant God-hater, would put on his sash to go out and give the Lambeg drum a traditional dunder. My father, Francie, stood on a firing-step on the Somme and ordered the Grandas of Duncher's lads into hell — and they went —'

' "With a song on their lips" '

'— knowing that if they didn't they'd never get their jobs back at the mill! A collective inferiority; that's what's wrong with the huers. And it's become pathological since the Trendy Left propaganda machine began chewing them up. Dr Goebbels' dream! A campaign that has the effect of confirming in the object a view of himself that he has always secretly held! That's the root cause of all their splits and schisms. It always reminds me of the Groucho Marx one — "I wouldn't set foot in a club that would tolerate me as a member" — or something.'

'What about Kate and the kids?' I asked (anything to coup him off his hobby-horse). 'Where will they be on Sunday night?'

'Out of harm's way, I assure you. Toby's moving them to the Big House today. All the action will be at the neck of the peninsula and at certain points along the shore — well away from the house, so they'll be safe enough... Now, here's the drill...'

I didn't take notes. I nodded and grunted at the full stops and did a closed-eyes, grimace of pain, 'engraving on the mind' thing at paragraph endings; all of which seemed to satisfy the silly bastard. His unabated enthusiasm confirmed what I had suspected all along: that all that guff about 'repatriation', 'withdrawal' and 'exchange of population' had been so much cover-up for a straightforward Military Intelligence plan for the extermination of two flocks of dangerous shitehawks with the one stone — the black militants to stave off the inevitable for another generation, the Irish to make way for an all-Ireland settlement well short of their various extreme ends. I doubt whether B-J or any other politician had a hand in such a dicey caper — except, perhaps, as sleeping directors in one of those international companies whose main concern is a harmonious Common Market. Having had previous dealings, I knew something of the niggardly budgets attached to most Intelligence operations; and to me the lavishness of Toby's set-up on the peninsula, not forgetting the peek I'd had at his honey-pot, had a strong smell of numbered accounts in Zurich.

Which was why I paid little attention to anything but the bare bones of the 'drill'. The success or failure of their plan did not concern me; all I desired was to ensure a maximum state of confusion on the peninsula as a cover for my own 'Operation Honey-pot'.

Not that I'd anything but the vaguest notion of how I was going to go about it. But through the blur of gin that Thursday midday in the Cavan man's boudoir I managed to extract certain useful facts, like the approximate whereabouts of Toby and Burton himself on the night (well away from the House, I was gratified to hear)...

'And his Royal Prickship?' I asked.

'Ah yes. Bertie —' Burton looked a trifle embarrassed, but continued: 'At the moment he's on the Isle of Man... Look here, Francie, I suppose it's all right to gen you up in the circumstances — but under your hat, mind... You see, it has become politic, practically overnight, to remove Bertie from the firing squad, as it were, and put him against the wall. He thinks he's over there as, as you once put it, a Judas Goat among the black Bolshies. The first he'll know about his change in status, we hope, is when a Gurkha kukri penetrates his Royal anus —'

'And what has caused poor Bertie's fall from grace? Shagging the wrong Minister or something?'

'The unmentionable,' breathed Burton: 'the mad bastard got stinking drunk at Cowes on Sunday night — he flew straight from here, remember — anyhow, he ended up at a party on the Royal Yacht and sometime during the night he went sleep-walking with a length of flex —'

'Ah Christ no!' I squealed, almost sober; 'not —?'

'No, no — but bad enough. The Royal chef — from Barbados — a genius — swinging from the yardarm when the Royals came on deck on Monday morning! You can imagine the furore! All hushed up, of course — but there's a Regal contract out on our Bertie: New Year's

123

Honours — a knighthood at least — and Toby fancies it strongly...'

He must have left shortly after this revelation — or I left him. I awoke in the black bed, alone with an empty gin bottle and two glasses. The two duff letters lay on the bedside table, but when I opened and tried to read one the crest and '10 Downing Street' was as much as I could bring in focus. I smote the Cavan man's purple carpet thrice with his antique delph po and Steffers appeared, clad only in a crotch-length blue silk thing I'd seen Jeremy flouncing about in from time to time. Her face was red and sweat-beaded and wisps of steam curled about her thighs. She'd been having a bath, she pouted angrily, as I summoned her to the bedside and bade her read me the letter.

Dear Mr O'Lig,

Further to our conversation in London on the 12th inst., I am pleased to confirm arrangements for the transference of certain materials to your organization. The said materials (listed below) will be off-loaded at high tide (2300 hours approx) on the 28th prox... in a cove known locally as 'Barney's Boul'... on the... 'Wee' peninsula... I trust you will be able to provide adequate transportation, and must stress... the need... for the ut... most security at all times. Materials are:- 200 Rifles (.303 calibre); 200 Self-loading Rifles (.308 calibre); 100 Sterling Machine Pistols (9 mm);... 20... 20... Mortars... 3 inch...'

An impressive list — actually three times as long as above, increasing in calibre until 'Best wishes' and B-J's signature, but that's as far as we got at that first reading. I have interpolated the rows of stops in the text to give some indication of the difficulties Steffers wrought under. I considered ending each row with an exclamation mark to further indicate her surprise at the situation which had arisen, but thought it might confuse. I too was surprised, and inclined at first to doubt the substance of the manifestation (balls or bladder). On the brink (the lip?) of putting the braggard to the test, I paused to inquire: 'Can you get a hold of your Da's car for a day?'

'Aw — ah — huh —!' she gurgled testily.

On Friday morning Punchy and I set out with the letters to prime and load 'Operation Honey-pot'. (I just don't want to talk about the few remaining bits of Thursday that I do recall. Suffice to say that an irate Cavan man spent the night on the sofa, from which he had evicted the convalescent Punchy onto the floor. Also, the rioting appeared to have ceased, or at least reverted to the hand-to-hand owing to a shortage of ammo caused by the absence of lines of supply — Punchy.) Steffers had gone off to see about borrowing the Da's car for a quick recce round the peninsula, specifically to ascertain that Toby's boat was still at its moorings and, if possible, to waggle her tits at the nearest gnarled old salt and find out if any plans were afoot to move it.

Convalescent, a Lazarus readjusting to terrestrial hell after a glimpse of the Elysian Fields, Punchy shuffled alongside me and girned: 'If you take my advice you'll jack the fuggin' lot an' git back to bread an' butter... All them weemin friggin' about — yer woman, an' dirty Teesy — an' Kate, fer Chrissake! —' I'd let slip about Kate earlier, almost precipitating a relapse — 'That dong of yours,' he forecast mournfully, "ll be the death of us all yit.'

'Do not speak ill of the all-but-dead,' I chided. 'Anyway, things are on the change, oul' han' — or haven't you noticed?'

Blind if he hadn't. Hard to believe that only ten days had passed since I'd paraded Steffers through the ghetto like the young Pompey doing a triumphal with the loot. Very few of the adults abroad in the rubble-littered side streets seemed to recognise us — we did, I suppose, have the look of walking wounded — but those who did tended to hawk and spit oysters if passing close enough, or to shake clenched fists in a way that had nothing at all to do with the solidarity of Workers and Small Farmers. The childer, of course, expressed themselves very succinctly...

Entering a street on the last leg of our journey to the Golden Calf we came upon a skipping game in progress. Odd enough at any hour for a generation of tots, any one of whom would immediately associate the word 'rope' with 'noose'; but before noon in the wake of a riot, startling. Then, on drawing nearer, we saw a tweedy man with a shoulder-held camera and a hooky pipe, a girl with a watch on a chain round her neck and a clipboard in her hand, and, crouched in a doorway, a sound mechanic.

'No, no, children,' the girl was saying as we came within earshot; 'not as it's written, not "Cayenne" pepper — "Carry-an' pepper" Much more —'

'Ethnic,' mumbled the cameraman.

Then the childer spotted Punchy and me. Before we could beat a retreat they had broken ranks and gathered round us on the pavement, howling such unscripted refrains as:

> 'Who stole the cheese outa the gravedigger's piece?
> Francie O'Toole, Francie O'Toole, Francie O'Toole!'

and:

> 'Who stole the poultice off the scabby child's head?
> Punchy Coyne, Punchy Coyne, Punchy Coyne!'

Recognising one or two down-looking male bastards in the crush — well over military age, eleven or twelve, with bulging pockets — I flashed the tobacco knife and Punchy criss-crossed the air with his Hamburg Ring, clearing a way through as they broke into another old tyme favourite:

> 'If you've kilt a British sodger, clap yer han's...'

which they did, rhythmically, self-hypnotically, little faces clenched in the same mindless fervour as their Ma's when performing on the bin-lids.

They had us cornered against a gateway and things were beginning to look a hair ugly when the tweedy cameraman took a hand and saved the day — for us, if not himself. 'Please children... Positions please...' he cried, pushing a way through, the camera perched on his shoulder like Robert Newton's parrot, making wandlike gestures with the hooky pipe. Then he fell, brought down by a tangle of power cables. Fatal. To lose your feet in that company is like an outback drover being dismounted in front of a mob of wild cattle: a matter of lost dominance. They were on him in a flash, giving Punchy and me a chance to do a quick flit. The roars of him were terrible to hear, even three streets away. A minute later his camera overtook us, borne by two of the down-looking elders, and by the time we reached the Golden Calf it was already the property of the lounge barman.

'Whad'ya think of that for two quid an' a gallon of scrumpy!' he exclaimed proudly.

'Very nice,' said Punchy, taking the all of four hundred quid's worth from him and tucking a note in the breast pocket of his bum-freezer. 'There's a fiver for it an' I'll see you get home safe the night.'

Oh, the resilience of the human spirit! The fracas had certainly put Punchy back on his mettle. The barman knew better than to argue, and even set up two Powers as a luck penny.

On asking Rory's whereabouts we were directed to a bottling store in the back yard of the premises and told to knock twice with knuckles and once with the boot. When we did so, a peephole framed a bloodshot eye briefly and a voice, unmistakably Rory's, screamed: 'Fugg aff! You pair of bastards niver brung nothin' but trouble.'

'All right, all right, old friend,' I said soothingly; 'Punchy said you were taking a back seat this weather, but I insisted on giving you the first say. Where is Rarity, by the way?

At this the door flew open and there he was; a hell of a state, worse even than the Cavan man's word picture — but, surprisingly, sober enough.

'Fuck Rarity, the skivin' bastard... What are you on about anyway?'

'Something that could put you back at the wheel, Rory. D'you mind that thing Punchy told you about? The British arms shipment for Duncher?'

I produced and passed the crested letter to him. After reading it to the last listed mortar, he ripped it in two, flung the crumpled halves to the ground and howled: 'Perfidious Albion!' as though coining a phrase. (He was genuinely hurt — as is any Irishman when England or the English deviate one degree from the Christlike. And this after an education in English perfidy from Cromwell to Henry Wilson which, you'd think, would lead us to expect the worst.)

'There'll be wigs on the green over this! I'll bring it up in the —'

He was going to say 'The House', but remembered in time that he had helped burn The House down. 'Christ, Francie, we can't just let them get away with it —'

I explained to him that we didn't intend to, and that we looked to him to organize an interception committee for Sunday night. I also suggested that with the aid of the letter, which I had rescued from the floor and smoothed out, he could pass it off as an intelligence coup on his own part and perhaps regain the initiative from Rarity. I could see he liked this.

'But I'm skint,' he whinged; 'that huer has cornered all my collections. An' you know Christ hisself couldn't move our lot outa the smoke without a few bob for gargle at least.'

I threw in the clincher: 'You didn't think we were doing this for charity — or the Wild Bitch of the Bogs — now did you, Rory?' I enquired suavely, pulling out the roll and starting to peel off ten fivers. His eyes lit up at the very hint of larceny. 'What do you think we'd do with all that hardware? Use it! I've the Welsh Nationalists all lined up for a cash deal on Monday, so you can consider this an advance on your cut of the proceeds.'

'I knew right well you wouldn't be handin' out yer own fivers,' he growled, pocketing them (an attitude I had anticipated). 'OK, we'll do our very best. But you'll have to give me a bit more gen —'

'That's Punchy's pigeon. He'll stay with you today and lend a bit of moral support — and a drop of the physical if necessary. I've things to do elsewhere.'

Duncher.

But before that I dropped into the Prince for a stiffener or two...

'Things is bad, Francie.'

'Couldn't be worse.'

'Are they all fuggin' mad, d'you think?'

'Mad for power.'

'You niver spoke a truer word!'

There was a great dearth of notables in the lunchtime throng. The vice squad man still plied his trade among the students. A stout young poet from the Ministry of Culture lectured a circle of gaping girls on the artistic — and profitable — by-products of communal slaughter. A spokesman for the Workers' Commune gulped double whiskies as fast as a delegation of liberal English vicars could buy and bartered a vivid eye-witness account of how a squadron of Chieftain tanks had opened up at point-blank range on the funeral cortège of 'The Faithful Five'. In one snug the 'In Depth' team from Lord Toronto's Sunday sang 'Eskimo Nell'; in another sat Burton and Chloe.

'Mr O'Dongo, darling!' cried Chloe, ravishingly well-pissed in a peach-coloured see-through thing and little else. 'Isn't it a fabulous scene! "O" has been telling me that the girls do short times in these snugs at night! Imagine! They must have hinged vertebrae, the poor things! I've suggested to "O" that we try a spot of research — but he's chicken, dry old stick!... Well, come and sit by me — and do try not to devour my boobs in that unequivocal way, you horny brute! It's very itch-making —'

'For God's sake, Chloe, give it a rest,' hissed Burton angrily. 'Be eternally grateful, Francie, that you never married a lady scribbler, especially one obsessed with the basic impulses of the male beast. Any gathering is an excuse for her to make sexy speeches in a loud voice and take note of how many within hearing distance start playing pocket billiards —'

'There's one away now!' cried Chloe delightedly; 'did you see him? That pimply fellow in the tight denims who went into the loo just then... Poor thing! Those trousers weren't made for surreptitious fondling... "O", do you remember the time I did the piece on the prevention of pubic moulting at Foyle's luncheon? My God, Francie, it was like the beating of giant wings under the table!'

I took off as quickly as was half decent — pausing to give my own giant wing a cold sluice under the tap in the yard. But not before I had given Burton an optimistic resumé of our progress to date and learnt that prognostications for Sunday night — weather, etc — were good. The only cloud on the horizon was the unspeakable Bertie who, it seems, had absconded from the Isle of Man and thus shopped Toby's prospects of an instant knighthood.

I completed my journey to Duncher by taxi. The fat little man who drove it thought he was going to drop me this side of the bridge, on the way regaling me with tales of atrocities committed on straying travellers by Duncher's Mohawks since the army checkpoint had been taken off. Sure enough, when we reached the bridge they were clearly visible on the other side, lounging on their motorbikes; but by this time my little man had seen me slip the single load into my fountain pen and had been persuaded to finish the journey. We passed Duncher's boys at 70 mph and I was kicking at the door of his tin tabernacle before they'd a chance to mount a pursuit.

The door didn't open, but I heard a shrill voice, recognisable as Teesy's, coming from somewhere inside. On circling the building I found the window of the small annexe in which I had had my last interview with Duncher and, face pressed up against it, Teesy. The window was tightly shut and reinforced with criss-crossed wiring. We had to shout...

'Oh Francie, I knew you'd come back! Are you here to get me away? He's me locked in with no clothes on... look...' One gigantic udder filled the window momentarily.

'Yes Teesy; never fear; you'll be free very soon, if I've anything to do with it. Where's Duncher now?'

'Up at the drillin' ground — it's the playground of a school just across the road... For God's sake hurry up an' do somethin' to get me away, Francie!'

I was turning to go when I remembered the threatened nuptials.

'Are youse married yet?'

'Aye — last Tuesday — in the sight of the Lord, he says. All I know is he's been doin' me twice as often. Oh Francie, it's killin' me!'

I found the drilling ground easily enough. Howls of command were clearly audible from the main road, and, as I drew nearer, the clash of a hundred metalled heels. The howls were Duncher's; he stood on a podium, resplendent in dark blue battle dress, Sam Browne belt and sword, the insignia of a Field Marshal glittering on his epaulettes; the heels belonged to a company of the over-thirties section of his organization, in smart khaki combat dress with Afrika Corps style caps, all forming fours, dressing to the left and slow-marching in response to his incoherent, cockney-inflected commands. Other persons in Australian bush hats — a General, a brace of Majors, four or five Captains — lounged and sauntered in front of the podium, slapping their thighs with leather-coated swagger-sticks and throwing quivering salutes to each other at the slightest opportunity.

The General, whom I recognised as a particularly foul-mouthed driver of a Corporation bin-cart, spotted me first. He paraded over, swagger-stick clubbed in his right hand.

'I know you, y'rotten Fenian baster —' he began.

'And I know you,' I interrupted, 'you non-conformist shite shifter. But it's the Field Marshal I came to see; so if you'll just pass the word I might not kick yer fat arse for ye.'

But for the high level of liquor in my tubes I'd never have dared. Luckily he turned out to be one of those large men who shoot their bolt with mouth and blood vessel, leaving nothing for that spurt over the top into action. Again, the suggestion that I knew him and his calling probably helped (they'd only recently stopped wearing dark glasses and masks on these outings), the thought of retaliatory Molotov cocktails in the night causing him to about turn without another word.

I still had to wait through the march past in quick-and-slow time before the troops were dismissed and the General muttered in the Field Marshal's lug. Duncher approached me, flanked by two thuggy-looking Captains.

'You've gall enough for a regiment!' he growled; 'just danderin' in here like it was a Boys' Brigade display! I'm beginnin' to think you're not all there or somethin'!'

'Now Duncher, all I want is one minute's private chat — no more. The last time I was here I told you about certain forthcoming events, one of which has happened already. The withdrawal of troops? So if you'll just get rid of your lads here, I've something else to show you.'

He did as I asked, waving the two Captains back among their mates while he and I retired into a doorway at the back of the school. Knowing him, I was surprised at this acquiescence — until we were alone and out of earshot...

'I 'clare t' God, O'Toole!' he hissed venomously. 'If it's the last thing I do I'll see you gutted like a herrin' for this!'

'For what? I'm doing you a favour and —'

'Have a look at them over there then,' he grimaced, tight-lipped, looking downward so that 'they' might be forgiven for thinking that he was inviting me to admire the shine on his ammo boots. 'They' were, I noticed, tending to stand around in muttering groups, glancing over at us... 'They'll swear, b'Jasus, I'm in the pay of the Vatican! There's a few unbelievers among them that has bin stirrin' up trouble about my new Missus, an' the like of you comin' friggin' about'll not help. What is it that couldn't wait till after dark, anyway?'

'This,' I said, palming his version of the Downing Street letter. I let him get well down it before saying: 'So you see the urgency of the matter. Sunday night doesn't leave a lot of time if you want to get cracking.'

'Git crackin' at what?' he sneered — but stuck the letter in his tunic pocket. 'Catch yerself on! — D'you think it's oul' Joe Soap yer talkin' to? Sure how do I know it's not you an' O'Lig tryin' an oul' come-on —'

'Ah, for Christ's sake, Duncher! I could see the sense in your being suspicious if the location of the landing was on the other side of the river: but in your own back yard! And look at the loot — it's a gift!'

'An' since when did you start bein' Daddy Xmas! Onct a Fenian, allus a Fenian, an' I can't see you —'

131

'But above all else, Duncher, I'm a thief. I can get two thousand, cash, for that load of hardware if I had it tomorrow. Half for you if you'll do it.'

It was a shot in the half-light. All I had to go on was his misdemeanours while Quartermaster Sergeant in the Rifles depot — and that's more an occupational disease than evidence of innate delinquency. I'd heard rumours, of course, about sidelines in arms, uniforms and the like, but nothing definite. With bated bad breath I awaited his reaction and, remembering the Head Constable's teeth, kept well back out of leaping range of his forehead.

'Say no more now,' he whispered, head down, pawing the floor with one boot; 'there's lugs out there could pick up mention of money a mile away... Phone me the night about eight. You've the number —' Then, poking my guts with his stick, he began to shout — 'An' that's another thing: total withdrawal, you said, an' there's still a full company of them Scotch Taigs protectin' that holy kiphouse down there. But you mark my words, the days comin' when that affront to ivery dacent woman in the district is gonna be pulled down roun' their Fenian ears —'

He went on in this vein for some time, to the evident approval of his eavesdropping High Command. After about ten minutes of it I managed to extract myself in good order — though the General, I could see, would have had it otherwise.

My little taximan had stayed, rigid, where I'd left him, heart afeared to recross the bridge without so much as the protection of my fountain pen. On the way back I noted a fresh gem of gable graffiti illustrating, perhaps, local unrest over Teesy: 'Duncher For Pope!' it advocated.

I walked back from the Prince to the chalet, passing the Golden Calf en route. I had intended dropping in to see how Punchy and O'Lig were making out, but on hearing strains of patriotic dirgeology from within I decided to leave well enough alone. Going by the volume — not forgetting that a fine tenor (Slack) and four bassmen were singing elsewhere — things seemed to be coming together nicely under Rory's largesse.

In the chalet I found Steffers stretched on the bed, resting after her scout round the peninsula in Daddy's car. She greeted me warmly; and afterwards (two hours) divulged her findings...

Toby's launch was still fast to its moorings, inhabited at present by two mechanics who were replacing a burnt-out bearing in the port side diesel. They, in the nebulous way of specialists, had told Toby that the job would take them until Tuesday to complete; an estimate which had seemed to satisfy him. But they intended to be finished by Saturday lunchtime, when, taking an essential small part of the starting mechanism with them, they would go off for a long week-end of coarse pleasures and return on Tuesday to collect their money. Steffers — grand gel! — not only had managed to find out the exact specification of the essential small part but also had purchased one on her way back! Further, she had ascertained that the fuel tanks were almost full and that there was enough food and water aboard for a lengthy journey.

I congratulated her on fine job well done, making no mention of certain black greasy marks I'd noticed on parts of her not normally exposed to accidental friction. I then went to the bog and gave Fagan his second sluice of the day, this time with a tincture of Jeyes fluid, just in case. A diesel mechanic's dose was all I needed.

At about seven o'clock Punchy arrived, semi-footless but cogent, to report that Rory was presiding over a booze and ballad session of Olympian proportions in the Golden Calf, but had run out of funds at a crucial moment.

'— We flashed the letter to a fair cross section of hardchaws an' so far they're all for it. Rory's even managed to put the boot back in some of the collectors — but he needs a few quid to keep it going through the night. That's the only time you'll git the big gelly boys out from under the bed. Could you manage a score, Francie?'

'Talking about gelly,' I said, peeling four off the roll; 'have you any plastic handy? — Enough for a small safe —'

'Toby's? Oh aye. No bother.'

I gave him the score and he scuttled off back to the high jinks in the Golden Calf. At eight on the dot I rang Duncher...

'Yis?'

'Is that you, Duncher?' (As if I didn't know.)

'Who wants till know?'

'Francie O'Toole. Remember? You asked me to ring.'

'An' how do I know you are who you say you are! Sure you could —'

'— I'm in no mood for fucking about, Duncher! For one thousand cash are you prepared to help hi-jack that load on Sunday night? If not, say so and I'll get —'

'— Now, now, Francie; no need to take that tone. It's just that you've got to be canny these days. There's them that would get up to anything to get their knives into me.'

133

'Aye. I see you're running a strong third to King Billy and the Pope on the gable walls over there.'

'Traitors an' informers on all sides! Yi'd niver believe it. But sure it was allus the same in this kip of a country — stan' up an' be counted an' there's allus some cunt waitin' to draw a bead on you! That's why I'm thinkin' of takin' the lil lady an' clearin' out for good. So a few quid'll come in handy —'

'— You'll do it! Good man, Duncher —'

'— Ah but here — it'll not be as easy as all that. I'd need a right few down there — an' it's them motor-bike ligs that are slanderin' me on the gables. Even at the best of times they git uneasy if they're outa sight of the gantries —'

'What about that fine body of men you were parading this afternoon?'

'On a Sunday! — double time! — yer jokin'! All right on week-days, they'll git over the wall for the likes of thon the day an' back in time to punch out; but you'd niver git them to chance losin' a Sunday — not if Jesus Christ hisself was to come danderin' into Bangor bay draggin' the Isle of Man after him!'

'Well, look here, do you think would fifty notes in advance help the situation, Duncher? A bit of a drop here and there might smooth the path.'

Pause.

'D'you know, Francie, it niver crossed my mind — but I see what you mean right enough. Look, if I send the wee fellas roun' —'

'Dead-on, Duncher — no trouble. And I'll give you a ring sometime tomorrow to hear how things are coming along.'

Scarcely fifteen minutes after ringing off the wee fellas appeared at the Cavan man's side door and the money changed hands. I let Steffers do the actual transference, for though I comforted myself with clichés about sprats, mackerels and bread upon the waters, the fact that I was one hundred and twenty quid down on the day seemed to me a bad omen for the next two. Illogical; but so, after all, are all forms of punting.

Then, just before the first rifle crack that signalled the setting of the sun, a short leather-coated person in large dark glasses came sidling into the bar, lingering near the door and sizing up the clientele in a way that caused the veins on the Cavan man's nose to throb visibly. Besides Steffers and I there were only two or three pensioners in the bar, so there wasn't a lot to size up; but this strange leather coat took so long about it that even I, half-cut, was beginning to feel edgy when, after a minute, the Cavan man's nerve broke...

'Can I help you, sur?' he screamed.

'Francie Fallis?' enquired leather coat. For one awful moment I thought that my first impression had been drastically wrong and that murder gangsters, without my knowledge, had suddenly started dressing the part.

'That's him there,' the Cavan man pointed, he and the barman ducking down behind the bar as though gripped by a sudden telepathic urge to start quarterly stocktaking.

Leather coat strode purposefully over to where I sat frozen to a tall bar-stool. Whipping off the dark glasses, he stuck out his hand and grinned. 'I'm Cooney,' says he: 'I've a bit of a legacy for you.'

Cooney! — the sub-contractor I'd used many times and never met... Slack and the French TV proceeds! I'd nearly forgotten.

'One-three-oh,' says Cooney, counting it onto the bar; 'I took mine out. He done right an' well outa them Frogs.'

Ten quid up! 'Never let the sun set'! A sign from beyond the grave that had the — illogical — effect of sweeping away any doubts I may have had about the forthcoming caper, buoying me to a crest on which I was to ride, supported by a quart or two of Gold Label and oblivious to all reefs, onto the rocks on Sunday night.

Cooney and I chased the pensioners; the Cavan man locked and barred the door; and we embarked on a swill.

Something that never ceases to surprise me is the number of people who still think that those legions of woolly-headed stone-clodders they watch on TV are normal. Far from it. They are, of course, the inmates of Header Hall, probably under contract to the horn-rimmed graduate who appears at the end of the clip mumbling cliches about 'The sickness of our times' etc. In the foregoing narrative I have mentioned them in passing several times; it is now necessary for me to give a more rounded picture, seeing as they were the reef we all bloody near foundered on!

Header Hall is a lay establishment, administered entirely by the Education Authority, for youths who had proven too much for even the redoubtable Brothers, amenable neither to the disciplines of learning or religion. The idea had been, from a law and order point of view, to provide a place where they could work off surplus energies for eight hours daily, in the hope that they would leave society in peace for the other sixteen. Consequently, the duties of the staff — a Headmaster and six teachers — had been merely to keep damage to a minimum and stay alive. That had been in peacetime...

At the outbreak of hostilities the first to go had been two of the teachers, both ex-army PT instructors, only one of whom had escaped with his life, if nòt all his limbs. The Headmaster, a Sligo man with no qualifications other than his courage and a winning way with a blackthorn stick, had then embarked on a career as a sort of Urban Guerilla's Fagin, ably assisted by his four remaining underlings. Rent-a-lout, as I know from my own early dealings with him, had been a goldmine in the three years prior to his retirement (to a cottage in Wales, address unknown). That had been a year ago, coinciding with the internment of his four associates — on information, I'm certain, provided by him. Since then the Authority had twice sent in squads of hand-picked sadists — with fatal results (in one or two cases the pupils made a *double entendre* of the old phrase 'exposed on a pike').

That's not to say that they were now completely leaderless. Their enterprise had attracted the attention of an international student anarchist group headed by a one-eyed, crippled, twenty-two year old Frenchman, their ranks swelled from time to time by visiting commandos from seats of learning as far apart as Berkeley, Calif, and the Sorbonne... No matter how intrepid the crew, TV — even colour — cannot transmit the full flavour of a Header happening. To be caught in the midst of — or worse, to be the object of — the foam-flecked reality is a shattering experience. Above all one remembers the 'heat of battle' made tangible in smell as they, bed-wetters to a man, reach the climax of their protest. Very hard on the eyes.

Whoever dropped the word to the Headers about the peninsula has a sin to answer for. Punchy still blames O'Lig, who, he says, got so carried away on Saturday that he let fall a whisper to his favourite linkman, who in turn formed a cartel of cronies to hire a third force and ensure a lively production. Right enough, when I went round to the Golden Calf that Saturday morning every camera in the country seemed to be there, either inside recording the unabating revelry for posterity, or outside interviewing the five or six tar-clabbered recalcitrants who decorated adjacent lamp-posts — a sure sign that Rory's star was in the ascendant. Rarity himself, a hoarse and raddled Punchy informed me, having been de-jodhpured and anointed anally, had been last seen galloping for sanctuary with the Friars over the hill, clad only in short bush shirt and socks.

I didn't actually enter the Golden Calf. I put my head round the door into the howling stoor of the main bar and Punchy spotted me. He signalled frantically for me to stay outside and then followed. There were people inside, he said, ex-internees and the like, who would disembowel me on sight. Never in his life had he seen such a Hosting of the Gael, the flower of the National Freedom Movement: men with eyes that glowed in the dark; men with cobwebs in their hair and a strong stench of marzipan about their persons; men with fingers missing, eyes missing, balls gone; all with a pathological aversion to the clamouring of wrist-watches, all mad drunk and busting for a charabanc ride to the briny with the chance of a bit of straightforward slaughter thrown in.

It sounded good. But the problem would be to keep them together and reasonably happy until blast-off. About this Punchy had had the grand idea of making a book on the big meeting at, I think, Chepstow, due to start in an hour and a half's time. (It was well after twelve. I'd had one hell of a night with the dacent criminal man Cooney, a rum drinker of professional status, who had laid me out on the sofa at four o'clock and dandered into the night, the Cavan man says, as steady as he came.)

The book idea had already been approved by Rory, who had promised a backing of fifty quid, which I now matched, knowing it would be safe with a time-served fiddler like Punchy. We then discussed transportation and decided on double-decker buses — six, to be hi-jacked, of course — and Punchy remembered some banners he'd acquired just before the Knights of Columbanus had dismantled the Ebenezer Gospel Hall — 'Jesus Saves' 'Ye must be Born Again' and (believe it or not) 'Behold, I come quickly!' — which he proposed draping along the bus's sides as a disguise once across the bridge. I left him with a reminder about the plastic and detonators and the information that he would accompany Steffers and I to the scene of action in her Da's car, leaving about three o'clock on Sunday.

Steffers was already on her way to repossess the Da's car — his No 3, if you don't mind! — which I'd thought preferable to a hi-jacked job, in case of last minute hitches. She had left in a very ratty mood. With all the comings and goings it had become increasingly difficult to maintain that my sole motive was a fortnight of bashing the bunk on Toby's boat. That morning, therefore, I'd told her that Toby and Burton were the masterminds of an assassination plot aimed at the leaders of the Irish Workers and Small Farmers movement, and that Toby's safe contained a list of names which I intended to purloin before our embarkation. After the affair of the Matron's knickers she'd have believed anything of Burton, but was piqued at having been kept in the dark. I dreaded to think of her reaction when confronted with Kate and brood — and vice versa; but I needed someone to drive the bloody boat; and anyway, why should I dread? — By that time I'd have enough ready cash in hand to be above intimidation by any one woman. Money, as some punter once said, is the great aphrodisiac; the hand in an empty pocket usually fondles a limp dick (I say).

On the way back to the Cavan man's a hearse drew up alongside me. McNinch, in top hat and morning suit, sat beside the uniformed driver. The driver had a Sterling machine pistol across his lap, and the black-blinded body of the vehicle, I was certain, contained a very lively cargo. (Better thinking than you'd expect from bulkies: in our city a hearse draws as much attention as a bus in Piccadilly Circus.)

'Well Francie,' beamed McNinch, 'what about that whisper you promised at our last meeting?'

'Nothing yet,' I replied, deciding on the moment that things could get dicey enough on the peninsula without him and his bullies.

'And Miss Hamilton? Well, I hope? I've given her Father a solemn undertaking that if you do not leave her as you found her the Division's tug-o-war team will trample you to a bag of Papish bone-meal in time for next year's Orange Lilies.'

Or words to that effect. He's one vindictive bugger, that McNinch; at this very moment he is trying his damnedest to extradite me for a list of crimes stretching back to 1935 — the year before I was born!... But as he was driven away that Saturday — after giving me a benedictive poke in the ear with the ferrule of his ceremonial umbrella — he was the least of my worries.

Once back in the Cavan man's I took root for the rest of the day. The extempore cabaret put on by the trio behind the bar was of an unusually high standard, due largely to the re-appearance of the good man Cooney, now sporting an off-white slouch hat, double-breasted pinstripe, black shirt and white tie — like an extra from *Guys and Dolls*. It turned out that he actually had trod the boards once — in the Unity Theatre, London, rhubarbing in a chorus of Kulaks comprised entirely of Irish ex-felons. We drank and talked of gaols and gaolers we had known until Steffers returned with the Da's car. Quickly sizing up the situation *vis-à-vis* the Cavan man's ménage and Cooney she prised me away into the back snug and there accused me of being a crypto-queer. I think it was then that I clubbed her, but I'm not at all sure. All I know is that on Sunday morning she had this mammoth steaker — which, by the way, she made no attempt to camouflage.

It wasn't the first time. I had clubbed Kate too the time she'd caught on that our Cavan neighbour was something other than the peculiar spoilt Priest she'd taken him for — 'A culchie turd-puncher!' had been her vivid indictment — and accused me of being his enamorado... It may even have crossed the dirty minds of some reading this; if so, let me put you straight on the matter...

Unlike most of my fellow inmates in good old Galwally I'd already had my end in (twice) the Christian way before being sent up; so, beyond a few sessions of mutual Bishop bashing (a competitive sport called 'Kentucky Whist') I emerged as innocent of the ways of Sodom as I'd gone in. Others didn't, and when I met them again during later spells of imprisonment and internment — eight years in all — they'd become 'institutionalised', as Social Workers say, meaning as queer as three bob pieces and as happy as pigs in shit, the source of all merriment, practical jokers of genius, lynch-pins in a chain of gossip and intrigue that made the long days a bit more bearable; in short, the only 'normal' people in the whole bleak kip. Which is why I still enjoy the society of odd fellows — as a lay brother, of course. You don't have to believe me. Kate never did: her last letter to me from Gormanstown, care of the Cavan man, had been addressed to 'Miss Gladys Fallis...' Hurtful cat!

I rang Duncher.

'Yis!'

'Hello Duncher. It's me again.'

'Who's "me"?'

'Monseigneur Daddy Xmas, who'd you think —'

'Oh it's you. Whad'ya want at this hour?'

'How's things going?'

'Not so duckin' fusty, if yer interested — but I'll manage. They're hard to shift — 'specially these motor-bike Tuaregs. Yi'd think with all that horse power under their arses they'd jump at the chance of a wee jaunt. But no — they'd sooner burn out a handy High Anglican than travel a mile to roast a Jesuit! Anyroad, I'm havin' a wee skelly at the map here an' I remembers this Mormon trainin' college that's down that way, only a spit from where the stuff's comin' in. So this mornin' I plants a yarn in the weekly newsheet over here, all about the Mormons goin' to sell the buildin's to the nuns. It's goin' the roun's of the pubs just about now — but from what I've heard so far they'll not be hard to persuade in the mornin'.'

'Hard luck on the Mormons —'

'— Frig the Mormons if I can git a good crowd headin' in the right direction!'

'That's the spirit, Duncher. If you get down there about ten pm at the latest I'll contact you.'

'The best laid plans —' as the Scotch Behan said... We weren't to know that at that very moment a 'friendly' fixture was drawing to a close in Hampden Park, Glasgow — between Rangers and Celtic; or that Rangers would be awarded a one-nil decision on a disputed off-side goal in the last minute. In the half-hour following the whistle fourteen died and hundreds were maimed. On hearing the news, Duncher's Mohawks paraded *en fête* down to the perimeter of the Little Flower. there to taunt the uniformed Celtic supporters within, flaunting placards which read: 'Rangers 14 Celtic 0' regardless of the fact that causalties had been evenly split between supporters of both teams.

Unfortunately, the day had been a festive one for the garrison of the Little Flower: the commemoration of some obscure skirmish in the Zulu wars in which the regiment had excelled itself. This took the traditional form of a dinner of boiled thistles *sautéed* in the blood of a black sheep, washed down by no less than one quart of fifty-year-old Glen Affric per man. The OC, a twenty-four year old vicar's son from Sussex, had passed out over a spoonful of clotted blood at midday and was being succoured by the nuns when the demonstrators appeared. Unrestrained, the troops opened fire, killing four at once; they then mounted a spectacular charge across open ground and polished off a further four with bayonet and razor before retiring in good order.

Consequently, at Sunday's hungover dawn the garrison began a day that is already being mentioned in the same hushed breath as Rorke's Drift and the Alamo. And poor Duncher had an uphill job to muster a few carloads for his peninsula expedition.

(The team managers of Celtic and Rangers stood side by side at a service for the fallen held in a neutral ground. In a press release both blamed *agents provocateurs* from Partick Thistle for the carnage.)

At the time of writing I've not had a jar (social) — as distinct from a drink (medical) — for four long months; since that last Saturday night bust-up in the Cavan man's to be precise. The memory is enough to set the back of my throat aching, so I'll not linger on it — or its horrific aftermath on Sunday morning — but take up from when Steffers, Punchy and I crossed the bridge at around three-thirty in the afternoon, Steffers driving, Punchy and I cowering painfully behind dark glasses in the back seat.

The bridge was deserted: no sentinels, no pedestrians, no traffic... 'Christ! They must hardly breathe on the Sabbath,' exclaimed Steffers, taking it canny in case of ambush, booby trap or mine.

'There's a lot of them doing something somewhere,' I said: 'listen —'

It was, of course, the sound of gun- and mortar-fire carried down on the water from 'The Siege of the Little Flower', but we didn't know that then.

'Duncher's maybe havin' a rougher time than he thought, persuading his wee fellas,' wheezed Punchy. That Punchy could hear at all was amazing. Since being delivered by a pair of O'Lig's hardchaws that morning, he'd had every appearance of being stone blind and semi-paralysed. But he had still managed to gabble a paragraph or two...

The stock of the Golden Calf had run out twice in the space of eight hours; two nearby off-licences had been looted and drunk to the dregs; the pressure on the extern of the local infirmary had been such that eventually they'd had to station a mobile stomach pump in the carpark; six double-deckers had been hi-jacked from the depot and loaded with enough stout to keep the pilgrim's blood count at fighting level till they reached the peninsula: and all at the ridiculously low cost of ten tarrings, two deaths by accidental discharge and one by heart attack. (The latter a grand old punter called Festy Doran who had killed three Tans in 1922 and lived well off the story since. Such was the turmoil, Punchy says, that Festy had been dead in his chair for six hours before someone noticed that the five cigarette butts stuck to his lower lip had gone out.)

'How's Rory?' I asked.

'Top of the world. Borrowin' money on the strength of future profits.Wearin' Rarity's ridin' boots an' bush hat — the spittin' image of a warden on a chain gang I used to know.'

Across the bridge safely, my suggestion that we pay a call on Duncher to see how things were going was vetoed by Punchy. What if we were stopped by a stray band of Mohawks and they uncovered the contents of his holdall in the boot? The thought of the orifices they would find to fill with a pound of highly explosive putty led me to agree with him... 'Anyway, sure it doesn't matter now how Duncher gits on,' he sneered; 'there'll be enough of our idjits down there to raise ructions.'

He should have known better — so, of course, should I. At the heels of the hunt the only party to muster a full, indeed overflowing, complement on the peninsula was the one that had not been called for...

Rory was to blame. As personal transportation, presumably to go with the riding boots, he selected an open-top Mercedes from O'Driscoll's chapel yard stock. Placing himself at the head of the six-unit convoy assembled in front of the Golden Calf, he performed a ten-minute posing session for press photographers before firing the signal shot to advance. The Mercedes shot off and crossed the bridge at 80 mph; the buses, crammed to the roofs like jars of demented tadpoles, lurched forward to a top speed of 20; and Rory, at the mercy of a pot-addled car nut who had never before trod the pedal of anything more nippy than a flogged-out Cortina, was in sight of the peninsula before the first bus had cleared the city suburbs. Had he taken up the rear, like a good commander, he might have averted some of the catastrophe — but not all: no power on earth could have saved the occupants of the last bus to cross the bridge, for instance, which on losing sight of the one in front, took a wrong turning and ploughed into a mob of Duncher's wee boys on the way to do battle at the Little Flower. If anyone survived that, I've yet to hear of him.

The only other bus to stray off course was one bearing relatively sober contingents from certain militant Holy Orders and the National Handball Association, patriots abstemious in all save murder. It did so later in the journey, taking a side road which came to a dead end at the harbour of a small fishing hamlet just south of the peninsula. The fleet was at sea, fortunately for the bus's Holy-bemedalled burden, or there would certainly have been another slaughtering match. In this case all lived to tell the tale of their humiliating treatment at the hands of the heretic fisher-folk: of how, descending from the bus unaware that their paralytic driver had missed the road, they had been set upon by a horde of muscular women, clad in gumboots and rubber aprons, who disgorged from an adjacent fish factory; of how, rendered incapable of retaliation or retreat by a bombardment of rotten fish guts, they had been dragged away one by one, green and puking, to be subjected to an unspeakable ritual usually reserved for the initiation of young girls in the factory; a ritual involving, among other horrors, the sexual apparatus of large codfish...

Of course, the root cause of all the trouble was that the drivers did not stint themselves at the gargle either before or during the journey. A third bus ended up lying on its side in a field of barley — appropriately — after the driver had become so carried away by the choir behind that he'd risen from his seat, turned to face the company, and had conducted two verses of 'A Nation Once Again' before the sluggish vehicle reached the end of a mile straight and left the road. Heaped together, the passengers seemed to have slept quite comfortably until a breakdown crane arrived in the early hours of Monday.

All that came later in the day. Steffers, Punchy and I reached the peninsula about four-thirty and had a quick recce round the perimeter road to see if there was any stir.

There wasn't; on land or sea. The gulls seemed to have taken the day off; no ship marred the horizon; the Isle of Man was behind a bank of low cloud. This latter bothered Steffers.

'If it comes this way we'll be buggered tonight,' she said, putting up a finger to the wind.

'God, it's one wild, wild hole!' moaned Punchy, shrinking back from a car window full of pleasant, domesticated landscape.

'Never you mind,' I said. 'Just get tinkering with them detonators and wires so's we'll not be futhering about in the dark at the last minute. Steffers and I have a wee job to do down on the boat.'

We had parked at the head of the jetty opposite the main gates to the estate. We boarded Toby's craft without difficulty, smashing a lock on a hatch cover so that Steffers could lower herself into the engine housing and fit that small essential part. I, in the meantime, investigated the luxurious appointments, had a crap in the dry toilet (aural and visual satisfaction), a large Scotch from the gimballed cocktail cabinet, and was

144

lying on a bunk having visions of sunlit meanderings through the canals of France when Steffers came in. A dab of grease on the front of her sweater added a touch of voluptuous perspective...

'Give yer hands a good rinse, woman,' says I, playfully, 'they're needed.'

She prefaced her reply by giving the member offered a sharp flick with her fingernail. 'No. Not here. You'd never know who'd come —'

'I have every intention —'

'I'm going for a swim,' she announced, flicking away, every flick less painful than the last, her eyes heavy as though with sleep, her lower lip pendulous and wet, transformed by lust into the image of first loony in *The Snake Pit*, '... in the nude, if you're interested.'

Of course I was. Always glad of a fresh experience to broaden the outlook.

Beside the jetty was a little beach, enclosed by high rocks and well concealed from the road. And there, for the first time, I saw the whole package unwrapped — helped to unwrap it — in daylight. The sheer volume was staggering; overwhelming even when stationary — and in motion ...! Running seawards, all the bits and pieces rotating wilfully, gathering such impetus that I feared for her safety as she careered into the tide. Bad enough going, but God! — coming back...

Impetuously, I ran down the beach to meet her — straight into a reel of X certificate Buster Keaton: for in the ensuing wet, salty tangle, due to over-enthusiasm on my part, I fell victim to a complaint known in nudist circles as 'sandy dick'. Very painful — and deflating; a condition not helped by the mirth of the one who'd caused it in the first place. Worse still... to get easement I decided on another first: immersion in the sea. So, trouserless and holding up my shirt tails — a hysterical sight going by the screeches of the only witness — I inched into the icy water until the injured party was well awash and — Christ! — turning black in a mini oil slick! How's that for the luck of the Irish?

Crude oil and sand: Fagan and dependants were a sorry sight indeed. And hilarious; I can see that now, but at the time I cut short Steffers' flippancies about the Society for the Reclamation of Befouled Wildlife and sent her post-haste to the car — clothed, of course — to fetch some cleansing cream from her bag.

I mention the incident as a watershed; a symbol; after it, nothing went right. Apart from the fact that the sea had shocked the last vestige of drink out of me — a handicap I later made up with the bottle of

Powers I'd secreted in the car — I had to sit half naked on that bloody beach for a full hour, chilled to the bone, while Steffers laboured over my belongings with cream and scissors.

By the time she'd finished it was after seven. The sun was well down and the bank of cloud out by the Isle of Man had moved appreciably closer. And by the time we had pilfered some grub off the boat and got back to something near normality with the help of John Powers, it was past eight and still no sign of life in the vicinity.

I instructed Steffers to deposit all personal luggage, including Daddy's charts of the North Channel, on board the boat in case we had to ditch the car in a hurry. Punchy transferred the explosive contents of his holdall to the poacher's pockets in his second-hand hacking jacket.

On board, I liberated another bottle of Toby's Scotch and outlined my plan of action — still with certain resevations... As soon as it was dark — or when the bottle was empty, whichever came last — we would drive back to the neck of the peninsula, there to take up a watching position overlooking the place where three roads converge into the single coast road — a place known, inscrutably, as 'The Three Road Ends' — through which all traffic to the peninsula must pass. This was where Toby had said all the action would be, so I stressed stealth and cunning. All we required was confirmation that O'Lig and Duncher had arrived in sufficient strength to keep Toby, Burton, the Simbas, the Gurkhas, Black Power and whoever else occupied for an hour or two. Then, back to the car, a quick dash back up the road to the Big House, blow the safe and —

'That fuggin' woman of yours'll be the jinx,' groaned Punchy — meaning Kate — before I could shut him up.

'Cheeky old bastard!' cried Steffers, taking it to heart. 'Proinsias, this is no time for him to start —'

'—But I —' Punchy began to plead...

'Shut up!' I roared, effectively. 'Say no more — any one of yis. Get that drink down and save your breath. I've a notion we'll have to do a bit of leppin' about before the night's out.' (Who's a prophet? — Within ten minutes of leaving the boat I was hoisting Punchy over the six-foot-high wall of the estate.)

It was exactly nine-thirty when we set off, and as black as the devil's anal tract. We were still about a quarter mile away from 'The Three Road Ends', following the wall that bounded a particularly foresty stretch of the estate, when Punchy, in the front beside Steffers, spotted the lights... 'Christ, that looks like a futball groun'.'

I looked, saw the blue sodium glare filtering through the trees, realized it was at 'The Three Road Ends' and told Steffers to pull off the road. One of my better snap decisions, as it turned out.

We could have walked the road for the last quarter mile, an alternative whinged by Punchy when scrabbling at the rough hewn granite of the estate wall and repeated by him at least half-a-dozen times during our passage through the trackless undergrowth between the trees; but I had a premonition about those lights — justified by later observation. For me especially, to have blundered into that particular céilí at the crossroads would have been suicidal.

I blazed the trail, with Punchy following and Steffers bringing up the rear. The air was stale and humid down there behind the windbreak of the wall, and we were soon in one hell of a mucksweat. My one vivid recollection of that long quarter mile is of my growing awareness that Steffers' cream had not cleansed all the oil from my jewels and that what remained was reaching a painful state of tackiness. In the later stages, though, nearing where the wall takes a sharp U-turn at the crossroads, I remember taking note of certain off-stage stirrings not connected with the cursing of Punchy, the panting of Steffers or my own thudding pump. And once, I thought, a pair of eyes, luminous, peered at me round the stump of a tree — a badger, I hoped.

From behind the wall the crossroads glowed like the orchestra pit in a music hall. As we drew nearer, any moment I expected a flourish of penny whistles (the National Instrument) in 'The Sweets of May', introducing an Arts Council revival of crossroads dancing (floodlit) as an attraction for insomniac tourists. Nearer still, it sounded like the pits at a twenty-four hour road race: engines revving, men shouting... Then, even as I grasped the top of the wall and hunted around for a toehold to hoist myself up, a sound and a voice arose to quell all others and to tell me, before looking, what it was all about... *Clack.* — 'Interview — Take One — Silence, please — Action! —'

At first look I was dazzled by a semi-circle of spotlights directed at a tableau just five yards out from the wall beneath me. Then, eyes clearing, the make-up of the tableau itself nearly sent me tumbling back into Punchy's arms with shock. O'Lig and the Duncher! — caught in a massive ambush by the media — organized, presumably, by Rory's favourite linkman, who now stood between them and mouthed his introduction to a phalanx of cameras... '...the confrontation of the century... two men who personalize the titanic conflict in this island, yet who have never met until this moment in time... in this grim and inhospitable setting ITN has spared no effort in bringing this meeting about in the hope...'

Focussing now, I made out the shapes of at least two double-deckers parked in the dusk behind the arc-lights... and a Land Rover with what looked like a Police sign... and, yes (Christ!) Sergeant McNinch in full regimentals, flanked by his bullies, posed in a central position between the buses and a cluster of people around a vehicle which bore the illuminated advert 'Caulkers Mission. Ye Must Be Born Again', part of Duncher's contingent (I learnt later that he had managed only a mini-bus and six carloads).

The protagonists themselves made the whole thing look like a rehearsal for one of those time fantasies beloved by producers in the early days of TV. A bush-hatted Rory, teetering tipsily in Rarity's too-small riding boots, as Ulysses S Grant, confronting Duncher, done up in his Field Marshal's gear plus an Afrika Corps cap as some sort of Rommel/Monty hybrid. They stood quietly while the linkman rabbited on with the intro: even the noise from the separate gangs around the transport was minimal enough to be called, in relation to that company, a hushed reverence.

'On my left,' said the linkman, 'the Right Honourable Rory O'Lig MP, Chairman of the RSVP party. Now, Mr O'Lig, first of all I think the viewers would like to hear your considered opinion, leaving aside politics for the moment, your considered opinion of your worthy opponent on my right, the Reverend Clegg.'

'Well, Robin,' Rory began, addressing the cameras, 'first of all I'd like to say how pleased we all are to have you back among us after your spell in Vietnam and to wish you *Céad Míle Fáilte*, a hunnerd thousand welcomes. As to your question, I can say here and now, categorically, that I've always recognised Bishop Clegg to be the true spokesman of the Protestant working classes. You know as well as I do, Robin, at the end of the day it's sincerity that counts, and as a deeply religious man myself, one thing I've always respected about the Bishop is the deep sincerity of his religious views.'

'It moves me to hear you say that, Mr O'Lig,' throbbed Robin. 'And now, the Reverend Arthur Clegg: your personal view, Reverend, of the Right Honourable O'Lig?'

Duncher (Arthur!) cupped his hands over Robin's around the proffered

148

microphone, bending over as though being given a lick of an ice-cream cone. He shouted: 'I've allus known Rory O'Lig to be a man of honour an' integerty. He an' I has crossed words in the public prints many a time, but niver swords. I know his han's are as clean of these sectarian bombin's an' killin's as my own is. I can say without fear of conterdiction —'

At this point my attention was diverted by a cold pressure behind my right ear — followed quickly by a hoarse whisper in my left...

'Easy, Francie... or I'll blow your devious head off now —'

Toby. Poised in a toehold beside me. I looked downward involuntarily and recognised Burton, notwithstanding the blackened face, holding a gun on Punchy; and Fred the barman half-smothering a struggling Steffers.

'I fully intended putting you down in any event,' said Toby, his breath in my ear causing my balls to tingle, 'but after this circus I was to do it slowly. For five hundred quid I'm due a bit of sport, don't you think? How much did those TV bods pay you?'

'It wasn't me,' I had begun to plead; and Robin the linkman was saying, 'And now we come to the nitty gritty, gentlemen — the sixty-four thousand dollar —' when the first white mini-bus, having already run over McNinch and his bullies, came ploughing out of the darkness through the bank of cameras and straight for him. O'Lig and the Duncher threw themselves to either side, but Robin was too slow. The mini-bus hit the wall full tilt with him spreadeagled across its bonnet, still clutching the severed mike, in which captive position he was then clubbed unconscious by the crutch of the first to emerge from the shattered vehicle — a woolly-headed, one-eyed...

'*En avant! Les garconnets arriérés!*' he cried as the second mini-bus tore through to telescope into the back of the first... then a third... all marked: 'Co Down Education Authority'.

'Gerratyafugginbasters!' came the chilling response as the doors burst open to spew the cream of Header Hall onto the road.

'What the hell's that!' breathed Toby — and I felt the gun waver at my neck. Leaving go one hand I gave him a hard elbow in the guts. The gun went off as he fell back on top of Burton, but the round went wild. Before he could recover I'd landed with both feet on his chest, which put him past caring for the time being. When I turned round the days of Burton's televiewability were already over; he squatted cross-legged on the ground, trying to hold his sliced nose together as Punchy advanced on Fred with a bloodstained razor. Fred bolted. Released, Steffers started screaming hysterically until I hit her a welt.

The lights had gone out on the other side of the wall. The volume of the Header war whoop increased with the thud of more mini-buses arriving, as did the sound of gunfire as the O'Lig and Duncher factions united to dig in around their transport. It would not be long, I knew, before either they were overwhelmed by sheer tonnage of murderous cretins, or the latter, in their fey way, would get fed up and go on the pillage. And there being a wall, they'd certainly climb it.

It dawned on Punchy... 'Sacred Heart! That's niver the Headers!'

'It is, oul' han', so we'd better get off-side quick. No use going back to the car now — we'll make for the house across the estate.'

Gnawing her knuckles, eyes like saucers, Steffers watched Burton doing the faith-healing, Yogi bit on his nose, mesmerised.

'Come on,' I said, grabbing her arm.

'Did you see what that savage did!' she shuddered.

'If you think that's bad stay around here for a while...' As though to stress my point the high-pitched squeal of some martyred cameraman came piercing through the bedlam over the wall. She started tunning through the trees. Punchy and I, pausing only to collect the Lugers dropped by the afflicted, followed, he with his ankle-length dexter gathered up waist high like an old lady going for a paddle.

Having a fair idea of the lie of the land I headed into the thick of the trees, trying to keep as straight a line as possible. I knew the deserted village lay somewhere between the crossroads and the Big House. If we could reach it the rest of the going would be comparatively soft.

The undergrowth began to thin out as we got further away from the wall. I found a rutted track which led through a series of small clearings scabbed with tree stumps. Spurred on by the noise of battle behind and the awful awareness, on my part at least, that it was not diminishing with distance, we were stumbling along at a fair lick when, in one of the abovementioned clearings, we were confronted by Meg.

Not really confronted, for she stood under some foliage on the other side of the clearing, about fifty yards away, a barely discernible shadow. I knew it was Meg when she growled; and then there were four or five other shadows low on the ground in front of her, snorting and snuffling, and her arm outstretched as though dragging on leashes.

I, naturally, stopped dead — and the others piled up my back. At that moment I must have been cocking the Luger; but all I remember is the hair rising on my neck.

'What's up?' hissed Punchy.

'Can we have a rest?' belled Steffers in a voice that echoed round the clearing. Whinging bitch!

Meg shouted and the four shadows in front rose up on two legs apiece and started across the clearing towards us at speed, hurdling the tree stumps like gazelles, eyes and teeth gleaming, steel flashing in their fists...

Simbas.

Without a word I kicked the feet from under Steffers and started firing — two-handed aimed shots, crouched à la Callan, real copybook stuff. They broke and started to dodge and zig-zag, but kept coming. Punchy's first shot almost matched mine; his third knocked one flying with a great gurgling scream. I picked the forerunner and kept pumping at him until he was so close I could see the ring through his nose, trying all the time to recall how many rounds in a Luger magazine. When he fell, riddled, I had to step back to avoid his kicking feet. Punchy got the one behind coming for me. I tried a snap shot at the survivor, who seemed to have left the ground a few yards in front of Punchy, flying at him with a short, bayonet-like thing extended. My firing-pin clicked. But Punchy, the old pro, had known the exact load of a Luger and had counted his shots; so when the Simba hit him, the bayonet penetrating the dexter, a Harris tweed hacking jacket, a corduroy smoking jacket, a Fair Isle choker (a great one for the golf club jumble sales, Punchy), a pullover, shirt and two pair of combs, but never touching flesh, Punchy had the razor already in hand. They fell together and rolled over once.

We helped him to his feet and retrieved his cap from under the dead Simba.

'Ach, in the name of Christ will ya look at the state of me oul' duds!' he girned. 'What kind'a life's this for an Oul' Age Pensioner! Wanderin' about fightin' mad niggers at all hours of the night... What the hell sorta jungle's this you've brought us to anyway?'

'You must have heard of Safari Parks,' I said, trying to keep my voice steady — no mean feat when everything else is shaking. 'It's just that this one tries to be that wee bit more realistic.'

'My God, Proinsias, these are black men!' wailed Steffers accusingly, she having spent all the action with her face buried in the ground.

'Just think of them as dead black Protestants if it makes you feel any better,' I fairly shrieked, 'and for fuck's sake get your skates on. Just listen to what's on our heels —'

'Gerratyafuggin*black*basters! —'

The Headers were certainly over the wall and had made contact with other sections of Toby's forces. There was no sign of Meg as we started across the clearing at a jog-trot. Away to fetch the beagles, I supposed.

On reflection, it must have been only a running spit from the scene of the fight to the deserted village, but what with watery knees, tacky balls and palpitations, to me anyway it seemed Irish miles. More than anything I wanted clear of the trees, which, as if not getting on my wick enough already, had started rustling and sighing nerve-wrackingly in a slight breeze. Once on the other side of the deserted village I'd at least know where I was going, with a nice clear track over the hill to follow.

'Deserted' village. It was this unconscious use of that adjective in relation to the village that threw me off guard. With Toby and Burton at the crossroads and the Simbas in the woods, it never crossed my mind that it would be anything but 'deserted'. But it wasn't. When the track we were on ended abruptly at the gable of the end cottage, I bloody near fell into a campfire surrounded by a handful of small darkies!

They hadn't seen me. But when I turned to duck back into the trees I trod on Punchy's foot coming up behind. He, naturally, bawled, 'Fuck ye!' and gave me an irate shove which landed me right out in the open again. The little men round the fire turned and stared. One, in the act of chopping a piece of wood, paused with a curved knife suspended in mid-swing: the sort of knife pawnshops had been stuffed with after the last war — kukris... Gurkhas!

Miraculously, none of them budged. The knifeman looked away and continued his downstroke; the others just sat staring and then, presently, began to grin and nudge one another, one or two making an international lewd gesture with clenched fist and hinged elbow, and I realized that Steffers had stepped into the firelight beside me. Emerging from my terrified trance, emboldened, I said: 'God bless all here,' in a loud voice, took Steffers by the hand and, Punchy limping behind, circled the fire and set off up the street. The little men giggled — but stayed put.

The place was alive with them. They wore tiny pill-box hats and, curiously, brilliant white tunics which made them stand out in the dark like glow worms. They sat in groups along the ruined pavement and around the cottage doors and made no move to intercept us. Just giggled. I began to wonder if I was rambling in the head.

Outside the cottage which had housed the arms cache and the Simbas what looked like a queue had formed. NAAFI? I wondered as we hurried past. Then from the lighted interior came a peal of familiar laughter — Chloe!

I hesitated, torn between the urge to headlong flight and curiosity. Tea and wads for the troops was hardly her forte. What then?

'What's up now, fer Chrissake?' hissed Punchy. 'Have ye lost yer road?'

'Oh don't tell me that, Proinsias!' whimpered Steffers. 'These wee men give me the shits the way they stare!'

Chloe shrieked. The queue giggled.

'Look,' I said, pushing them out in front, 'straight ahead up into the bushes yonder. Once you're clear, wait for me —'

Punchy grumbled, but went; Steffers was glad to follow. Ignoring the cat's eyes of the queue I marched up to the cottage door. It opened just then and a Gurkha came out, adjusting his pillbox to a jaunty angle over his ear. Chloe shouted, 'Next, please,' and the man at the head of the queue — no youngster, with stripes on his sleeve and waxed moustaches, like a doll soldier made in Japan — gave me an aggressive elbow as we entered the cottage neck and neck. He was the first not to grin; quite the opposite — he hooked his thumb meaningfully towards the door.

'Mr O'Dickens, darling!... Never mind Havildar; he's a friend.'

She lay on a mattress on the floor, wearing the same flimsy peach thing as when I'd last met her — up round her neck! Oh, and shoes. The black G-string I gave her credit for at first sight turned out not to be. Rolling over, with a pencil she cancelled out a third set of fives on the wall beside her. 'Only another seven,' she sighed, 'to equal that cat Milly Drooper with the Spanish onion drivers. You see, Charlie, I've got this fabulous contract for 10,000 words with *Nova*. God, but it's hard work though! They're like brown ferrets... brown ferrets?... Hey, that's not bad! Wait'll I make a note, Havildar... whoops! Steady...'

No respecter of the creative impulse, that Havildar. Whilst I gaped and she gabbled, he had been unharnessing. I left him ferreting away — and judging by the noises coming from Chloe the work was also congenial. She wouldn't mind, I thought, getting enough material for a novel when the Headers arrived.

It must have been the glare of so much white flesh, but once outside I was blind again. I followed the tunics and teeth of the queue, which seemed to have grown considerably, hoping they led to the old roadway. They did; at the last tunic I tripped on a lump of ruined pavement and would have gone arse over kelp but for grabbing this tunicless blob... 'Sorry, mate,' I muttered, making to push on.

'Great God! O'Toole, old chap! What on earth are you doing down here?' cried Major Giles ('Banger') Wilkington-Pike. For it was he — in combat gear, blackened face and woolly cap, flourishing a mess tin. I was beyond words: he rattled on like a man just out of a month's solitary.

'Up to your neck in it with these Oxbridge MI12 bastards I'll bet. Eh? No names no pack drill, old boy, but if I'd known that mad cunt Toby Mann had an interest I'd have sent in my papers... What do you think of my shock troops? Eh? Like a bunch of ship's stewards! Usual War House balls-up, of course — sent the bloody pipe band instead of the rifle company. Believe it or not, Francie, most of these poor fuckers think they're on a barbecue in the Scotch Highlands! Half-a-dozen of O'Lig's animals would eat them alive. By the way, you came out of the cookhouse just then — what's on? Not more of that curried shit of theirs, I hope. I spotted the queue and thought I'd grab a bite before we moved on. When I asked for a cook/batman they all pretended they couldn't speak English, malingering wog midgets —'

'— Header Hall —' I managed to get in.

'What?... Oh, I see what you mean. Yes, we're well out of that, old boy. The coloured brethren are bad enough, but after seeing the bits of poor Briggs that —'

'—They're here, Major.'

'Who?'

'The Headers. They're —'

'Now look here, Francie old chap, you've got it all wrong. These are Gurkhas, from the Edinburgh Tattoo... Are you sure you're quite all right?'

'I am,' I said firmly, starting to ease off into the darkness, 'and I'm telling you that the Headers will be here in about five minutes. I'm off.' Leaving him standing, I ran along the road in what I hoped was the right direction. Behind me I heard his mess tin fall clattering on the broken pavement and an explosive 'Great God!' It had dawned on him... Just before I reached the bushes where Punchy and Steffers were waiting, there came the thud of ammo boots behind me and the Major puffed alongside.

'Retreating, Major?' I gasped.

'Withdrawing to reappraise position. The Nepalese yak-shaggers can fend for themselves — they can't talk white, so no use me giving them orders. Which way do we go?'

That was all I needed...

'We'd better split up,' I said. 'They're liable to be all over the place. You go that way —' pointing into the wilderness well away from the Big House, '— we'll meet up on the road. I've a car parked.'

'Roger. Good thinking. Stout fella, Francie.' He ran off into the darkness — full tilt into every tree trunk on the way by the din of anguished cursing and threshing that arose. I rejoined the others and we started over the hill to the Big House.

Burton's two-way lecture that Sunday had made the journey between house and village seem like miles, yet in about ten minutes Punchy, Steffers and I were crossing the car park to the main entrance. There wasn't a car or invalid carriage in sight, so I supposed that Toby had given notice to the geriatrics prior to the event. The house itself was in total darkness: not what I'd have expected with Kate and litter on the premises; so perhaps they weren't... Hope springs eternal.

The front door, being half-glazed, was no match for Punchy's elbow. The shattering glass made one hell of a racket and we stood silent for a moment in the dark hallway awaiting a response. When none came I told Steffers to have a scout around the upper rooms while Punchy and I made a beeline for the Warden's den.

She didn't like it. The happenings of the past hour had left their mark on her, emotionally as well as physically; she'd lost a considerable amount of her cool along with one shoe and most of one leg of her jeans. But I insisted, not wishing to tarnish her idealism with the sight of all that free money. Besides, there was always the danger that the gombeen Prod in her would emerge to claim a share — and that wouldn't do...

I needn't have bothered. Even before opening the door of the Warden's den I smelt gelly in the air. The light switch didn't work — and when Punchy struck a match we saw why. It had been used as we had intended using it — to detonate a charge. My little honey-pot lay in the centre of the shambles: gaping open; empty.

'Whatever rotten cunt —' I had begun to compose, when the match went out. Punchy — singed — cursed. A scream echoed in the distance — Steffers? I whirled round, sensing something — and froze solid. A

155

pair of eyes, yellow, luminous, floated towards me... and then they too went out — or to be less subjective about it, I did, due to a hefty clout on the forehead from a Watutsi knobkerrie.

When this sort of carry-on happens in fiction, the victim usually comes to in the next chapter either in lone captivity ('— the dark silence was almost palpable —') or getting his head bathed ('— the caress of perfumed hair on my —'). I came to suddenly in a cramped bedlam, my blurred vision full of Kate's hate-twisted face, my ears ringing with her accusative screech — 'He's pished heself, the dirty pig!'

So I had — but sparingly. She hit me again — her first it was that had jogged my lobes into place — and then someone dragged her off. As my vision widened I saw that it was all happening in the lounge of Toby's boat; by 'all' I mean Kate struggling and spitting in a half-nelson being applied by Punchy, Steffers sobbing (Kate had clobbered her also), my kids screaming encouragement to their mother (on catching my eye Concepta spat at me), and — in the name of Christ! — Teesy Hagan! in her little black, good-livin' dress, taking Kate's part by trying to catch hold of Punchy's most delicate parts from behind. (The puzzled look on her face as she groped vainly up that tangle of rags!) The black man who squatted at the door leading to the wheelhouse seemed highly amused by it all.

...Oh, and the boat was afloat — boisterously. Every now and again the sea was doing its damndest to get in through the small round window above the bunk where I lay. And the bunk itself seemed determined to be rid of me, rising and falling at a hell of a rate and bringing me to an awareness of my stomach, which had been gimballing about down there for God knows how long, waiting for me to waken and let fly. I was preparing to do so, fingers poised for throat priming and bent, vindictively, on coating as many of the assembly as possible, when Bertie came stooping through the wheelhouse door.

Like the sentry, he was wearing combat dress; but instead of a Thompson he carried a riding-crop. At that moment Kate's voluminous cherry-coloured arse — she was wearing trousers — loomed clear of the struggle. Bertie let her have it... and again. She erupted, shrieking, flinging Punchy and Teesy in all directions, and went for him. A terrible sight; enough to send shudders up me even though I, for once, wasn't the object. But Bertie — stout fella! — stood fast, smiling coolly, and she never got near enough to lay a claw on him. He lashed her hands, bare arms, thighs and finally arse again until she turned and fell howling among the childer. For the first time I could hear the throb of the engines over the din.

'That will be quite enough of that,' said Bertie, waggling the crop. 'I cannot have the lives of black persons endangered by the squabblings of you honky trash. You, Madam, I will have garrotted if you speak above a whisper.' Kate snuffled and drew the kids around to form a barrier between him and her. She probably imagined 'garrotting' to be some form of heinous gynaecological torture.

'Ah, Mr O'Toole!' cried Bertie, sending me a glint of precious metal. 'You've returned to us. Good. Now perhaps you'll join me in the wheelhouse for a long overdue chat. You too, my dear.' This last to Teesy, who smiled and lowered her gaze shyly.

I got up with some difficulty, and when up had to be supported by Punchy and Steffers for a moment. Kate growled far back in her throat like a farmyard collie and, as I followed Bertie into the wheelhouse, Concepta hissed : 'Oul' pee-the-bed.'

There was another black fellow at the wheel. The heaving about was much more violent than in the lounge, and I had to grab hold of Teesy to stay upright. The helmsman squinted through a windscreen on which the wipers were fighting a losing battle. I began to wonder if Bertie had brought me out to tell me he was going to abandon ship. He hadn't...

'I say, you've widdled yourself, old chap!'

The helmsman grinned.

Teesy giggled.

I lost the rag. 'Never you mind my waterworks, Sambo. Just tell us what a clever black cunt you are and we'll all clap.'

He lifted a Thompson which had been propped beside the chart table, levelled it at my button, and cocked it. I took a firm grasp of Teesy's shoulder with a view to getting behind her if his finger moved inside the trigger guard. 'Have a care, Paddy the pig, or I'll play you a tune on my banjo,' he said softly.

'Oh no... please,' cried Teesy, trying to wriggle out of my grip. 'I'm sure Francie didn't mean no harm, yer honour.'

It created a welcome diversion, causing the muzzle of 'yer honour's' gun to waver and then droop floorwards. 'Not to worry, Teresa my dear,' he said, 'I have no intention of hazarding the structure of this craft for the brief pleasure of ventilating Mr O'Toole's dung coloured carcass. Besides, I have other plans for him. Come over here, Mr O'Toole, if you please.'

He laid the Thompson aside and turned to the chart table. 'We are here,' he said, making an X on the chart, 'approximately ten miles north west of the Isle of Man. I intend following a course which will take us... south, along the western coast of the island — the lee side in these present conditions. And somewhere along there, Mr O'Toole, we shall part company.'

'You mean the mast will then be steady enough for a lynching,' I said.

'Oh dear me no; a worse fate for you, Mr O'Toole,' he grinned. 'I shall return you to the bosom of your family and release you, along with your mistress and the ancient degenerate. Look out there —' He beckoned me over to a window behind the helmsman and pointed. A small open boat cavorted wildly on the end of a long rope in our wake. 'That's your lifeboat. It may be standing room only, but it's the best we could do at short notice. The sea will be much calmer close to the lee shore, of course.'

My relief — it seems incredible now, but even a watery grave was a better prospect than a length of flex and a kicked bucket — must have showed on my face. 'You can thank Miss Teresa for your life,' he said. 'But for her persuasive ways you would have gone overboard a mile out from the jetty. But then, as she pointed out, it isn't as if you're going to live happily ever after.'

I saw what he meant. I thought then of asking him, as a favour, to deposit Kate and brood on some lonely Manx beach, but decided not to. Instead, I turned to Teesy and offered profuse thanks.

'Niver mention it, Francie,' she said, very prim and hurt, 'even though you didn't go out of your way when I needed help.'

'And what about mutual friend Duncher,' I inquired hastily. 'How did you manage to shake him?'

'Easy. The last I seen a coupla Headers were playin' futball with him. I took off along the road an' Bertie here picked me up.'

This Is Your Life, Teesy Hagan, thinks I...

'And very useful she turned out to be,' commented Bertie fondly. 'when it came to dealing with your terrible spouse and her spawn — an eventuality I had not allowed for.'

'The beginning of a beautiful friendship ... strolling hand-in-hand into the sunset — with the pot of gold under your oxter... Eh, Bertie?' I couldn't resist it even at the risk of provoking another lunge for the Thompson. But he didn't rise.

'If you mean that she's not joining you and yours in the dinghy, you're quite right, Mr O'Toole,' he said, smiling richly. 'Miss Teresa has elected to stay on board, which she can do for as long as suits her.'

Or you, thinks I to myself. But then... I noted Teesy's expression as she looked at him and I wondered if even he, sadist, butcher and power maniac, would be a match for her.

I returned to the lounge and acquainted the inmates with the change in transportation which would take place, Bertie had added, in thirty minutes or thereabouts.

That's one half-hour I wouldn't care to live through again — not that I was very much alive at the time, what with the knock on the head causing my consciousness to come and go like a TV picture in an electric storm and my guts hitting the back of my throat at the bottom of every trough. Any detailed description is beyond me. If you've ever been drunk on warm stout during a rough crossing from Liverpool on the August Bank week-end, as I have, imagine then that the boat's sinking and you're caught in the middle of a riot in the steerage bar. It'll give you some idea of the atmosphere.

But for Punchy's protective presence I don't think I'd have lived to see the dinghy. Kate didn't actually lay hands on me again, but the unceasing obscene clangour of her tongue ('Putrefying fuckbag!' —just one gem) had a terrifying effect on the childer. Snapping and spitting they shoaled in and out of my delirium like piranha fish, restrained from doing their daddy terrible harm only by the fiercesome glowering of Uncle Punchy. Indeed, my return to full consciousness came at the end of the half-hour when, with Punchy already in the dinghy and me still on the boat's deck, two-year-old Malachy — culchie ghett! — took the opportunity to sink his teeth in my wrist.

I was helping Bertie to lower the brute over the rail into his mother's waiting arms ('Watch my chil', y'black baster!') when it happened. 'It's a wise child...' murmured Bertie. 'Now, O'Toole,' he went on, 'yonder is the Peel light. Only three or four miles — but against the current, I'm afraid, so you'll have to apply yourselves to the oars or —'

'Francie, for frigsake hurry!' cried Punchy from the dinghy.

'Your decrepit villain appears eager to be away, so let's not detain him any longer. Goodbye, Mr O'Toole.' — This accompanied by a nudge from the Thompson.

No sooner had I fallen into the stern of the dinghy than Punchy and Steffers, seated behind an oar apiece amidships, started pulling like mad away from the boat's side. In the light that radiated from the boat I could see that Steffers' eyes were clenched tight and her lips were moving as though in prayer. And even when the boat revved up and roared off into the darkness — the last human sound I heard from it was one of Teesy's high-pitched, suggestive giggles — the pair of them laboured away purposefully.

I took stock of the situation. Compared to conditions a short while ago the sea, as Bertie had promised, was as flat as stale stout. I could see the light he had mentioned and, as my eyes grew accustomed, the length of the dinghy with Kate and the kids huddled, ominously quiet, in the bow behind the straining rowers. But that was all I could see; and the cold began to bite through my lounge bar navy-blue; and my head throbbed... Up shit creek, proper; skint, homeless, sober — an all time low.

Only when the roar of Toby's boat had died away completely did the rowers let up. Steffers slumped over her oar and sobbed, 'My God... Oh my God!' in the most pitiable fashion, which I thought was a bit much for a big healthy girl after barely five minutes exercise. And when Punchy struck a match and consulted his giant gold hunter I was driven, even from the sump of despair, to remark: 'Are yis trying for some sort of record?'

'Wait,' he hushed me. 'Just about —'

'Oh my God!' sobbed Steffers. 'I tried to stop —'

Thud. Like someone slamming a heavy door in the distance...

'Hurray!' yelled Punchy. He was standing up, waving his cap. 'Take that, Rastus! Ya black bastard!'

The dinghy rocked sickeningly; Kate cursed; the kids whimpered; I screamed: 'Sit down for Christsake... What's got into —'

'The plastic, Francie, the plastic!' he cried delightedly. 'Under the bunk up agin the bulkhead. Pow!...'

'But Teesy!'

'Fuck Teesy! No fancy coon's gonna pull the wull over my eyes an' git away with it. Anyway, it's hardly a pound — just enough to blow a big hole. They'll probably all git out of it — more's the pity. But it'll sure put a spoke in Rastus's wheel! Eh?'

Bertie had himself to blame, for it was he who had started off to search

Punchy and given up in nose-wrinkling disgust after penetrating to only the second layer. The plastic had been pancaked between the shirt and upper combs, the safety fuse wound round his left leg.

'Savages... savages!' sobbed Steffers.

'Da Hagan'll have yer life,' snarled Kate.

'You're one bloodthirsty oul' divil,' says I.

'An what in the name of Christ did yis expect!' exclaimed Punchy, astonished.

The coaster picked us up two hours later, in the first grey glimmer of dawn. We had been drifting for most of the time (I had taken an oar to warm myself up and, once warm, had fallen asleep and lost the oar over the side) and the sea had begun to show signs of renewed life. So it was with great relief that I threw my leg over the coaster's rail... until, that is, the bearded runt of a skipper opened his mouth in greeting. My heart fluttered...

'Where are you from?' I interrupted his adenoidal flow.

'Dub-al-in,' he whined.

'Where are you heading now?' (Fearfully.)

'Dub-al-in.'

Unfortunately, Kate was within earshot. She flung herself into his arms, screeching: 'God bless you, sur! You'll get a medal from the Pope hisself if you deliver that pair of bastards there to the Castle. They're wanted for floggin' guns to the Protestants.'

Well, not for that — but they did want us to help with enquiries into other matters. And they got us, that very day, after Punchy had shopped any hope of a personal appeal to the skipper by giving Kate the full benefit of his right hobnail on her left kneecap. On her first and only visit to me in my present residence she stayed long enough to mark me for life with her metal crutch, which she had sharpened specially for the purpose. Since then she has contented herself with smuggling the occasional poisoned cake and hiring short-term men to duff us up in the bogs. (But fear not: Punchy has managed to corner a fair segment of the snout market in our block. Any duffing that's done, he and his concessionaires do it.)

Teesy, very much alive, floated into Douglas harbour that same day, stark naked, lying on the remains of a bunk from Toby's boat (where she'd been, I like to think, when the plastic went off). 'Venus Hagan Tells All! shrieked the *Mirror*, announcing the serialisation of *My All*

For Ireland, in which I am sadly maligned.

Steffers is back at the University. She wears black, chain smokes, never smiles, and has achieved fame as the first Irishwoman to say 'fuck' on the box. *Hibernia* called her 'the Maud Gonne of student action'.

McNinch, one of the five generally known survivors of the peninsula, was promoted Inspector, received the Police Medal from the Queen, and is devoting his life to my extradition.

Duncher married his wife at long last and emigrated to Montreal, where he leads a campaign for the repatriation of all Frog Popeheads to their Motherland.

O'Lig is in the custody of the merry Friars over the hill.

Colonel(!) Wilkington-Pike wrote me a cheery letter from the Imperial Staff College, where he is at present director of Urban Guerilla Studies. In a PS he tapped me for a subscription to help re-form the Gurkha pipe band.

The filming of Chloe's book, *Bang, Bang, You're Dead*, written in a Swiss clinic, is dogged by industrial disputes with Equity over the hiring of Header Hall's worst to play the mob scenes and the consequential danger to Union members.

Toby and Burton, the latter under another nose, almost certainly survive somewhere.

O'Driscoll visited me on his way to an ecclesiastical bun-fight in Maynooth. He heard my confession, slipped me a half-bottle of Powers and twenty Woodbine and, when I showed him a draft of Chapter Twelve above, hit me with a bog oak crucifix which hangs on the wall of our cell.

All the fut sodgers perished, of course.

The publishers acknowledge the financial assistance of the Arts Council of Northern Ireland in the publication of this book.